TURNED OUT WELL

TURNED
OUT
WELL

JEANNIE
PENEAUX

EDITED BY MARGARET DEVERE

To the readers within the JAFF community,
with thanks for your encouragement and support

Contents

Tactful

Fitzwilliam Darcy, amongst his equals in society, was well known for the reserve of his manner and his entirely understandable hauteur. He was, after all, a wealthy man and naturally aware of his impeccable lineage. Generally speaking, he was held to be a good sort of fellow, if a little high in the instep and rather too attached to his dignity to add much liveliness to a social gathering.

It had come largely as a surprise, then, to find that such a man had wed an Unknown Young Lady from Hertfordshire some three months ago and was only now bringing the new Mrs. Darcy to London for the season.

Opinion was divided with regards to Mrs. Darcy. Those who had already met the lady allowed that her manners were quite unexceptionable, and the gentlemen at least could comprehend that Mr. Darcy had fallen for a pretty face. The fact that she had the evident support of both the earl and his famously difficult-to-please sister, Lady Catherine de Bourgh, silenced most of those who might otherwise have considered her to be beneath their notice.

Elizabeth Darcy also dressed well enough, the society matrons decreed, and although she was clearly not an ardent follower of what was fashionable, one would be hard-pressed to find a cause for criticism in the elegance or quality of her dress.

The first ball that Mrs. Darcy gave at Darcy House won her considerable favour. Those select three hundred and fifty persons honoured with an invitation praised her as much for her considerable charm as for the excellent supper they had sat down to. No one was quite sure how or even why, but Mr. Brummell himself had graced the evening with his presence and thus the event was thereafter considered to be a very great success.

Also present at the ball were the remaining Miss Bennets of Longbourn. To the unvoiced surprise of her new brother, Miss Catherine Bennet was pronounced to be acceptable company, and to his outright astonishment, Miss Lydia looked quite set to become all the rage when she graced London with her come-out.

Despite her husband's severity of opinion regarding the idleness of Beau Brummell, Mrs. Darcy could not help but like him. She had been anticipating every ridiculous eccentricity of apparel that society had to offer displayed in one being. Instead, she had been presented with a neatly dressed, quiet-spoken gentleman with nothing about him to invite mockery. Having heard tales of His Highness the Prince Regent and *his* excesses, she was rather taken by surprise by the understated elegance of the man who famously set the latest fashions which Prinny followed so enthusiastically.

They had been introduced in Hyde Park one morning when Elizabeth had been strolling on the arm of the Earl of Matlock. Mr. Darcy had been shut up in his study with his man of business, and Mrs. Darcy had been entirely charmed by her new uncle's arrival on her doorstep, announcing that she must be taken out and Seen.

He made for amusing company, even if she did think the height of his lordship's heels made it rather difficult to walk properly. His undisguised dismay at her practical suggestion that top boots might provide him with more comfort amused her so much that she let out a trill of delighted laughter. Two gentlemen, whom the earl and Mrs. Darcy were just about to wander past, turned with interest at the musical sound.

"My Lord Matlock, good day to you!" hailed the one, his eyes on the pretty young woman with his old friend.

"Good morning, Danby. How do you do, and Mr. Brummell, back from Brighton so soon, I see. I am enchanted to see you again, sir. Mrs. Darcy, may I present Lord Danby to your notice – I was at school with his lordship some...some considerable time ago. Also, our renowned arbiter of taste, Mr. Brummell. Gentlemen, Mrs. Darcy is my newest niece."

Elizabeth curtseyed and the Beau bowed slightly. "I am pleased to meet you, my lord. And of course you also, Mr. Brummell."

Beau Brummell was looking at Mrs. Darcy's hat, a simple enough creation that suited her very well. Lydia had sent it to her, lovingly wrapped up in a bandbox with quantities of tissue paper. A slight curling brim framed her face to perfection and delicate lace roses adorned it. Nothing else was needed. Lydia had written a brief crowing note to her sister that she must love her very dearly to part with such a triumph.

"Madam," he pronounced, "may I compliment you on your choice of hat. Rarely have I seen such restrained good taste on a such a young head. You are to be congratulated."

Rather thinking the man must be a coxcomb to be so invested in her bonnet, Elizabeth smiled sweetly and thanked him with amusement dancing in her eyes. "I fear I should be the most wretched sister in England were I to take such a compliment for myself, sir. My youngest sister has a certain talent for clothing. I daresay she will be pleased to receive your assurance of her genius."

Mr. Brummell smiled but was clearly disappointed that the person responsible for creating the hat was not present. Elizabeth swallowed a laugh and, nodding to the gentlemen, said that they ought to continue their walk. As the gentlemen were once more bowing, she smiled at them.

"I believe my husband has said that you must certainly be included on the guest list for our ball, Lord Danby – I shall be quite delighted to see you there. Mr. Brummell, if you would like to meet my gifted younger sister, you must come also. I shall have an invitation sent to you. Good day!"

The two walked on. Elizabeth felt her husband's uncle shake with silent laughter and tilted her head inquiringly.

"My dear Mrs. Darcy, I knew that you should be a delightful addition to the family as soon as I laid eyes on you. I do so like to be proved correct. I do not think I have ever seen Beau Brummell so casually invited nor so readily dismissed. I should not really be surprised if you have piqued his curiosity. You will be quite Made, my dear!"

Elizabeth shrugged at this, and shrugged yet again when she related the events of the walk to her husband.

"*Brummell*, Elizabeth? What can you have been thinking of? It is your ball, of course, and you must naturally invite whomsoever you wish, but have you a yet unrelated desire to become a grand society matron? I had not realised it, my love. No wonder my uncle was so amused."

He greeted the man very courteously when he strolled in on the night of the ball, however, and assured him of his welcome. Brummell was one of the last to arrive, and Mr. Darcy had already excused Georgiana, Catherine, and Lydia from the receiving line.

The ballroom was a blaze of light, and the chandeliers shone like diamonds above the glittering beau monde. Once the last of the guests had arrived, Mr. Darcy led his wife out to dance. Mr. Brummell made his way around the edges of the ballroom, occasionally bowing to his acquaintances and once or twice greeting a young lady desperate for his notice.

He was in due course introduced to the new Mrs. Darcy's sisters, and, having bowed to Lydia, looked her over and stopped short in appreciation. Lydia had spent much time selecting her gown that evening and had done herself no disservice in the effort put forth. She looked every inch a debutante in white damask with a simple strand of pearls clasped about her neck. Her height, of which she was so proud, was shown to advantage by the three-quarter-length lavender overdress that had been perfectly matched to the shoe roses peeping out from beneath the lace edge on her dress. Her brother, Mr. Darcy, had made a supposedly amusing remark about her being a seller of purple, which Lydia found to be a lacklustre compliment. She supposed that his lack of charm did not bother Lizzy, however, for her sister had laughed lightly and fluttered her fan at him.

"I gather, Miss Lydia," said the Beau, clearly deeming her ensemble adequate after peering at her through his quizzing glass, "that you are the sister who sent Mrs. Darcy that exquisite hat."

Lydia was a little distracted by the beautiful cut of Beau Brummell's coat.

"La! Was it the one with the lace roses? I said it should suit you well, did I not, Lizzy? I am so very rarely wrong. Mr. Brummell, I vow that your coat is as near to perfection as I have ever seen."

Elizabeth was a little scandalised by this forwardness, and her eyes widened, but the Beau was pleased to be amused by this young lady who so clearly understood Good Taste. She spoke so earnestly that it was made evident to him that she was focused as much on the cut of his cloth as on his person. He smiled. Beau Brummell had an unusually charming smile which he used to great effect.

Lydia blinked.

"I wonder if you are permitted to dance, Miss Lydia?" he said gently. "I should very much like to speak with you about those delightful lace roses."

"No, not here, alas!" she said, wistfully looking at the dancers. The beautiful Mrs. Bingley was leading the set with her husband, attracting nearly as much attention as the unexpected presence of Mr. Brummell. "Mr. Darcy says that I must wait until I am older, though I am permitted to stay until supper."

"In which case, Miss Lydia, I shall take it upon myself to reserve a dance with you in a year or so when you have your season. I would wager," he added with a knowing smile, "that you will enjoy it immensely."

The next morning, the Darcys sat with their guests for a belated breakfast. Lydia, still behaving very well, had contrived to arrive in time for Mr. Darcy to seat his tired-looking wife.

"I do hope, Lydia dearest, that you will not do anything foolish," said Elizabeth eventually, after her second cup of tea.

"So do I, Lizzy!" replied Lydia irrepressibly. "But what did you have in mind that I should not do?"

"It would not be wise to fall in love with Mr. Brummell," advised her elder sister.

Lydia opened her eyes very wide. "Well no, of course not; I want to speak to him about fashion. Love? Why, he is quite Old!"

Mr. Darcy set down his coffee cup.

Her voice quivering slightly, Elizabeth paused before answering.

"He is only a year or so ahead of Fitzwilliam, Lydia."

"Well, yes, which just proves it, does it not?" said the youngest Miss Bennet, entirely unaware that her brother was rapidly on his way to taking insult. "I do not have any designs on Mr. Brummell, Lizzy. He is quite safe from me."

"I was rather more concerned that you should be safe from him, my dear, but if you say that you are in no danger I am quite content."

Lydia laughed. "He is a very good judge of what is beautiful, you know. As I was not to dance, speaking with him of the dreadful errors of judgment some of your guests made was as entertaining a time as I could have had. We had a jolly game of it between us. We are quite decided that Miss Bingley ought to have left off the second plume on her headdress, for apart from that she acquitted herself quite well."

Mr. Darcy's lips tightened and Elizabeth intervened.

"How glad I was to have the support of my family at my very first ball! I should not have enjoyed it half so much if at least some of my sisters had not been there. Fitzwilliam, might you take me to the park after we have finished? I did not go out at all yesterday morning and you are still *quite* my favourite escort."

Her husband, aware of Elizabeth's intent, permitted the diversion and drily replied that he was relieved that three months of marriage had not caused her to tire of him.

"Oh no!" said Mrs. Darcy, sending him an impertinent smile and then a tender look, "not yet, my love, *not yet*."

UNDERCURRENTS

Miss Catherine Bennet of Longbourn was of a shyer disposition than her sister Lydia. She had often watched, with a kind of awed fascination, how her younger sister seemed to make friends with so little effort. Lydia appeared to have been born with a self-confidence that was entirely foreign to Kitty, who, when reaching fourteen, had felt entirely crushed by her own awkwardness. Before this, the difference between them had not been so very evident except that Lydia generally led the two of them into some sort of mischief. It had been a delightful childhood, really – long days of being permitted to entertain themselves however they wished so long as they did not get underfoot. Very often, Lydia would befriend boys of their own age and Kitty was naturally included in those friendships – for some reason the youngest Miss Bennet was a great deal more entertained by playing with the Goulding or Lucas boys than with their more delicate sisters. Until her daughters reached a certain age, Mrs. Bennet was content to turn a blind eye, knowing full well that the suitors of marriageable ladies often came from the playmates of their youth.

Young Master Goulding, when Kitty had turned eleven years old, had felt that her education was entirely lacking and so had quietly – while Lydia had been playing boules with his brother – taught her how to plant a facer with great effectiveness. She caught on quickly and in one lengthy lesson had mastered the basic mechanics. By the time an afternoon had passed, the pair of them sported very fine sets of colourful bruises up each arm, Kitty having cravenly squealed at the suggestion that they actually aim for each other's noses. She was pronounced to be a jolly good sport by the lad, and kept to herself the unladylike knowledge for whenever it might prove useful.

Alas, at fourteen, no such opportunity had occurred, and by the time Lydia had overtopped her by several inches, leaving her quite the shortest member of the family, Kitty began to feel so self-conscious in her burgeoning femininity that she could do little more than curtsey politely to William Goulding for several months, avoiding him whenever possible. She wondered, when she looked back on her girlhood, if he remembered teaching her to throw a punch one sunny afternoon at Haye Park.

It had not taken her long to find great comfort in imitation. What Lydia did with such ease, Kitty copied assiduously. Eventually, she discovered that her younger sister's shadow was not so hard a place to be in company, but was increasingly uncomfortable at home of an evening, when all she wanted to be was Kitty rather than an extension of Lydia.

When Kitty was seventeen, the Bennet fortunes underwent drastic improvement. Not only did Mary unexpectedly secure the future of Longbourn by marrying Mr. Collins, but Jane, the very next year, married Mr. Bingley, and Elizabeth, outshining them all, wed Mr. Darcy of Pemberley shortly thereafter.

Kitty was invited to London before Lydia, on account of her seniority, and the long-wished-for London season, earned by nearly six months of decorous behaviour, was hers to be enjoyed.

Except that she did not. Without Lydia there to distract young men, Kitty found balls and parties not nearly so wonderful as Mama had promised that she would. Where Lydia took joy in making new acquaintances, never once fearing that she should be disliked, Kitty fretted her way through each and every introduction, greatly fearing the censure of her new acquaintances. She endured as best she could the schedule that had been set for her, and could honestly say that whilst she did not disgrace herself, neither did she precisely shine amongst the refined elegance of the ton.

Unexpectedly, the promise of respite came for her halfway through the season when Elizabeth knocked on her chamber door one morning and entered.

If Elizabeth Bennet had been a pretty, lively girl with a ready wit, Elizabeth Darcy was a creature of beauty, glowing with happiness and possessed of a delightful talent for repartee that had rapidly brought her great popularity as both hostess and guest. Marriage suited Lizzy; however severe her husband had seemed, under Elizabeth's laughing and affectionate gaze he softened considerably – even Miss Darcy, who had previously allowed no fault to be attributed to her brother, declared that he was not so daunting a man as he once had been.

"Kitty, are you still abed?" smiled Elizabeth. "I cannot scold you for it; last night's ball finished monstrously late, did it not? Fitzwilliam assures me that Harding had to undress me while I was half asleep!"

Kitty stretched and agreed. The maid had drawn back the drapes, and dappled sunlight shone in onto the rose-coloured counterpane. "It was a very grand ball though, Lizzy. I cannot help but think Lydia would have enjoyed it tremendously and likely would have danced every dance."

"Very likely. Lydia has the knack of getting dance partners, but we must not forget that you had many charming partners yourself, Kitty."

"Oh, I suppose not. I think some of them were a little too charming, so smooth spoken that I could hardly be expected to believe half of the pretty compliments they paid. Mr. Colchester was so very rehearsed that I felt dreadfully awkward. I am afraid it showed, Lizzy."

"My wise little sister! I cannot praise such discernment enough. Some men, dearest, are altogether too smooth spoken – one cannot but suspect that it is the result of long practice. You do right not to be too trusting. Of course, that does not mean that the compliments paid to you are undeserved, does it?"

Kitty made a moue of discomfort. "I...I do not exactly sparkle, though, Lizzy. I cannot truly relax, feeling as though everyone is staring at me to criticize the countrified nobody. I do not...I do not think that I should like to live in London all the time."

Mrs. Darcy looked offended. "I beg your pardon, Kitty? You are a Bennet of Longbourn, my dear, hardly a blacksmith's daughter, and without wishing to boast, your connections are excellent."

Kitty smiled at her sister's attempt at pomposity. "Oh, do stop it, Lizzy – such talking doesn't become you at all."

"Shall you be very unhappy to leave for Pemberley next week, Kitty? Instead of remaining for the whole season, I mean. Fitzwilliam wants to take me into the country for...that is, we have reason to believe that you may become an aunt again by the end of the year. "

"Lizzy!" shrieked her sister, now wide awake. "A baby – how absolutely splendid! I should love to see Pemberley – when may we leave?"

Elizabeth laughed. "Not until next Friday, I fear. We simply must attend Lady Patterson's rout party on Thursday. She was Fitzwilliam's Mama's oldest friend, you know; it would not do to offend her."

"Oh, Lizzy, I can endure any number of parties knowing that the end is in sight. Thank you."

Lizzy frowned. "Well, I am sorry that you have found it so dreadful an ordeal. Perhaps you might even enjoy this last week now that your reprieve has been granted. I shall tell Fitzwilliam that Friday will be a delightful day to travel."

For Kitty, the unlooked-for consequence of the imminent removal to Pemberley was that she entirely forgot her awkwardness, so focused as she was on seeing her sister's grand home and not having to endure any more stilted conversations.

Mr. Osmond-Price, who was the least intimidating young man that she had met in London, approached her that evening at Madam Joubert's ball and begged the favour of a dance. Mrs. Darcy gave a pitying nod to his stammered request and watched as the pair of them made their way to the dance floor.

"A-are you enjoying the evening thus f-far, M-Miss Bennet?" asked the poor young man, having been cursed with an impediment of speech since his youth. Kitty felt sufficiently sorry for him, for he must feel quite ten times as awkward as she, that she forgot a measure of her shyness and attempted to put him at his ease.

"Ye-es, but my sister has told me that we are to remove to Pemberley next week, which I think I will enjoy even more. There are ever so many people in London, aren't there?"

Mr. Osmond-Price bowed in his turn and made the first steps of the dance. He danced well, with a good sense of time and a natural grace.

"I a-am s-sorry that you w-will be l-leaving us, M-miss Bennet; shall you n-not r-return?"

Kitty made her curtsey and followed the pattern of the dance. She did like to dance – it was the easiest part of a ball for her. Each person moved in the manner that was already laid out in front of them. All she was required to do was remember the steps and enjoy the exercise.

"I do not think we plan to, no. My younger sister Lydia will come to town next season, I believe. She will enjoy it tremendously."

"A-and wh-where w-will you go?"

Kitty made a turn, surprised. "I had not given it much thought. I suppose I will go to Pemberley with Mr. Darcy and my sister and then go home to Hertfordshire. It will be much more comfortable for me, to be in a more familiar company. Do you like London, sir?"

Mr. Osmond-Price raised his sandy-coloured brows and looked at her. "D-do you kn-know, M-miss Bennet, n-nobody has e-ever a-asked me that b-before." He considered his answer while leading her down the dance. "I-I do n-not think I do. M-my home is in N-Norfolk, you know. I...I have b-been w-wishing to m-make improvements to it but M-mama said that I should find a w-wife in town first."

"I have not ever been to Norfolk. Where is it?" asked Kitty, not having paid the least heed to her atlas as a girl.

Mr. Osmond-Price did not seem to mind. He was a young man, no more than twenty-three, and rather liked to impart his knowledge. So few people had the patience to listen to him try to get his words out, and the others tended to doubt that his mind was perfectly sound. Little Miss Bennet did not seem to feel that impatience, nor did she look at him with any disgust. He rather suspected that she was taking a kind pity on him but did not find it offensive in her. Her dark hair was piled high on her head and her eyes rested on him attentively as he briefly outlined the geography of his home county.

Fletchley Grange was a fine old house, he told her. The stone in Norfolk was a light colour and when the sunshine fell upon it, the Grange never looked so delightful. A river ran through the grounds and he liked to row his boat on it when he had the time.

Kitty smiled, imagining it. "I have not ever been on a boat. It sounds delightful."

Mr. Osmond-Price found himself grinning enthusiastically at her, and once the dance was over, led her back to her sister while haltingly telling her of the many mishaps one might have on a river. Having rarely enjoyed a dance so much as the one with her, he summoned up the courage to ask Mrs. Darcy if he might call on Miss Bennet in the morning and take her out for a drive in the park.

Mrs. Darcy politely responded, "You are of course very welcome to call on us, Mr. Osmond-Price. Tomorrow is our morning at home so it would be no inconvenience. Mr. Darcy will wish to be consulted as to the drive, but I daresay he will agree if Miss Bennet may take her maid." She threw Kitty a surprised look, seeing how her sister blushed but did not look alarmed at the prospect of this poor young man calling on her.

"I will...I mean...I shall see you tomorrow, Mr. Osmond-Price," said Kitty, shy again now that they were under observation. "I will ask Mr. Darcy to show me where Norfolk is on a map, I think."

Mr. Osmond-Price went away after that, quite enraptured with her and flattered by such interest.

The next morning at the fashionable hour, Kitty and Mr. Osmond-Price set off in his carriage for a drive around the park. Her maid sat up on the box with the groom and did not trouble them. Kitty smiled at the young man, who was perfectly ready to be encouraged.

"Does your mother remain in Norfolk, sir?" she asked after they had struggled their way through opening preliminaries.

"Y-yes, m-my father, he does n-not have good health; the a-air in London does n-not a-at a-all s-suit him."

"Oh," said Kitty, unsure what to say next.

Feeling quite masterful, Mr. Osmond-Price rescued her. "He does n-not m-mind s-so much, I do n-not think. He prefers it. M-mama holds a great m-many parties; they do n-not s-suffer for loneliness."

It was a successful outing. The pair of them rapidly found that they were quite at ease in each other's company. Kitty was glad that he did not attempt to pay flowery compliments, and Mr. Osmond-Price was equally glad that she did not seem to expect it. He told her quite bluntly, at the end of the drive, that he thought her a "c-capital girl," and Miss Bennet had looked so pleased that, judging by the brightness of her smile, he might have compared her to a summer's day or something equally poetic.

He called on her the next day, and the day after that, and by the time Wednesday had come he was in a fair way to being very much in love with her. She seemed to like him very much, and appeared so sweetly delighted to see him that he forgot his bothersome stammer and for the first time felt like any other young man in a room. If Miss Bennet did not mind that he did not talk as other young men did, well, neither did he. If she thought him pleasant company, he was very glad of it.

He wrote to his mother that evening, declaring his intentions towards the young woman. Her fortune might be negligible, but he was well enough able to provide for a wife regardless of it, and her connections were clearly excellent. The Darcys were a very well established family, after all. Doubtless Mrs. Osmond-Price would be content to know that her only son was making a good effort to bring home a wife by the end of the season.

The next day, with Mr. Darcy's blessing, Catherine and her maid were taken by Mr. Osmond-Price to the Thames to see the boats. He had some idea of asking Mr. Darcy's permission to pay his addresses to her once they returned to Darcy House, but rather thought he had better see one last time if she appeared willing before he made a fool of himself.

Alas, as they were strolling along, a pair of young bucks happened to overhear Mr. Osmond-Price stammering to his pretty companion about how a rudder worked. Seeing an apparently clueless young man as an opportunity for sport, they called out to catch his attention. One of them loudly declared that such a pretty little miss ought not to be in company with a man who could not even spit his words out, and the other, laughing loudly, called Mr. Osmond-Price the most dreadful name that Kitty had ever heard.

Very rapidly the situation got out of hand. Mr. Osmond-Price attempted to escort Miss Bennet away from such "vulgar p-persons" but the men followed them. One of them, in quite the brightest yellow trousers that Kitty had ever seen, compared poor Mr. Osmond-Price to something quite unpardonable and pushed him hard on the shoulder.

Aghast at this unprovoked attack, Kitty stepped forward.

"How dare you! You are...you are mannerless and unfeeling brutes and I wish you would go away. If *I* do not mind hearing him talk of rudders and oars and such, who are *you* to object to me hearing it. Go away, I say!"

The man, not liking to be given a dressing down by a female, approached very close and loomed threateningly over her. Mr. Osmond-Price, quite red with anger and shame, lashed out at him and knocked him over with tolerable science. Naturally, the second fellow, who sported a ridiculous pair of tinted gloves and whose corsets groaned as he intervened, threw the second punch. Caught by surprise, Mr. Osmond-Price fell to the ground.

Seeing Mr. Osmond-Price quite outnumbered and no one else around within calling distance, Kitty saw little option but to even the odds.

In fairness to her suitor, he had given a very good account of himself, but he could not fight the other two from the ground. Seeing one aim a kick at him, Kitty shouted in outrage. Furious beyond anything she had ever felt, Kitty rounded on the man in the yellow trousers, drew back her arm, and dealt him a well-aimed blow to the eye. Quite caught off balance by the lady, the man fell over his own feet in trying to put some distance between them, and landed with a heavy thud.

Kitty's maid, by this time, had begun screaming in hysterics and drawn the attention of other onlookers. Mr. Osmond-Price rose rapidly from the ground and dispatched the other foolish fop very efficiently. The two men departed from the scene with swollen and bleeding noses, and Kitty watched them go with blazing eyes.

"M-miss Bennet?" said a very shaken Thomas Osmond-Price. "I-I ought to return y-you home."

The anger in her eyes faded and Kitty sniffed once before she inevitably began to cry. They returned to Darcy House in miserable silence, and Kitty watched with slumped shoulders as Mr. Osmond-Price, *her* Mr. Osmond-Price, made his way into Mr. Darcy's study.

Elizabeth, having soothed the hysterical maid, came to find her sister. A sisterly arm slid about Kitty's shoulders and she was pressed in close to Lizzy.

"I could not entirely make it out, dearest, but Briggs seemed to think you had struck a man down. She is a very silly creature, I fear."

Kitty gave a wail and groped for her handkerchief. "Oh, Lizzy, those two *dreadful* men came and said such things to poor Mr. Osmond-Price and pushed him and so I told them they must *stop* and then Mr. Osmond-Price defended me and...and yes, I punched one of them when he was pushed to the ground and although *he* won't want anything to do with me now, I am not in the least bit sorry I did, for I *cannot* see that I should have done anything else."

Quite shocked, Elizabeth gasped, "Do you mean to tell me that you did knock him down, Kitty? I cannot even imagine it."

An icy voice from the doorway spoke. "I am glad to hear it, madam. I do not think that a gently bred lady such as yourself *ought* to be able to imagine such things. Miss Bennet, I should like to see you in my study immediately, if you please."

Kitty gulped and then sniffed again. Elizabeth pressed her own clean handkerchief into her sister's hand and sent her furious husband a pleading glance.

"Fitzwilliam...."

"Not now, Elizabeth."

Poor miserable Kitty trudged into the study. Mr. Darcy shut the door behind him with an ominous click and held a chair out for her before seating himself behind the desk.

"I cannot think, sister, that you can have any explanation that will sufficiently excuse such behaviour as I have been hearing of this morning."

Kitty fixed her eyes on her toes and would not look up. She thought that she would rather be facing anybody's wrath but his. Her mother would have screeched at her, her father would have derided her, but this frigid, *polite* accusation was entirely dreadful. He made her feel that she had been in the wrong, that no woman of breeding ought to even think of forming a fist, let alone landing it neatly in a man's eye. She had little option but to go into inconsolable hysterics and whip herself up into such a state that Mr. Darcy eventually admitted that there was little purpose in exhausting his limited patience by prolonging the interview.

He rose from his desk and crossed to the door. Opening it a fraction, he requested that the servant outside summon Mrs. Darcy.

Upon her sister's entering the study and throwing a deeply reproachful look at her husband, Kitty cast herself into Elizabeth's arms and sobbed yet harder.

"Hush now, Kitty, I am here; I will amend all. Calm yourself, dearest. I am certain that Fitzwilliam did not intend to upset you so."

"*I* upset her?!" interjected a now irritated Mr. Darcy. "Thank you for assuming my innocence, madam."

"Well, what *am* I to think, Fitzwilliam, when she is so very unhappy after being in here with you for only a few minutes?"

Kitty gulped and, with an effort, ceased her wailing.

Lizzy spoke soothingly and stroked her hair gently. "It is well now, Kitty; it cannot be so very bad after all, can it?"

Kitty coughed and could not speak.

"It certainly *can* be so bad as all that, Mrs. Darcy. Your sister punched a gentleman in the face in a public park. It is beyond anything I have ever heard of. I do not care to think what damage this may do to Georgiana next year if it gets out. I knew that your parents had permitted her to run wild, my love, but…."

Mr. Darcy was not permitted to finish uttering his ill-judged words, for the two women, arms about each other, raised their heads in unison and looked at him with such burning anger that he was brought to understand that they had taken grave offence. Never had they looked so alike to him as in that moment.

Like any sensible man, he realised his danger and trod carefully. "I apologise. That was not what I wished to discuss. I wish to understand, Catherine, how such events as Mr. Osmond-Price has related to me could possibly have come to pass. I should like to hear an explanation, please."

With an icy anger that Elizabeth thought quite marvellous, Kitty responded with some disdain. "You have already declared that there cannot *be* an explanation, Mr. Darcy. I cannot, therefore, see any purpose in wasting my breath by providing you with one."

To her satisfaction, Mr. Darcy looked very surprised. It was hardly astonishing that he should be so – she had always been so meek and shy around him since coming to stay as Mrs. Darcy's guest, so very afraid of making some dreadful misstep and being sent home in disgrace. Well. Now she had made a dreadful misstep, and she found that she did not care what he thought of her or her upbringing.

Elizabeth, her eyes burning with anger, turned and spoke softly to her sister. "Will you tell me, dearest? I cannot think that anything but the direst provocation could have caused you to act so – and I can presently perfectly comprehend a wish to hit a man, my love, but – oh, *do* tell me, Kitty!"

Nobly, Catherine swallowed her injured pride and nodded. "Very well, Lizzy. I will tell *you*. Since you have asked me so *reasonably* and have not *assumed* that I must be entirely at fault without even having *asked* me."

Mr. Darcy sent her a level look.

"Two horrid men approached us, entirely uninvited, and said the...the vilest thing to Mr. Osmond- Price – I do not wish to repeat it but they knocked him down and he had not done a thing to deserve it and...oh, Lizzy, I couldn't *bear* it and so I tried to stop it. William Goulding showed me *how* when we were children and I have not ever needed the knowledge until today. I know it is not at all ladylike but I would do it again – yes! I should do it a *hundred* times more if it meant that he should not have to face such awful injustice alone ever again."

With such an impassioned speech she retreated once more into Elizabeth's arms and buried her head in her sister's shoulder.

Elizabeth held her close. "I see. Well then. I do not hold with violence, dearest, but I can quite see that you felt utterly helpless when Mr. Osmond-Price was so shabbily treated. I *daresay* I might feel the same if Fitzwilliam were set upon for something he could not help."

"Yes, that is it exactly, Lizzy, and now...I know he will never wish to speak to me again because he will think I am wild and dreadful just like Mr. Darcy does."

Mr. Darcy grimaced. "I beg your pardon, Catherine. I ought not to have spoken so. It was wrong of me." His mouth twisted once more when she looked at him in astonishment. "Yes, I *am* capable of apologising when I have erred – as your sister is well aware. Mr. Osmond-Price is to call tomorrow. I shall see what may be done to smooth things over. Elizabeth, I should like your opinion on what is best to be done, if you would share it."

His irate wife almost smiled at such wisdom, but, still annoyed, contented herself with a frigid nod.

"I think it might be best if *I* speak with Mr. Osmond-Price on the morrow, Fitzwilliam. Fret not, Kitty; I do believe that I am quite capable of arranging this to everybody's satisfaction."

Mr. Osmond-Price, the next morning, was shown into a very pretty yellow sitting room and invited to take tea with the charming Mrs. Darcy.

"Mr. Osmond-Price!" exclaimed she, with great warmth. "How happy I am that you have called. I most particularly wished to thank you for your heroic defence of my sister yesterday afternoon. To be set upon in such a fashion must have been most distressing, I do not think Kitty has ever been so upset."

He bowed politely to the lady and accepted the tea she offered him.

"I a-am m-most s-sorry t-to hear that M-Miss Bennet has been m-made unhappy," he said, cautiously. His wounded vanity at having been thrashed in front of the woman he loved was soothed a little by the knowledge that Mrs. Darcy seemed to think him quite the hero.

"Oh, you must not mind her so much, Mr. Osmond-Price. Kitty feels loyalty very keenly. I think she would not have been *so* unhappy if it had been anybody else," said Mrs. Darcy, delicately. Mr. Osmond-Price was not yet old enough to have learnt to hide his feelings very well. He looked up at her then with such obvious hope that she felt quite sorry for him. It was well that Kitty would take the poor boy off the marriage market, for anybody might take advantage of such a youth. Fortunately, she had his best interests in mind. "I shall be frank with you, Mr. Osmond-Price. My dear sister is not so concerned with the inevitable loss of her reputation as with the loss of your own good opinion."

"M-Mrs. Darcy!" exclaimed the boy, "can y-you b-be serious? I w-was c-certain that s-she m-must think me such a w-weak fellow for having been s-so easily t-taken by s-surprise and kn-knocked d-down. I think M-Miss Bennet is...is...is s-splendid. M-my own M-mama, y-you kn-know, once shot a m-man for injuring m-my father. Do y-you think she w-would take me, M-madam? Even a-as I a-am?"

Mrs. Darcy smiled gently. "Mr. Osmond-Price, I think a gentleman who can show such a splendid account of himself as Kitty reports can find sufficient courage to speak to the lady himself. Suffice it to say that if you will rescue my poor sister's reputation, I shall myself be quite indebted to you."

Mr. Osmond-Price grinned, his sleepless, agonised night immediately forgotten with the possibility of showing heroism. "W-would y-you permit m-me to speak t-to her now, M-madam? I w-would not l-like her to r-remain d-distressed if I c-can help."

"That is very gentlemanly of you indeed, sir. She is in the study with my husband at present. Shall you come in with me?"

Mr. Osmond-Price, feeling quite significantly more cheerful, nodded. He liked Mrs. Darcy, he decided – she had a delightful way of making him forget his speech impediment, not unlike her sister.

Kitty was sat in the study poring over a map of England. She had not been able to locate the particular part of Norfolk in which Mr. Osmond-Price lived, but had found a river that he had once mentioned to her and was tracing it down to the sea with a delicate fingertip. Mr. Darcy, who was at the desk, looked up when his wife entered and looked a little less tense when she nodded to him.

"Mr. Osmond-Price has kindly called on us this morning, my dear."

Mr. Darcy rose and returned his visitor's bow with a slight one of his own. "Good morning, sir; you are very welcome."

Miss Bennet had looked up from the map when they entered, and was blushing when she stood to curtsey. She had very carefully chosen a dress of pale green that morning; the gentle shade suited her colouring very well, and she had draped a light wrap about herself to complement it.

Mr. Osmond-Price thought that there was never a finer girl. He did not mind that she was not a great beauty – he had quite decided that he definitely preferred pretty girls to intimidatingly beautiful ones; and he did not mind that she was uncomfortable in society – he was not fond of it himself.

"M-Mr. D-Darcy, s-sir. I sh-should like t-to have a few m-moments w-with M-Miss Bennet, w-with your permission."

Mr. Darcy, not a cruel man by nature, nodded and guided his wife toward the door. "You may have ten minutes, Mr. Osmond-Price. Catherine, should you wish for us we will be in the music room. Mrs. Darcy has been promising to play something soothing to me."

They exited and the door clicked shut behind them. Kitty looked decidedly embarrassed.

"I a-am s-sorry that you have been unhappy, M-Miss Bennet. Y-your s-sister s-said that y-you thought I might have thought l-less of you b-because y-you hit that f-fellow." Kitty nodded miserably, and, moved to compassion, feeling more manly than he had ever done before, Thomas Osmond-Price heroically approached nearer to her. He saw the map book turned to the Norfolk Broads and it gave him the courage to smile at her.

"W-well, I think y-you a-are s-splendid."

Kitty, who had been staring at her hands, looked up in shock.

"You mean you don't *mind*?" said she, unable to comprehend it.

"W-well, do y-you m-mind that the cad kn-knocked m-me down s-so e-easily?"

"I mind very much that he hit you at all, Mr. Osmond-Price. I do not think I have ever been so angry. When you leapt up and hit him again, I wanted to cheer, I was so pleased. I am sorry – I know that hitting young men is not in the least ladylike. My brother read me a very stern lecture on the subject."

"I w-want to m-marry y-you, M-miss Bennet. Y-you a-are quite the finest girl in the country; I a-am s-sure of it. M-mama t-told me that I sh-should find a-a w-wife this s-season and s-she w-will b-be e-enchanted that I have."

Kitty shook her head. "She won't be if she gets wind of my having hit a man in a public park, sir." Then, belatedly realising what he had said before that, "Oh! Truly? I should like to be your wife more than anything, sir but...but I d-do not know that I should."

Mr. Osmond-Price grimaced. "N-Now don't y-you s-start s-stammering, K-Kitty – one of us is q-quite e-enough. The only reason y-you sh-should s-say 'no' is if you s-simply can't b-bear to hear m-my wretched v-voice t-taking an age to s-say what it is I m-mean. I can understand if y-you do feel that w-way, though I sh-shall b-be sorry for it all m-my life."

Kitty shook her head emphatically. "That is not it – no! I am worried that I have no dowry and worried that I am not very easy in large crowds and...and even though I think you are quite the nicest man I have ever met and I should be so very sorry not to see you any more, I don't want to serve you an ill turn by saying 'yes' when it is not the best thing for you."

Mr. Osmond-Price, deeply impressed by this romantic self-sacrifice, rolled his eyes. "K-Kitty, don't b-be n-noble – it is m-my happiness t-too, y-you know."

"Oh," said she, clearly not having thought of this before. "I see what you mean. All right, then, *yes*. I should like to marry you, if you please. Will you take me on a rowing boat on the river?"

He grinned, relieved. "Y-yes, I'll take y-you b-boating, K-Kitty. W-we'll have ourselves a-a s-splendid outing. Y-you don't m-mind b-being c-called K-Kitty all y-your life?" he added, taking her hand in his.

She brought his hand up to her lips and kissed it quickly. "I can't think of a nicer thing than to forevermore be K-Kitty. I was...I was so ready to leave London but a few days ago and now I am an engaged lady. I do not want to leave you."

She found herself being led by the hand to the door of the study. Strains of music could plainly be heard when they reached the hall; clearly, Mrs. Darcy had changed her mind about playing soothing music to her husband and was enthusiastically hammering away at the pianoforte. Kitty did not recognise the composer.

They paused before opening the music room door, and Mr. Osmond-Price took her other hand in his.

"W-we sh-shall b-be a-allowed to write to each other wh-while y-you a-are a-away. I w-will w-wait till then t-to s-say what is in m-my heart. Y-you should have...y-you deserve t-to b-be told w-without having to w-wait for m-me to m-manage to g-get the w-words out."

Kitty shook her head at this. "I will read whatever it is you write, Mr. Osmond Price, but I do think you ought to know...."

Much to his frustration, she was quite unable to tell him just then because the door opened and out stepped Miss Darcy. She jumped a little to see the two of them standing there, and laughed at their surprise.

"I beg your pardon – I was not expecting anyone to be so close to the door. Were you about to enter? Elizabeth is inclined toward rousing music today; Beethoven is her composer of choice."

"Yes," said Kitty, "we will go in now."

A week later Kitty was sat with a small pile of letters beside her in the rose garden at Pemberley. Lizzy had laughed merrily when the footman was obliged to bring in two silver trays worth of correspondence for the four of them at the breakfast table. As soon as possible, Kitty had escaped to read her correspondence.

The first was from Lydia.

"Mama is in transports of delight over your engagement, Kitty. You will let me come and be a bridesmaid at your wedding, will you

not? I have the most charming new shawl that needs a very special first outing and I do think I had better save it for a special occasion.

I was not able to speak to Mr. Osmond-Price (such a very grand name to be sure!) for Papa said that he needed to go straight back to London and I was in Meryton at the time. Mama says that she thought him very gentlemanly, though, and has even now gone to Lucas Lodge to crow to Lady Lucas."

Kitty opened the next with a smile. Papa was not at all fond of writing, much like Lydia, and so to have received letters from the two of them must be counted a great triumph.

"I have given my consent to your young man, Kitty. Your sister wrote to me assuring me that you were in favour of the match and I am altogether fairly pleased with him, for all that Norfolk is such a great distance away. What joy you have bestowed upon your mother, my dear – she will be forever talking of her dearest Mrs. Darcy, Mrs. Collins, Mrs. Bingley, and now her dear Mrs. Osmond-Price. Let us hope Lydia distinguishes herself similarly when she heads off to London next season or she will be quite put in the shade."

The last letter, which she read once she had quickly skimmed over the congratulatory epistles from Jane and from Maria Lucas, was from Mr. Osmond-Price himself. Kitty opened it with trembling hands.

"My dear Kitty,

Does it surprise you – to see your name written in my hand, doubtless hearing, in your ears, it being read by my own voice and for it not to be a stumbling, slow thing but very smooth?

I have long relished the freedom that my pen gives me to communicate unhindered what is in my head. I hope that once we are married we will not often be apart, but I will enjoy the excuse to write so to you, telling you quickly all the things that I wish I could say with all the eloquence of an orator.

I think you know already, without being told, that I love you. One day, perhaps after we are wed, I will stutter it in your ear and perhaps you will care for me enough not to laugh, and so I shall repeat it often thereafter.

I owe Mrs. Darcy a great debt; when I came to call that last morning, I was utterly convinced that you would want nothing more to do with me. I had been told, Kitty, for so long, that every young lady desired a man who could speak well, look well, and fight well. I failed on the first, barely scraped by on the second, and to my humiliation had fumbled on the last in front of you.

I am sorry for it, not that I think those two men by the river were justified in any way, but rather that it was not the first time others have taken exception to my impediment, nor do I think it will be the last.

Your brother, who gave me a very rare trimming for having endangered you, had the right of it there. If you are in my company much, you will encounter such people and their prejudices. It matters not to them that it is only my tongue that is defective – to them I must be a simpleton through and through. I am afraid, my dearest Kitty, that you will often have your sense of justice offended if you are to be my wife.

What Mr. Darcy could not, for some reason, comprehend, is that your defence of me did not trouble me in the least. I thought you – I still think you – the most splendid, capital girl I have ever encountered. I think that many women would have merely gone off into hysterics (like your maid, whom I do hope you will not bring to Norfolk), which is not in the least bit helpful. I will tell you one day the story of how my Papa met my Mama and she wielded a gun in his defence and he proposed the very next day. Perhaps he will like to tell it though. He has always said how pleasant a thing it is to not fee alone, to know that there is a woman beside him who will forever be on his side as well as by it.

I understand it now. I never did before.

Yours &c."

THE GRANGE

The newly wed Mr. and Mrs. Thomas Osmond-Price arrived in Norfolk after nearly five days of travel. The bride was assisted down from the carriage, and with great interest surveyed her new home. Her husband, pleased to have reached Fletchley Grange whilst the light was still good, looked with pride upon his ancestral home and asked Kitty if it was not the prettiest great house she had ever laid eyes on.

His new wife, entirely willing to oblige him, admired the sprawling building. To the left of the drive was a wide, meandering river, not so close so as to cause any difficulty with flooding, Thomas had assured her, but providing an interesting view, and Kitty longed to go with her husband on the promised boating expedition as soon as might be arranged.

"Thomas, it is all that you said it is. May we...might you take me on a boat – oh, not tonight, but perhaps tomorrow?"

The Grange itself was a handsome building, built of a light stone, and with the sunlight shining on it as it was now, was entirely charming. It was not Pemberley – nothing was, but Kitty, who had been rather intimidated by Elizabeth's enormous responsibility, found that she infinitely preferred this. Larger by far than Longbourn, but not so big as to feel empty, it was on first impression exactly what she would have wished for herself.

"Here a-are m-my M-mother a-and Father, K-Kitty."

Sure enough, the large oak door to the house had swung open, and a plump, red-haired woman burst through it, followed at a more leisurely pace by a man who had a very strong resemblance to Thomas, albeit with a little more grey at the temples and a good deal more weight about his face.

The elder Mrs. Osmond-Price was a comfortable-looking woman, a little taller than Kitty and more heavily built. She was dressed simply in a light printed muslin, with her red curls largely covered by a little cap pinned neatly over the crown. Her round face beamed at the two of them and she came forward with her arms stretched out.

"Ehh now, let me see the daughter my Tommy has brought me home. Well, aren't you darling, then? You'll be worn to the bone by that journey – Derbyshire to Norfolk! You'll have a nice hot supper and then bed. We shall have you right as rain in the morning." Kitty, who had been preparing to drop a tired but respectful curtsey to her new Mama-in-law, was stopped from doing so by the lady wrapping her arms about her and planting a kiss on her cheek. Catherine looked to Thomas who was smiling fondly at the kindly whirlwind who had by now moved on to kiss him.

"W-we w-were a-an extra d-day on the roads, M-Mama. K-Kitty does n-not c-care for e-excessive s-speed."

Mrs. Osmond-Price laughed. It was a deep laugh for a female, but mellow and very pleasing to the ear. "Well, that is something good then! I have been telling this boy of mine for many a year that he must not travel at such reckless speeds about the country, else he will end his days breaking his Mama's heart."

Mr. Osmond-Price had by now come near and took Kitty's hand. He bowed over it with a gentle courtesy.

"You are very welcome, my dear. Your new Mama has been looking out for your carriage since daybreak. Had we more hills in Norfolk, I am sure she would have sought higher ground so as to get a better view of the roads."

He had a pleasant, slow voice. It was deep and a little gravelly. Mr. Osmond-Price spoke as though there was nothing in the world to hurry him along. Kitty smiled at him and pressed his hand as she curtseyed. After so warm a welcome, she forgot a little of her shyness and natural nervousness. These people loved Thomas and appeared entirely willing to love her too – it was a pleasant thing.

"Thank you, sir. I am glad to be out of the carriage, for all that it was very comfortable. I have not ever travelled half so much as I have this past year."

"Well, come in, my loves – how pleasant it is for me to now have a son and a daughter. I love the Grange in any season, but I like it best of all when it is full of people. I shall go out tomorrow and make sure that all the families about will come for a little party to meet you – won't that be merry? Tommy, my lad, do see your wife in. Kitty, Tommy will show you to your rooms. There is a lovely view of the river, and you may change and come down for a little food."

The young couple entered and Kitty found that all she saw of the principal rooms of the house as she passed them was very pleasing, if a little less modern than Longbourn. Her rooms were charming. The furniture, although heavier than was fashionable in London, was of good sturdy quality and very comfortable. Thomas held her hand up the stairs and paused to introduce her to a passing maid.

"This is m-my w-wife, G-Gibson. Sh-she w-will like a b-bath d-drawn up this evening, I sh-should think. G-Gibson w-will s-see to it, K-Kitty."

Kitty marvelled at how informal the Grange was. There was little possibility of her parents using Christian names in front of a servant. She did not necessarily see his address as wrong – merely different. She suspected that if there were indeed fewer rules to remember in her new home, she would be less fearful of misstepping and so would feel comfortable much sooner.

Mrs. Osmond-Price was pouring hot tea from a large pot when the pair entered the sitting room. She looked up and smiled warmly when she saw them.

"I must learn how you like your tea, Kitty. Oh, you will not mind if I call you Kitty, shall you? Thomas called you so in his letters and so I feel as though you cannot be anything else. How dreadful it would be if we were to live in the same house and be always addressing each other as though we were strangers rather than kin."

Kitty, eager to please and be pleased, sipped the hot tea that had been handed to her.

"Yes, that is just right, Mrs. Osm– Oh! Shall I call you 'Mama'?"

She was not the sort of girl to ordinarily suggest such a forward thing, but there was something so kindly about Thomas's mother that she found her usual shyness did not hamper her as it usually did. Thomas smiled at her as his mother replied warmly, "Indeed you shall, my lass; indeed you shall. I can quite see that we shall get on splendidly! You must call Mr. Osmond-Price 'Papa' too. He might look like a stern fellow behind that bushy beard of his, but you mustn't think he is – I'd not have married him if he were."

Kitty looked at Mr. Osmond-Price, who was sat in a large wing chair beside the fire, and observed that he did not look in the least bit offended by his wife's words; rather, he nodded in agreement, a slow merriment lurking in his eyes.

"Aye, that certainly is true, Kitty. I practically had to beg her to wed me, and me the catch of the county."

Thomas, a very similar gleam of amusement in his eyes, spoke. "M-Mama w-was a t-tavern m-maid before P-Papa w-wed her."

Kitty blinked, extremely shocked and entirely unsure of what to say. She had realised that her new Mama did not speak with the same air of gentility as her own Mama, but she had supposed her to be a gentlewoman.

"Oh!" she said, after a fortifying sip of tea, "is that where you met?"

"Tell the s-story, P-Papa," urged his son.

"It's more your mother's tale than mine, lad," protested Mr. Osmond-Price.

The lady shook her head, "Aye, but I'll readily own that you are the tale teller of the two of us. You'd better tell it, my dear; you know our Tommy won't be content until you do."

Mr. Osmond-Price stroked his beard thoughtfully. "Well then, Martha, you'll hand me my pipe then, please. You'll not mind, Kitty? It aids the concentration, this old pipe of mine."

Kitty, intrigued, shook her head and replied that she did not mind in the least.

The man leant forward in his chair to receive his clay pipe from his wife, and settled himself back again comfortably after a nod of thanks to his lady. A look was exchanged between them, fond and affectionate, as though they would both of them enjoy a brief visit to the past, even at their age.

Mr. Osmond-Price looked at the expectant faces turned toward him and barked a laugh. "Oh, very well! You all remind me of my hounds a-beggin' for table scraps!"

He lipped at his pipe once or twice and patted his pockets. He extracted a flat tin box and opened it up with great unhurried care before he began his tale.

"Martha here was a tavern keeper's daughter – not one of these dreadful flea-infested places, of course, but a *respectable* establishment. The tavern keeper, Robert O'Brien, had come over from Ireland with a good amount of knowledge in how to brew a good ale and how to keep his customers cheerful. He bought a fine plot of land and built a pretty inn on it – nothing overly fancy but neat enough in its own way. There was no tavern in that particular Norfolk village at the time, but it was not far off from a river and as a result the custom and the town both grew. He wed a Norfolk lass, which made him very popular with the locals, you understand, and soon Mrs. O'Brien brought Martha into the world. She was the only wee one they were blessed with, but *how* they were blessed! She had a knack for thinking on her feet – still does in fact – which was invaluable in such an occupation as she grew up in.

"But I stray from my tale; you must nudge me, darling, if I meander too often. If you would just wait a moment while I refill my pipe I will gather my thoughts and get back on track. There now, look at you all staring at me as though you had none of you heard this before! Our Kitty has some more excuse than my Martha or Tommy, I think."

His fingers, deft with long practice, refilled the old pipe, and he sat back comfortably in his chair.

"Well now, it was a dark night – a new moon, in fact, and so cloudy that not even the stars could shed any light on the road. The tavern was a blaze of warm light and a welcome sight to me. Your mother, with her pretty red curls, was a sight more welcome than anything. Ha! I might as well have handed my purse over there and then, had I not, Mrs. Osmond-Price? For she wrangled her way into it soon enough, with the offer of a fine hearty meal and a pint of her father's best brew.

"I was travelling home to the Grange, having had business in Cambridge, and I had been kept far later than I intended, but I put my business out of my head and settled down to enjoy an excellent meal. Martha had made the steak pie herself and 'twas a good one – you'll be wanting to sample some of that, little Kitty, the next time your mother-in-law decides I deserve a treat. Aye, she laughs at me, daughter, but I promise you that she has a kind heart and so will not make you wait too long."

Kitty looked to her husband. He winked at her and drew her closer to him on the seat beside him. She leant against him a little and smiled happily. It was delightful to be sat thus.

"I don't know how it was that a band of thieves had known I had a bag of money. Perhaps they accurately guessed the weight of it when I brought it out to pay your Mama, but at any rate, they made a target of me that night. I had paid no mind to them, Martha being such a comely lass, but I was later on told that they had sat in the corner furthest from the fire, drinking steadily and weighing up the room. Martha was serving them and, after she had wiped her tears of farewell away once I had left – yes, my dear, I do jest; you hadn't even registered the weary old man passing through, had you? – she overheard them speaking of me and gathered their plan was to attack me on the road.

"She's a kind-hearted thing, always was, I think, and it didn't trouble her that I was nothing to her. As far as Martha was concerned, right was right and wrong was wrong, and she'd not stand idly by while a man was robbed of his money and left for dead on the blackest night that ever there was. She gathered two of her father's guns and a quantity of rope concealed within a thick heavy cloak, and made her way to the river. Ingenious moment that, I always think it, every time I retell it; the road would've been too slow, but a boat – well now, the river below the inn wended its way to a bridge. By road it was a couple of miles but the river made it half the distance. She had heard the thieves talk of overtaking me at this bridge, knowing that I must pass over it on my way home, and so she set herself up there first.

"She arrived at the bridge, mooring her boat out of sight beneath it, just as one of the gang had pulled me from my horse and had given me a clout over the head with a cudgel – an unpleasant feeling, I promise you. She, quite enraged at the injustice, made aim with a gun and caught the fellow nicely in the neck. I still feel relieved that the wretches carried sufficient flaming torches to provide her with enough light for accuracy."

Martha, as lost as the rest of them in the tale, let out a soft snort. "Never held with kicking a man when he's down; still don't. I was in such a rage to see that villainy that I had fired before I even knew I meant to. Makes my very hands shake to think of it, looking back."

"Well now, there was such a furor! First, it was assumed that I, although unconscious, had made the shot, then accusations of treachery were bandied about, and then eventually they assumed that the woods were haunted. Your Mama, I can tell you, took great advantage of this! Aided by the echo of the stone bridge, she made a low, eerie-sounding laugh. I woke up to the hearing of it and I may tell you that the very hairs on my neck stood up in fear.

"That dreadful, echoing sound must have frightened them properly, for they left me where I was and mounted their horses as fast as they could get on them! I do not know if guilty consciences had much to do with it, but I have always thought that they must have been a superstitious bunch of men, to be so affected."

"Ha!" laughed Mrs. Osmond-Price. "You were white as a sheet yourself, sir – don't be pretending that you weren't vastly relieved to see me when I crawled out from beneath that bridge!"

Her husband looked a little abashed, but did not respond to her good-natured taunt and continued with his tale. "Regardless, your Mama had been hard at work as they were arguing about the shot, and quietly tied a rope low across the road between two trees. As they all went off as fast as they could, they fell foul of it and all but one of them came off their steeds. The one left mounted did not turn to look back, but the others that lived stayed nice and unconscious while my Martha tied them to trees ready for the law to find them on the morrow. She even remembered to relieve them of the gold that they owed her Papa, not having paid their shot before they left to set upon me. An resourceful woman, I tell you.

"I fainted again after that and she loaded me up on my horse. How, I will never know, for I was not a small fellow even then, and then she led us back to the tavern. She was hailed as a heroine by the other patrons, wiping out a plaguey gang of thieves in one night as she did. You may imagine, my dear, how I felt when I saw the darling girl in the morning and heard the whole story.

"'Martha O'Brien,' I said, 'you have done me such a splendid service in guarding my life tonight that I will not set foot out of this door until you promise me that you will always do so.'

"Bless the lass, she did not know what I was about, and, laughing at me, told me that should I run into any more trouble to just send her a message and she'd come right away. It took her some persuading to realise that I wanted her for a wife and even then she thought my blow to the head was responsible.

"Eventually she realised I was in earnest, and, feeling some responsibility for my life having saved it, she gave me her promise. Best decision I have ever made, for all it caused an uproar. No one can resist my Martha for long and she soon won 'em all over, didn't you, lass?"

By the time her father-in-law had drawn his tale to a close, Kitty was entirely enrapt in the story. She sat for a moment in silent appreciation before giving a little sigh and whispering, "Oh, it sounds so...so *romantic*! I...Mama, you were terribly, *terribly* brave."

Mrs. Osmond-Price blushed a little and shook her head. "I'd not change it for the world, for all I thought that dear man over there was having fun at my expense when he asked me. I've not regretted it, not for a single day."

"You s-see w-what I m-mean, K-Kitty – y-you rescued m-me every bit a-as m-much as M-Mama did P-Papa. I didn't write of it, s-sir, b-but I have b-brought a-another husband-rescuing heroine t-to the Grange."

Mrs. Osmond-Price looked in some surprise at the diminutive girl whose head was fondly resting on her son's shoulder. "A husband-rescuing heroine? What on earth do you mean, Tommy?"

"Oh, m-merely that K-Kitty s-saved m-me in London. K-Kitty, y-you tell it – n-no one w-wants to w-wait for m-me t-to s-spit it out."

"Oh, Thomas," said Kitty sincerely, "I will if you want me to, but why do you not tell it? I for one am quite content to listen to you, even if takes the rest of the evening."

Martha Osmond-Price was not a woman who often found herself near tears, but as she heard her new daughter-in-law speak so to her boy, her eyes grew damp, and her voice was dry and hoarse when she added her agreement. She met her husband's eyes and knew from the sheen on them that he was thinking precisely the same as she was. Their boy, their darling boy who had forever struggled to speak, had made a wise choice of bride. Tommy had thought all his life that he would need a bride who could speak for him when he could not, but in Kitty he had found something infinitely better – she was a woman who would listen to him.

The fire crackled in the hearth as the family took yet another cup of tea. Mr. Osmond-Price's pipe scented the air, and every now and then, as Thomas spoke in halting words, his Mama would pass around a plate of biscuits. Outside, darkness fell and Kitty rose to light the lamps, feeling entirely comfortable doing so without being invited. Outside, the river flowed and occasionally a tawny owl hooted from its treetop nest. The river would be explored tomorrow; a lazy day might be spent floating along the water; perhaps the newlyweds would take a picnic to enjoy on a grassy bank in the sunshine.

When Thomas finished his tale, his Mama was rosy with laughter. "I can send you off tomorrow on a boat without a worry that any mischief will come to you, Tommy. Little Kitty will see you safe!"

And so she did.

INTACT

Her ladyship sat quite alone that evening. She had rung the bell and given orders that dinner should be served, more out of long-standing habit than any desire for sustenance. In truth, she had not desired food for many a week now, but with an iron will had eaten each evening regardless.

It was important for the servants to see the continuation at Rosings Park, even after its heiress had been taken to the churchyard.

Anne was gone. It was a black, empty thing, this grief – she had not been prepared for it, for all her words to the contrary. Her strength had been sorely tested at the last, beside her daughter's bedside, watching her sleep more and more until that last wakeful quarter of an hour which she had cherished and loathed in equal measure. She had lingered on longer than the doctor had thought she might and was ready to cease the struggle.

"I am quite prepared, Mama," said Anne, in a breathless, reedy voice, "I shall go on ahead to heaven, where I will be stronger than I have ever been and you will meet me there too – one day. Only, do hold my hand,

Mama; I confess to feeling a little frightened of stepping through this last door."

Catherine leaned forward in her chair and clasped Anne's thin hand in her own. It was all so wrong, that she should be sat here marvelling at how frail she was; surely their situations ought to be reversed.

"Anne..." her voice cracked and she cleared her throat before trying again, "Anne, if I could come with you, if I could take this journey for you, I would."

Anne's eyelashes fluttered against her white face. "I know it, Mother; you are so fearless – I have wished...wished that I were more like you."

Lady Catherine de Bourgh grimaced. She did not explain to her child that she had been terrified beyond anything she had ever experienced since, a few weeks previously, the doctor had gravely pronounced the likelihood of Miss de Bourgh's imminent demise. If her daughter thought her unafraid and strong, well, so she would be.

"I will hold your hand for as long as you wish me to, Anne. I shan't leave you."

There was little else spoken between them, and for all the world it was as though the doctor were not five feet away and the maids were not waiting in readiness for orders, either side of the door. For Catherine, it was as though the two of them were entirely alone in this circle of light about the bed. She thought back to Anne's birth, in a similar room in this great house. She had commanded then, in no uncertain tones, that she desired to be left quite alone before the doctor commenced prodding her, and for that little time, it was just her and her unborn child in a similar circle of light.

Catherine sat forward in her chair and twined her fingers through Anne's. She had been present for the birth and so would she be for the death. Her back ached, but she ignored it and continued to hold on even as she watched her child's chest rise and fall with increasing difficulty. It would not be long now; she had seen enough of death in her life to know this for certain. She had sat with her Mama when she passed, she and her sister bearing each other company as their father, uncaring, had ridden out to his club. She had sat beside her sister's bedside too, when George Darcy had summoned her by express. Childbed fever was responsible for that premature departure, and all that Annie had been worried about was that her sister Cathy should watch over her son and daughter. A ridiculous request, really – surely Annie had known she need not have even asked.

Well, she had. She had done her duty by them and now they were doing theirs by her. Belowstairs, Fitzwilliam waited with his wife and sister. He was newly married but that had not made a jot of difference to him. He was ready and waiting, he said, to relieve her burden in whatever way he could. He would attend Anne's funeral; he would see her casket lowered and ensure that all was done properly. She could trust him for that, however little she liked to be absent from anything that concerned her own girl.

Then it was over. The last breath, a last little cry – so reminiscent of that first, weak little wail she had made when she entered the world – and she was gone. The doctor approached the bed from the other side and felt for a pulse. It was unnecessary and she told him so.

Catherine released the hand and stood stiffly. She did not shed a tear. She would not yet – she could wait, for a little while, until she was in her own room and she had dismissed her maid.

"Mrs. Jenkinson, you will be so kind as to keep vigil for Miss de Bourgh. My nephew will relieve you in an hour or so."

Yes, she could trust him for that; he was so like his mother.

She stood, entirely numb, for a moment and looked at her daughter. She reached forward and gently closed the lids of Anne's grey eyes before drawing up the sheet to cover her. She paused, fearing to appear foolish, and then drew up the quilted coverlet anyway. Anne had so disliked feeling cold.

Darcy rose from his chair as soon as she entered the drawing room. "I sent Elizabeth and Georgiana to bed, Aunt Catherine. They were not pleased with me but I thought it best. Shall I give orders for their maids to awaken them?"

Catherine sighed. "There is little point, nephew. She is gone now. We are but a few hours off the morning. Mrs. Jenkinson will keep vigil until daybreak, and then, if you will do so afterwards until seven o'clock, I am sure they will take their turn after they have recovered themselves."

"Will you try to rest, Aunt?" he asked in his deep, quiet voice. He was such a reliable boy, always had been.

She shook her head. "I do not think I could presently. I shall seek occupation instead. I will write down my wishes as regards the funeral. You will see them carried out, will you not, Fitzwilliam?"

"You know that I will," replied he, steadily.

Later that evening, after she had exhausted, dry-eyed, every avenue of distraction that she could find, she entered her own private sitting room and firmly dismissed her maid.

Slowly, she dropped to her knees beside her bed and closed her eyes.

"The Lord giveth and the Lord taketh away."

She shattered then, entirely taken over by heartache. When she arose from her knees some unknown time later, she was almost surprised to find that she was still intact. Her heart felt sore and bruised but it still beat. Her eyes stung and her throat was painfully tight but breath still came when she inhaled. Her hands, feet, and arms obeyed her when she made to move to the door. It did not feel as though she ought to be whole and alive and yet she was.

Lady Catherine made her way downstairs via a less-used staircase and stopped short when she heard her name mentioned from a side room.

"Made of iron *she* is, Lady Catherine; don't suppose she'll *feel* a thing, not in the way most people would at their daughter lying dead."

Shock made her pause and then a sweet voice surprised her even more.

"You will tell me your name, please."

"Mrs. Darcy! Beg pardon, madam, I didn't see you...."

"That is plain. Your name."

"P-Parker, Mrs. Darcy."

"Parker. You will go upstairs to your quarters and collect your belongings. The housekeeper will see that you are paid for any work you have done in this house thus far."

"You're *dismissing* me?" The servant sounded incredulous, even a little challenging.

"Certainly I am dismissing you." Mrs. Darcy's voice did not lose its sweetness, but there was a decided edge of authority there now.

"You can't!" Parker clearly did not know when to admit defeat. Lady Catherine stood still and listened. If she wasn't very much mistaken, Mrs. Darcy was about to prove her mettle.

A soft, irritated sigh was heard to escape Mrs. Darcy.

"You doubt my authority?"

"Yes!"

Had it been any other day, Lady Catherine might have twitched an eyebrow at that, but instead she continued to listen, her expression blank. She thought vaguely that she ought to be able to summon some sort of indignation.

"Her ladyship is currently occupied with far more important affairs than a slanderous servant girl. Mr. Darcy is used to acting in his aunt's stead when necessary, and, as his wife, I will assist *him* with the mundane necessities of running the house until such time as Lady Catherine wishes to resume command. I repeat, Parker, you will collect your things and leave. I do not tolerate gossiping housemaids. In fact, should you put me to the trouble of importuning my husband in this matter, I shouldn't wonder if your honesty were called into question as well as your loyalty. It would be dreadful, would it not, if you found it difficult to find other work on account of untruths being whispered abroad. These things have such a dreadful habit of sticking."

Silence fell.

"Yes, Mrs. Darcy."

Lady Catherine withdrew into an alcove as footsteps approached the door and the girl, Parker, passed by.

"And what is your name?" asked Mrs. Darcy.

"Benson, ma'am." This spoken very respectfully.

"Benson. I will permit you to remain on this staff with only a warning. You ought not to have tolerated such vile slander against your mistress. In the future, I hope you will remember to show your loyalty by renouncing such talk as soon as it begins. You will complete the cleaning of this room on your own."

"Yes. Thank you, Mrs. Darcy."

"Very well. I was informed that the housekeeper was here. Where is she now?"

"She left a few minutes before you come in, madam."

"I am not accustomed to chasing servants about a house. I had better summon her to me. Continue, Benson."

Catherine turned on her heel and disappeared down the corridor before her niece could exit the room. She need have no concerns about the ability of this young woman to manage a large house; she had the knack, it seemed, of managing servants.

Twenty minutes later, Mrs. Darcy entered the music room and nodded to her new sister, who was seated at the pianoforte. Lady Catherine was sat beside her nephew and looked up at her entrance.

"Your housekeeper was most helpful, your ladyship; there will be sufficient rooms ready if the earl arrives accompanied. It is to be hoped that he does not delay many hours – I fear the weather may turn."

"My housekeeper was likely petrified that she would be turned off should she disoblige you, Mrs. Darcy."

She did not quite smile at her new niece's look of surprise, but the faintest prickle of amusement disrupted the thick melancholy that enveloped her.

"Upon my word, Lady Catherine! Your communications at Rosings must be the envy of the army intelligence committee."

Darcy sent a questioning look to his wife.

"I dismissed one of Lady Catherine's servants not twenty minutes ago, Fitzwilliam. I apologize, your ladyship, if I have acted as you would not have wished."

The older woman waved this off. "You acted, Mrs. Darcy, precisely as I would have done in the same circumstances. Let us say no more about it, save that my nephew did well to listen to my advice to wed you in April. Now, you have the full list of my wishes for the morrow, Fitzwilliam – there is little use in delay, after all. Let it be done with, and quickly. I will relieve Mrs. Jenkinson for an hour or so now. Mrs. Darcy will ring for tea when it is required."

With that, she briskly quit the room.

Elizabeth looked at her husband. "The burial is for tomorrow then?"

He nodded. "Yes. Come here, my dear, and sit beside me." Elizabeth did so, with a quick glance to Georgiana, who was engaged in playing a stately melody. "Fitzwilliam," she said in a low voice, "I have been concerned about something – Lady Catherine will not be obliged to leave Rosings, will she? I mean now that Sir Lewis's heiress…."

Her husband's brow, which had creased at her question, cleared and he shook his head, "No. The de Bourghs are cousins to the Fitzwilliam family. My uncle Matlock officially inherits Rosings but he will not hear of her leaving. She also has the use of a house in Bath for the duration of her life, not that she uses it often. Perhaps she will now – the society would be good for her when she comes out of mourning."

"I suppose she has remained at Rosings for so long on account of Anne's fragility. Well, I am glad that your aunt will not be homeless at least. I could not help but ask – Longbourn is entailed, you know."

"Yes," he said quietly. "I know."

'Oh, of course. Papa would have mentioned it, I suppose."

He reached up and smoothed away an errant strand of his wife's hair. "You need not worry about such things now, Elizabeth."

Lizzy smiled at him and rested a light hand on his shoulder. "I cannot abandon all of my lifetime concerns, Fitzwilliam, merely because I have entered into wedded bliss! It will take at least another year of happiness for me to be mended to your satisfaction."

To her surprise, he did not smile at her teasing; instead he took her hand and kissed it. "It has hardly been the blissful start for you that I would have wished – merely a week in London and then here to deal with this."

"I would hardly be anywhere else, my love; did I not promise to be your wife? I am entirely content to be wherever you are, even if it is here in such an unhappy situation. Besides, I have been useful, have I not?"

"Yes, yes. My aunt would not say lightly that she is glad of you, which she did before you came in. I hope you did not have to endure any insolence from the servant you sent off."

"I do wish you will tell me how she can have found out so soon, Mr. Darcy!"

"Her ladyship did not enlighten me as to that, Mrs. Darcy."

"Oh, I do so dislike mysteries that I am not a party to. No, my love, I sent the girl off for some very unpleasant talk regarding her mistress. It was a small thing, though I confess I might not have interfered if I had not felt so angry. No, no, you must not frown at me so soon after our wedding, Fitzwilliam – it quite takes away from your delightfully proportioned features. There! A smile is far better; I must reward you by ringing for the tea tray to be brought. Georgiana, shall you abandon Mr. Dowland for tea?"

A day later, and tea was sent for once again. It grew cold in the pot. Lady Catherine was borne company by Mrs. Darcy, Mrs. Collins, and her niece Georgiana, as Anne was taken, one final time, from her home. There would be no more partings – this was the last.

The ladies said nothing, merely sat in silence as the mother became lost in her own memories. Catherine did not merely dwell on her daughter but also on her husband, her sister, and her own mother. It seemed as though she could not keep her thoughts from straying to her other losses. Mama's had been a hard parting; she had been young and resilient though, and of course, Annie had been with her then – it was not so lonely. Then Sir Lewis had died but a few years later, and although she would not have said that she was in love with him, she had regretted that his life had been so short – perhaps she could have loved him if he had lived. It was occupation that helped her in those lonely years; the business of taking hold of the management of Rosings with an iron fist had been a pleasant and satisfying distraction if truth be told. She had rather enjoyed her widowhood, in a way; there was so much more freedom for a widow of means than even for an earl's daughter with a husband. Anne had kept her distracted too, of course; although she was not a maternal sort of woman, there was something rather pleasing at looking at one's child and seeing familiar features or gestures that she knew had been hers first.

She really ought not be feeling so shaken as she was. She had known, for years now, that Anne had not been strong, and the doctor had given sufficient warning. Still, it had been a shock when she finally admitted to herself that she would outlive her girl.

Catherine sat, lonely and yet not alone, and felt every one of her fifty-three years; she wondered when her turn would come, when the Lord would determine that she had lived quite long enough. At that moment, she looked forward to it. Perhaps tomorrow, or the next day, she would stiffen her spine again and declare roundly that she was not weak – she was a Fitzwilliam and she would go on living.

Time passed, and the men returned. There was a trace of mud on the Reverend Collins's boots. She noticed it and felt quite sick. It had been that same soil, that same dirt, that her Anne had just been committed to. She swallowed, staring at it, and swallowed again.

Matlock came close, and, taking her hand, he said quietly so that no one else could hear, "It is done, Cathy. You cared for her well."

Blindly, she clutched at her brother's hand and nodded once, abruptly. She looked to Darcy through blurred eyes.

"Did you lay the rosemary?"

He bowed, ever grave and ever serious, "Yes, Aunt."

"Well then. Well."

She sent them all off three days later. There was no real need, after all, for them to be there and she wished, for a time at least, to be as alone physically as she was in her heart – she would accustom herself. Perhaps she would set herself a marker, a time in which she could indulge in her grief before putting off her blacks and rejoining the world. Mrs. Darcy paused before her as she took her leave.

"I will write to you, your ladyship, once we are returned to Pemberley. You promised me once that I might have your advice and I shall certainly seek it."

In the vague recesses of her mind, Catherine rather suspected that she was being managed, oh, kindly, but managed nonetheless. She looked at her favourite nephew's wife, slim and pretty and full of promise, and nodded graciously. Of course such a young thing would need advice – it showed great intelligence that she should seek it from such an experienced quarter.

"You must not fail to do so, Mrs. Darcy – I have some idea of visiting you, perhaps when there is promise of a child." Yes, assuredly, she would determine the end of her public mourning for her girl when her niece produced an heir for Pemberley.

One corner of her mouth lifted in almost amusement when Elizabeth turned scarlet and hesitated before replying. "Lady Catherine, you need no invitation to Pemberley. When you are ready to leave Rosings we will expect you."

She would not readily admit it, but such kind sentiments pleased her. Clearly, she was becoming one of those sentimental old ladies whom she herself viewed with such contempt.

Lady Catherine de Bourgh watched the carriage depart and turned back into the house. She stood for several long minutes in the hallway, staring at the clock. The footmen closed the front door, blotting out the wintry grey light. She ought to call for the lamps and candles to be lit but she would not.

With steady, measured footsteps, her heels meeting the tiled floor with a firm clicking step, she made her way to the drawing room. She would dine properly this evening, however little she felt hunger. She would call for candles then.

Inside her head, she counted, as she sat, each empty room in the house. This drawing room, the Indian salon, the great dining room, the family dining room, the library – they stretched on in her mind's eye, large and grand and entirely empty.

She might as well have been calculating the size of the void within her own heart.

TACTLESS

Chapter One

The year that Miss Lydia Bennet of Longbourn had been long wishing for had finally arrived. There would be no more impatient waiting and no more long wasted hours of dreaming and planning. She was to receive what she had long been promised and she desired greatly – her very own season in London.

Mrs. Darcy had six months ago given birth to a son at Pemberley, and great was the rejoicing throughout Derbyshire where the Darcy family was so well respected. Lady Catherine de Bourgh herself had been present for the birth, having for some time been desperately seeking a use for herself of some sort since the death of her own daughter Anne. She descended upon the house with the express determination that she would not go away until she had ensured that Mrs. Darcy had been safely delivered of her child. Seeing that her ladyship's officious interference was born out of the desire that Elizabeth not feel the grief of losing a child, Lizzy herself gave her entrance to the birthing chamber.

Lydia, who had been invited to spend the summer at Pemberley so that she might become more familiar with Miss Darcy (who was to also make her curtsey that year), had been greatly bewildered by all the fuss that was made by everyone over the small matter of producing an heir to the estate, and wondered for the first time if the Bennet ladies had been so very unfortunate in their circumstances given their father lacking a son. Certainly, Mama had wailed about it constantly – so constantly, in fact, that Lydia had largely ignored her whenever Mrs. Bennet began talking on the subject.

Lydia was not by any means a great thinker and so did not permit it to bother her for long, but when invited to admire young Master Darcy the next day, she dutifully peeped at him and congratulated her tired-looking sister. Having learned a good deal in the last two years, she did not remark that the baby seemed to her to be an ugly red-faced little thing. Elizabeth herself seemed so enraptured by him that Miss Bennet thought it would be unkind to point out his defects when his Mama was so happy.

Fortunately for Lydia, she was able, with absolute sincerity, to admire the set of rubies that Mr. Darcy presented to his wife to mark the occasion. She laughingly helped Lizzy to put them on, even as her sister was propped up in bed in her nightgown, and for a moment it seemed just like old times, except that not one of the Bennet girls had ever possessed such jewels.

Lydia stood back to survey the effect. "I do think that there could not be a better colour on you, Lizzy. Mr. Darcy, I applaud your choice."

Having grown a little more used to his youngest sister-in-law and how seriously she took matters of style, Mr. Darcy bowed, and, looking at his wife, said that his choice had indeed been excellent. He was rewarded with a very sweet, if weary, smile from his wife, which went unheeded by Lydia.

"You should not wear them with that nightgown though, Lizzy; it is too white – you need a yellower cream to set them off properly."

Elizabeth, clearly having become altogether too used to such luxuries as she enjoyed, had already lost interest in the subject and was once again staring at her son, softly stroking his bald head. Lydia hoped that his baldness was soon amended – it did not suit her to be in possession of an ugly nephew. It was most unfair on the poor boy, given that both his parents were so well favoured. Even Mary had produced a delightfully pretty little girl, all blonde hair and large brown eyes by the time Lydia had set eyes on her neice on the first anniversary of her birth.

Lydia excused herself when Lizzy started to compare young Master Darcy with other members of her family. "He has the look of you, I think, Fitzwilliam – he is gazing at me so imperiously!"

Mr. Darcy, fortunately enough, did not appear to notice the insult, and smiled indulgently at Elizabeth.

"I must go and bestir Georgiana. She will almost certainly wish to come and see you, Lizzy; she was in such a fret last night when we heard you...well, never mind. I shall fetch her."

Lydia found that there was not a great deal to do at Pemberley. She was not very much like Elizabeth, who would contentedly walk for hours or read or play the pianoforte – Lydia had limited patience for any of that, and, having walked the gallery once or twice, admiring one or two of the dresses and shaking her head at the rest, she grew decidedly bored.

She found, therefore, that she was perfectly willing to borrow an old habit from Miss Darcy and go out riding with her when it was suggested. Lydia had learnt the rudiments of horse riding at Longbourn, of course – they all had, but only Jane had ever ridden for pleasure. Lydia improved a great deal over the weeks that she was in residence at Pemberley, and was rewarded with the realisation that if she was to ride in town she would require a riding habit of her very own, and set about thinking of the styles and shades that would suit her best. Although Miss Darcy clearly favoured severe black for riding, Lydia wanted to be a little different and spent much time in deep consideration of whether she ought to choose an emerald velvet or a sapphire.

The season commenced for the Darcys, after much excitement and a tedious journey, with an invitation to a ball given by the Earl and Countess of Warwickshire, an elderly couple who, having never had children, still came to London each year for the season and very much enjoyed themselves on the whole. Lord Warwick was hard of hearing by now, and his put-upon wife was obliged to shout very loudly if she wanted his attention. This was a rare occurrence, however, for although compatible in terms of their shared enjoyment of society, they had neither of them spoken more than a few civil words to each other every day for years now.

Lydia had chosen for herself a deceptively simple gown of white sprigged muslin, worn over a silk rose underskirt with a demi-train. She liked a slight train – the style suited her height, and also one was obliged to loop it up for dances, allowing onlookers to admire the pretty matching dancing slippers beneath.

Miss Darcy wore white silk with a strand of her late mother's pearls about her neck. She had looked to Lydia for her verdict on the ensemble, a summer in Miss Bennet's company having convinced her of her superior taste, and having received a nod (one could not accuse Lydia of being reticent in giving her opinion), had gone from looking petrified to merely very nervous.

Mrs. Darcy, it had to be admitted, was the very epitome of loveliness. She wore the most delightful cream silk gown, richly embroidered with gold flowers, and completed the whole with her ruby necklace. The dark gems sat against her skin, turning it to alabaster, and somehow her eyes seemed darker and more vivid in her face.

Lydia had done more than nod. "Lizzy! You look quite magnificent, not a bit like my sister. I could not have chosen better for you myself."

Mrs. Darcy was in a sparkling mood that evening. She laughed lightly and her earrings danced fetchingly in the candlelight. "I could hardly have spent sixteen years in your close society, Lydia, without having learned one or two things about how I ought to dress, could I? But Harding deserves the credit, I fear – she has quite outdone herself. Well, Mr. Darcy, am I quite tempting enough to dance with tonight, do you think, or shall I be confined to the wall? Your cousin has promised me a dance if you will not, and I daresay Mr. Bingley will take pity on me too."

Mr. Darcy leant down and murmured something in his wife's ear, causing her to blush and Lydia to frown.

"No! Oh dear, no! Lizzy, on no account must you get too warm or embarrassed tonight – it quite spoils the effect if your face turns the same colour as your necklace."

Miss Darcy let out a nervous laugh, and Elizabeth, more used to Lydia, rolled her eyes.

The ball was all that Lydia could have wished for. If she discounted her sister's ball, at which she had not been permitted to dance, it was her first real London society event and it lived up to every expectation.

The ballroom was quite enormous, and lavishly decorated, with a gilt ceiling and elaborate chandeliers. Lydia thought that she would forevermore compare every ballroom to this one, so pleased as she was by it.

She stood, as instructed, beside Miss Darcy, trying to contain her excitement. Miss Darcy was not so similarly afflicted.

"Oh, Miss Bennet, how can you look so brave? I am in a quake! What if no gentleman asks me to dance? What if one does and I forget my steps or say the wrong thing or worse still say nothing whatever? Oh dear."

Lydia looked her over and took pity on her. Lydia was a cheerful girl, and liked others around her to be as contented as she. If Miss Darcy was not likely to enjoy herself, she must be persuaded to – at least a little.

"You are Miss Darcy of Pemberley. I vow that once word gets around that you are out, you will be inundated – all you need do is pick whichever gentleman you like the best and make the others wildly jealous."

Amused, Mrs. Darcy interjected, "I do not think Georgiana will enjoy that quite so much as you would, Lydia. Georgiana, although the case was a little too bluntly put, my sister is quite correct. There is nothing whatsoever lacking in you – all that you must do is decide if you like any gentleman who courts your favour. If none of them are worthy, send them to your brother who will assure them of their and send them on their way. I am sure he will like to do that."

Mr. Darcy, who had been looking almost bored, smiled a little at this, for all he was pretending not to have been listening. Assumed deafness was his favoured technique for dealing with his wife's sister – it helped him gloss over her more shocking pronouncements and caused fewer quarrels with his wife.

"Mr. Darcy, Mrs. Darcy, Miss Darcy, and Miss Bennet!" called the servant, before they were greeted by the earl and his lady.

The countess presented a mere Mr. Warwick to the young ladies. He bowed with great finesse and requested a dance with Miss Darcy, if she would be so kind. Heaving a sigh of relief, Georgiana managed to accept without stuttering overmuch, and wrote down the first for him on her card.

Mr. Darcy did not look pleased, and Lydia at first assumed some misguided desire that his sister never grow up, but, overhearing the whisperings between her sister and brother-in-law, she learnt that Mr. Warwick, although seemingly eligible as he was the heir to an earldom, did not have a good reputation.

Lydia, privately watching him from across the room, thought that whatever people might say about him, it did not make him one jot less handsome.

She was, aesthetically speaking, correct. Lydia, after all, had an excellent grasp of beauty and Mr. Warwick was unusually well favoured. Dark hair brushed into careful disorder, a tall well-built frame, and regular well-proportioned features were to his credit. The straight black brows drew attention to very light green eyes. If any fault was to be found in that face, it would be in the too thin lips that looked as though they would form cruel words all too easily.

He was forgotten, as swiftly as he had been assessed; if he had had the bad taste and manners to ask Miss Darcy to dance and not include Lydia Bennet, then he was not worth thinking of. She looked about the room for anyone she knew and smiled winningly at her other brother-in-law, who waved and made his way through the crush to meet her.

Charles Bingley, convivial as ever, bowed deeply to his sisters-in-law and shook hands with Darcy.

"Bingley, I had not thought you had yet come to town yet – how do you do? Is Mrs. Bingley here?"

"Ah, yes; she is with Caroline at present, speaking with Mr. Pond."

"Nathaniel Pond?" asked Mr. Darcy, frowning again.

"No, his younger brother – Bertrand, I believe. He was some years below us at Cambridge."

To Lydia's delight, they were then rescued from such dullness by Mr. Brummell, who, having heard them announced, had slowly made his way over to them, as he had been forced to greet many acquaintances en route.

"Mr. Darcy, Mrs. Darcy, and Miss Bennet. Good evening."

They bowed, and Mr. Bingley, suitably impressed by Mr. Brummell, coughed behind his hand. Mrs. Darcy took the hint and introduced him. Sadly for Mr. Bingley, Mr. Brummell was not pleased with the careless tying of Bingley's cravat, and so bowed very coolly and almost immediately gave his attention to Miss Bennet.

"Miss Bennet, we meet again. Dare I hope that you might spare me a dance tonight? You were forbidden at the time of my last request, I recall."

Dimpling, Lydia opened her little dance card. "Mr. Brummell, you may have any dance you choose – I have not had a single request so far and I have been here for all of ten minutes. I was beginning to feel as though I should have to hide behind the curtains, lest anyone see me partnerless."

Mr. Brummell smiled. "That would have been a waste of a delightful gown to be so concealed, Miss Bennet. I shall write my name down for the first, if you do not object. I must have a word with Mrs. Drummond-

Burrell before the set is made up, and then I shall come and find you. Fret not, Miss Bennet – I said last time we met that you should enjoy yourself and I shall see that you do."

Lydia sighed happily, pretending blindness at her brother-in-law's severe expression. It was the best way, she had decided, to deal with Mr. Darcy – if she affected not to notice his disapproving countenance, she suffered far fewer arguments with her sister.

Many people stared at Mr. Brummell leading Miss Bennet to the floor; he danced but rarely and for him to deign to do so with a miss in her first season was a very great honour. Lydia, sensible of the kindness that had prompted him, smiled winningly at him and, after they had begun the first steps, looked about her.

"Oh dear," said she, "the elderly lady in the puce velvet."

Mr. Brummell, delighted to find that Miss Bennet was every bit as interesting as she had been the last time he saw her, looked as directed, and a spasm of pain crossed his features.

"The Dowager Duchess of Beauleigh. I have hinted once or twice but sadly even my influence will only go so far. It is quite her favourite colour – she wore it as a bride. It used to be even worse with her hair when it was still copper."

Lydia looked horrified. "No, Mr. Brummell, surely you do jest. Copper hair? With that shade? I am grateful to have been spared. Now it is your turn."

He, feeling quite ten years younger, glanced about him. "I have it – the fellow speaking to the Earl of Warwick. I do not know his name, nor shall I be troubling myself to find it out."

The gentleman in question was of an unfortunate form, being dreadfully narrow in the shoulder and his valet having persuaded him to pad out his jackets with wool. Alas for the nameless fool, the padding on the one shoulder was uneven, lending him a decidedly twisted silhouette.

Their game having got off to a splendid start, the two of them enjoyed their dance tremendously. Mr. Brummell was heard later that evening to praise Miss Bennet for having both excellent taste and being a delightful dance partner, and she very soon found herself as popular in London as she had ever been in Meryton.

The rest of the evening was a decided success. Mr. Brummell, having opened the ball with Miss Bennet, had ensured her popularity, as might have been his aim, and she was thereafter besieged with young men requesting introductions and desiring to dance with her. Lydia was a young lady of great energy when it came to dancing, and did not sit out a single dance. Between partners, she was returned very properly to her sister's side, but in truth they barely had time to exchange a word, so in demand as she was. She was taken down to supper by a Mr. Kentmire, whose family originated from Northumberland. He was handsome enough but far too quiet for her tastes; still he ensured that she could sit near Miss Darcy, who had sent her a beseeching look when they had entered the dining room, and between them they kept the conversation flowing well enough.

What Lydia could not help but notice was that Miss Darcy did not particularly favour Mr. Warwick for his attentions during the evening – she appeared decidedly uncomfortable after their dance and whilst she was too unsure of herself to avoid him obviously, to Lydia at least it was clear that she did not care for his well-practiced flirtation.

Miss Darcy was, however, entirely fascinated with Mr. Kentmire's descriptions of India. He was, Mrs. Darcy had discovered from the Earl of Matlock during the quadrille, a Nabob, quite enormously wealthy from his travels and now looking to settle down in England. Lydia did not think him so very interesting – she had little patience for people who forever spoke of things she had not seen. He was a gentleman of medium height with wavy sandy-coloured hair. His eyes were brown, his skin was tanned, and Miss Bennet quickly determined that, although pleasant enough to look at, there was nothing striking about him, neither in conversation nor in his face. She received a quelling look from her sister when she had murmured that although the cloth of his coat was of an excellent quality, it had clearly been bought with little thought to whether or not it suited him. Unsubdued by Mrs. Darcy's attempt at sternness, she added that the waistcoat had clearly been chosen at random and would have suited almost anyone in the room better than him, but if Miss Darcy could bear to look at it throughout their dance, then she would not gainsay her.

They returned, at a dreadfully late hour, to Darcy House, and with a very brief exchange to wish each other good night, tumbled into their respective beds. Lydia Bennet slept the sleep of youth, being so utterly content with her present lot in life that not a thing in the world could have persuaded her that she was not the most blessed girl in all of England.

Chapter Two

It became clear, as the weeks passed and they attended balls and parties nearly every night, that Mr. Brummell had been quite correct. Lydia did enjoy the season. She was tireless in her enthusiasm for shopping, for choosing a gown, and for dancing with admiring gentlemen. As had been expected, Miss Darcy had many suitors, her thirty thousand pounds and excellent family proving to be a very great lure to many men, second sons especially. Her most determined suitors were Lord Henry Sewell, who was the youngest son of the Duke of Oxford, Mr. Kentmire, who remained quietly resolute, and Mr. Warwick, who did not seem to notice that Miss Darcy was in a fair way to being in love with the badly dressed gentleman from India.

Lydia too had her fair share of success. She had never fretted that she might be cast into the shade by Miss Darcy's fortune and accomplishments, for she had managed to be very popular in Meryton in spite of having to compete with the incomparably lovely Jane and the delightfully amusing Elizabeth. In short, Lydia expected to be liked and so she was; she gave little thought to how she accomplished this, and sallied forth every evening confident that she would not lack partners.

Miss Darcy, being of a timid disposition, envied Lydia this heedless confidence. The two young ladies were perfectly friendly with each other but were unlikely to become the closest of companions. They rode out together and shopped together and, at Miss Darcy's request, were often seated near each other when dining out.

As a result of being constantly with Miss Darcy, Lydia found herself often thrown into company with that lady's suitors. This occasionally proved pleasant – Lord Henry, for example, delighted in asking for her opinions in matters of style. More often, however, Miss Darcy's admirers proved very irritating. Ordinarily, the gentlemen approaching the young ladies asked Lydia for a dance only after they had gained Miss Darcy's acceptance for a set. Sometimes she was glad of it, for it meant that she danced nearly every dance of an evening, which she was always pleased to do, but more often she wished that they would let her alone and permit her to keep her dance card free for some of her own admirers. Lydia was a popular girl and found herself in as much demand in London as ever she had been in Meryton. Sir Daniel James, Mr. Barnabas Winterbourne, and the honourable Mr. Frederick Sheldon all formed her own little court. She liked Mr. Winterbourne the best – he had recently sold out of the army, and entertained her with his descriptions of Spanish formal dress. She might, of course, have found such information from a book but she preferred to be told – it painted a picture more readily in her mind that way. Sir Daniel James was pleasant enough and by far the richest of her admirers; if he had not droned on so very much about his estate near Bath, she might have encouraged him a little more. Although Lydia was not given to thinking meanly of herself, she rather suspected Mr. Sheldon of merely amusing himself and alleviating his boredom by attempting to break her heart. That did not bother her especially, given that she felt herself in no danger from him – he was polite enough, if a little too practiced in his civilities.

Nonetheless, it irked her immensely that Mr. Warwick consistently abstained from the empty civilities of Miss Darcy's other suitors. She did not wish to dance with him, although she would have enjoyed dissuading him from wearing a particular yellow floral waistcoat again, but it pricked her pride that he did not ask. It was as though Miss Lydia Bennet was so far beneath his notice that she was invisible to him. He was polite enough to the Darcys but had scarcely spoken more than three direct sentences to Lydia throughout their whole acquaintance. Lydia did not aspire to be the embodiment of all virtue like dearest Jane, but if one thing riled her temper more than any other, it was being ignored. She took to imitating him in his greetings as a means of amusement. If the heir to the earldom of Warwick barely bowed to her, she responded by offering a miniscule curtsey in return. The private game kept the worst of her ire in check.

She, while dancing with Mr. Brummell (he was a fast friend by now), one evening requested that he give Mr. Warwick a setdown for having the dreadful taste to inflict such an ugly waistcoat on society, and was disappointed when he could not oblige her.

"I wish I could, Miss Bennet. You cannot imagine how often I have longed to, but he is such a volatile fellow. I am almost certain he would call me out, which is not a thing I would enjoy. Such dreadfully early hours!"

Lydia discovered that Mr. Warwick had fought many duels in his career as a wastrel (for by all accounts he was forever outspending his allowance in disreputable establishments), and once or twice the earl had been obliged to step in and deal with a family so that they did not kick up too great a fuss over a particularly unpleasant injury.

She had been very amused to discover, from Mr. Brummell himself, that a wager had been laid concerning the two of them, supposing that they would make a match of it. He had not been offended when she had rolled her eyes and wondered aloud what they could have been thinking of.

"I think you are very well, Mr. Brummell, and I have never once found a fault with you in terms of your apparel, but I am quite decided that I shall be a dreadfully expensive wife. If you find a man who is handsome and charming enough and is able to support a woman of very good taste, you must send him along to me. I do not even mind if he is untitled, you know."

Mr. Brummell laughed, thinking that she was as like-minded a female as he had ever encountered. He promised to do so, and handed her off to another of her admirers (who in truth would have admired anyone that Mr. Brummell endorsed) for the waltz.

Mr. Kentmire, heartened by Miss Darcy's shy encouragement, invited the Darcys and Miss Bennet on an expedition to a maze at Hampton Court one sunny week halfway through the season. The proposed outing was accepted very readily by Mrs. Darcy, who had an inkling as to where her sister-in-law's preference lay. Mr. Darcy seemed almost resigned to the fact that his sister might marry soon, and, at his wife's urging, attempted to make conversation with their host for the day. He found in Mr. Kentmire a sensible man, very shrewd in some respects but not driven by a passionate nature. Mr. Kentmire had decided that it was time he returned to England in order to look for a wife, and, his own father having married after the space of one London season, thought he could do little better than to follow his parent's example. He had thought of purchasing an estate soon, having the capital available and wishing to settle, but he was unsure as to which county he preferred. Mr. Darcy, at some gentle prompting from Elizabeth, had told him that he could do no better than Derbyshire, and that if he wished to explore the northern counties, he might do so from Pemberley in the summer if he chose. Lizzy had teased him at length on the subject of his bias and laughingly offered Hertfordshire as a very pleasant alternative if he did not care for dreadful winters.

"For I have lived in both counties, you know, Mr. Kentmire – my father's estate is near a town called Meryton – and I would even go so far as to defy my husband regarding the relative beauties of Derbyshire and Hertfordshire."

Mr. Darcy, with surprising charm, Lydia thought, delighted his wife by smoothly remarking that both he and his friend Bingley were quite enamoured of the Hertfordshire beauties. Perhaps he was not so severe after all, if he could turn so pretty a compliment readily enough.

Hampton Court had a very fine hedge maze, the like of which Lydia had never before seen. She grasped the point of the exercise very swiftly, and her competitive spirits aroused, she challenged Miss Darcy and Mr. Kentmire in a contest to the middle. Mrs. Darcy, not to Mr. Darcy's surprise, joined in with the fun and said that she and her husband should be waiting at the centre for five minutes at the very least before anyone else had solved the puzzle.

Thus, Miss Bennet set off through the entrance with much haste, before her brother-in-law could raise any objection. She made several turns at random, quite forgetting which way she had turned and passed a pleasant half hour darting between the hedges and eventually made her way to the centre of the maze, and, to her astonishment (for, after Mary, Lizzy was ordinarily the quickest to solve a puzzle) found that she had arrived first. She sat on a bench in the sunshine and waited for the others to arrive.

She raised her brows when Mr. Warwick strolled through the topiary archway. He hesitated when he saw her waiting on the little white seat and watching him guardedly.

He bowed infinitesimally, and Miss Bennet minutely inclined her head to him, disdaining to rise.

"Are you here with Miss Darcy, Miss Bennet?"

So he was aware of her name then. How gratifying – she would not have guessed it. He did not look at her as he spoke, his eyes on the arch.

Impishly, Lydia could not resist needling him. "Oh, I daresay she is quite lost by now with Mr. Kentmire."

He did not appear to be distraught by this information.

It crossed Lydia's mind to enquire as to the company he was with, but she did not like to pretend an interest she did not feel and so did not.

They remained in silence for some minutes until Lydia grew impatient with it. Mr. Warwick clearly found the flat greenery of the hedges more interesting than the lowly Miss Bennet. He really was a very rude man – she might not have thirty thousand pounds and be very well connected but she deserved more civility than he was currently offering. The problem was evidently not with her, given that nearly every other member of the society she had encountered had been very courteous to her, particularly when it was revealed that she was a favourite of Mr. Brummell.

What Mr. Warwick needed was a crushing setdown.

Miss Darcy came around the last corner then, on the arm of her most favoured suitor. Lydia enjoyed that. Mr. Warwick bowed, and Miss Darcy ceased her laughter and managed a confused dip in response. Mr. Kentmire retained the young lady's arm and made a half-bow in Mr. Warwick's vague direction.

The two men eyed each other, and Georgiana, very aware of the tension, looked about her for a means to avert any potential unpleasantness. Lydia felt a little sorry for her.

"I suppose Mrs. Darcy and your brother have gotten quite lost, Miss Darcy." she said lamely.

Georgiana gratefully agreed that the maze had indeed proved too much for her brother's famed sense of direction.

Mr. Kentmire, sensing an opportunity, said, "I am glad he is ordinarily very good at finding his way, for otherwise I shall not especially trust him to show me around Derbyshire when I visit you at Pemberley."

This apparently succeeded in annoying Mr. Warwick, for his black brows twitched together for a moment, and Lydia watched Mr. Kentmire attempt to stifle his grin with absolute delight. She decided then and there that Mr. Kentmire must marry Miss Darcy, if only to annoy the ungallant man with the pale eyes.

Mr. and Mrs. Darcy then came upon them.

"Oh, Mr. Darcy, look – we have been beaten to flinders. Tell me, who had the triumph of getting here first?"

Lydia rose from her seat and curtseyed in a grand manner while her elder sister looked on with sparkling eyes.

"Well done then, little sister. I have been telling Mr. Darcy that we ought to have cheated and bribed someone to tell us the key to the maze lest we be quite lost forever. Perhaps next time we will do so, if my husband can bear the dishonour of winning unfairly."

Mr. Warwick turned to Miss Bennet, "Did you do so, Miss Bennet?" he asked, in dismissive tones – evidently sure that she could not have won otherwise.

Lydia grinned, which seemed to irritate him further.

"I should be obliged if you would furnish me with it, then. I should like to return to the entrance and rejoin my party."

Lydia opened her mouth to disclaim that she had done any such thing and then, seeing the clear contempt in his horrid green eyes, she changed her mind.

"Certainly, Mr. Warwick," she said demurely. "If you will take a left turn after each third right, you will likely find the key as helpful as I did."

"Thank you," he said curtly, and, bowing to the rest of them, left the center of the maze.

Elizabeth looked at her sister. "When can you have had an opportunity to gain the key, Lydia?"

Lydia's eyes danced and she looked for a moment every inch Mrs. Darcy's sister.

"Oh, I did not, Lizzy, but Mr. Warwick seemed so certain that I could not have done it without such assistance that I could hardly enlighten him, could I?"

"Lydia Bennet!" cried her sister, undecided whether to praise or condemn the deceit. She cast a sidelong glance at her husband, who was smiling in amused appreciation. "Well, I daresay he may have deserved it."

"Most certainly he did, for he is not especially gallant!"

Lydia did not know how long Mr. Warwick spent wandering that maze, following her false directions, but the four of them were led out almost unerringly by Mr. Darcy, who was possessed of an excellent memory, and they did not see the dark-haired man on their journey.

Lydia saw him two days later, at a ball given in honour of the prince regent's birthday, and was annoyed on Georgiana's behalf that he had not taken the hint the other day and ceased his persistent attentions to her. He approached, almost as soon as they entered and, once again not noticing Miss Bennet's existence, requested the supper dance from the heiress.

Lydia had had quite enough and decided that she needed to speak plainly – poor Georgiana looked very uncomfortable. It was too bad of the man, she thought, to spoil what ought to be a pleasant time for her friend.

She cornered Mr. Kentmire first.

"La! Mr. Kentmire, Miss Darcy has been so riveted by your exploits in India – I am sure she could listen to you speak on the subject at great length."

Mr. Kentmire, a little unsure what to do with such a line of conversation, murmured that he was glad that Miss Darcy had not found him boring.

"Oh no, not a bit of it, sir. What a pity it is that Mr. Warwick managed to ask her for the supper dance – it would have been such an opportunity for her to hear more."

Not quite catching on, Mr. Kentmire politely agreed that he was just as disappointed at the loss of opportunity.

"I know, Mr. Kentmire, and I do pity you – I cannot think what is to be done." She looked at him with wide eyes.

"Er – what would you suggest be done, Miss Bennet?" he asked.

"I vow, sir, I am so pleased that you *asked* me."

Mr. Kentmire looked at her blankly and Lydia looked heavenward for patience.

"Poor Mr. Warwick will have to entertain the two of us ladies from Darcy House, as no one has yet asked me for the supper dance and Miss Darcy and I are quite determined not to be separated this evening."

Lydia was quite astonished that such a slowtop should have been able to make such a vast fortune in India, given how oblivious he was to her unsubtle hints. The silly man was so occupied in looking longingly at Miss Darcy (who had taken her excellent advice regarding the china-blue damask silk) and feeling so self-pitying that he could not see that the solution was before him.

Lydia tapped her foot impatiently and concealed a yawn.

"Oh!" said Mr. Kentmire, at long last, "I should be most grateful, Miss Bennet, if you would grant me the pleasure of your company during the supper dance."

"Why, thank you, Mr. Kentmire; I should be quite delighted," said Miss Bennet, not troubling herself to conceal her irritation.

He looked abashed but smiled at her. "I beg your pardon, Miss Bennet – I have been woefully distracted. I do hope you will forgive me."

Well, at least he owned it. She looked over to see that Georgiana was watching the pair of them very carefully. She was far too well bred to display any vulgar jealousy, but Lydia supposed she must be feeling some sort of unhappiness at seeing her favourite in deep conversation with Miss Bennet. Silly goose. It was one of the reasons Lydia did not favour female companionship – other than her sisters, at any rate; girls were so annoyingly grasping when it came to ownership of a young man. Lydia herself had never felt so wanting in male attention that she could not bear to see any of her suitors talking to another pretty female, and could not quite understand why it was that others were not as she was.

After enduring a dance with Mr. Kentmire, who was not a naturally good partner, Lydia was more than ready to be seated for supper.

She rapidly led Mr. Kentmire to one of the oval tables that had been set out in the dining room and declared that they could not do better than to settle themselves near an end so that she could sit closer to Miss Darcy. Mr. Kentmire, catching on to the spirit of the thing, permitted her to have her way and went about fetching her a plate of food.

She waved to Georgiana when she entered the ballroom on Mr. Warwick's arm, and gratefully the timid girl walked over.

"Good evening, Mr. Warwick," said Lydia, sounding bored. "You see, Georgiana, I have saved you a pair of seats just as I had promised."

She was very pleased with the success of her machinations. Judging by the look on Mr. Warwick's face when Mr. Kentmire returned to the table to take his seat, she had been a little too obvious for concealment, but upon reflection did not much care. Once having finished her supper of duck and peas, she made sure to engage a passing acquaintance in a very lively conversation that forced her to withdraw her chair a little and turn from the table, thus ensuring that Mr. Kentmire and Georgiana were able to carry on a conversation very easily without needing to bend to talk around her. She was pleased to see that Mr. Warwick was all but ignored. Not that he gave her the satisfaction of showing his annoyance – indeed he was leaning back in his chair, largely unconcerned, but taking advantage of Miss Darcy's good manners whenever she turned to try to include him in the conversation.

"Oh, I say, Lady Beatrice! I have not seen you in an age. Did you enjoy the card party at Lady Patterson's last evening? I had heard that you were there, you see, and was sorry to have missed it. We had been to Hampton Court in the daytime and were entirely done in. Have you met Mr. Warwick? I am quite certain that he has been looking across the room at you in admiration of your headdress – it is vastly becoming."

Lady Beatrice, a talkative blonde with a sad tendency toward freckles, looked at the surprised Mr. Warwick and blushed. Clearly she was flattered to have attracted the notice of so handsome a man as he. Even as rude as he was, Mr. Warwick was unable to do aught but nod in agreement with Miss Bennet's assertion that he must have been looking in Lady Beatrice's direction.

"It is a very fetching shade, is it not, Mr. Warwick?" prompted Lydia.

He favoured her with a distinctly chilly glance and muttered "Indeed" in Lady Beatrice's general direction. The blonde required little encouragement – if the heir to one of the richest earldoms in the land had noticed her, she would work very hard to keep that notice.

Lydia gleefully watched as her ladyship engaged the reluctant gentleman in a one-sided debate regarding the merits of the extra height provided by ostrich plumes. She was not put off when he disclaimed knowledge of such things, and instead provided him with ample opportunity to comment intelligently on the height of hat that he preferred.

He had no other option but to apply to Miss Bennet for her hand in the next dance to get away from her, and Lydia very much enjoyed declining.

"How honoured I am that you should ask me, Mr. Warwick – alas, my card is now entirely filled this evening since Mr. Kentmire so kindly asked me for the supper dance. How unfortunate! Doubtless there will be some other young lady quite delighted to dance with you, if only you ask in time. Oh! I must go to have a word with my sister. Mr. Kentmire, would you be so kind as to excuse me? I have just this instant remembered that Mrs. Bingley asked me to find her during supper when I saw her earlier today."

With that, she glided off, with Mr. Warwick occupied with Lady Beatrice and Mr. Kentmire with Miss Darcy.

Later on, at the close of the ball, while she was waiting in the hall for the Darcy carriage to draw up in its turn and Mr. and Mrs. Darcy were fussing over Georgiana, Lydia found her elbow taken in a firm grip and was steered to an open space a little way from them.

Mr. Warwick did not appear to be in a very pleasant temper. She looked at him inquiringly.

"I can only attribute your uncalled-for interference between Miss Darcy and myself at supper to unchecked jealousy."

Lydia depressed such conceit by laughing at him. "Jealousy? Of dearest Georgiana? You wrong me, Mr. Warwick. How highly you do regard yourself."

He appeared to find this very surprising and smiled unpleasantly.

"Mr. Warwick, although I think that being soundly rejected would do you a great deal of good, I shall warn you that you had much better withdraw your suit – she does not favour you, you know."

He looked irritated by this assertion.

"I do not even believe you admire her overmuch – not as Mr. Kentmire does, anyway."

He raised his eyebrows. "What has that to do with anything? You cannot know, being from relative obscurity as you are, that those of rank do not marry for such romantic nonsense as is being spouted so often nowadays."

Lydia wrenched her elbow away from his grip. "I suppose you think the best thing about her is her fortune," she hissed at him, goaded.

"When joined with her lineage, yes." He did not look in the least bit apologetic. "I have no desire to discuss this with you, Miss Bennet."

"You, sir, are a fool. There are many excellent qualities in my friend, and if you looked as though you might value her for those qualities, I should not interfere, but it is very clear that you are only interested in money and connections – which is simply horrid."

He was silent, but his contemptuous look spoke volumes.

"I do not in the least bit care if you have run out of money. Miss Darcy deserves far better than a man who sees only what she may add to his pocketbook. Now, if you will excuse me, my sister will be looking for me."

And with that, she turned on her heel and left him standing alone.

Chapter Three

Two days following the ball, Miss Darcy and Miss Bennet, followed at a discreet distance by the trusted groom, John Mibbs, took a morning ride through the park. It was before the fashionable hour, but neither lady was of a mind to care that there was no one about to see the pretty picture that they presented. For all that they had enjoyed themselves thus far in the season, it was a pleasant thing to be sometimes away from the crowds of people in London.

Lydia looked very well in her blue riding habit – it was the primary reason she had decided that she should expand her riding abilities last summer at Pemberley. The cut of the habit did her figure justice and she particularly liked the flowing lines of the skirts. She was not a particularly accomplished horsewoman, but she had sufficient will to direct a dumb beast hither and thither, and once permitted by her brother-in-law to progress to a canter, found it less dull than she had expected. Georgiana was in low spirits that morning and addressed fewer remarks than usual to Lydia. Miss Bennet, never at her best when rising early, did not attempt to engage in lively conversation. Still, they were glad enough of each other's company.

The three riders had just brushed along the far edge of the park near the road when they found themselves in company with other riders. It was not until they heard the groom exclaim in alarm that the young ladies turned their heads to look at them. The riders wore dark scarves about their faces and had their brimmed hats pulled down low so that only their eyes could be made out.

They had their sights fixed on Georgiana. One rider pulled out a pistol and levelled it at the groom, who checked his mount abruptly; another man rode very near their suddenly very alarmed quarry. Georgiana had frozen in stiff wide-eyed terror, and could only whimper in fright as the man tried to pull her from her mare, but her legs were locked into her saddle and the man could not unseat her.

Lydia, shocked to her very core, did not trouble to think. She rode close to her friend and raised her crop, and brought it down as hard as she could on the attacker's hand. He let out a grunt and instinctively recoiled. Emboldened by her success, Lydia emitted a wordless yell and brought the crop down again about his head. Abandoning the attempt to lay hold of Georgiana, he turned on Lydia Bennet and cuffed her hard about the face.

It smarted – there was no denying it. She had never been struck so in her entire life, and she was white with outrage and fright. But Lydia Bennet was no coward – *she* would not freeze in useless terror. If these men meant them harm, she would give them as much trouble as she could and count each lash she dealt them as a victory. She raised her crop again and struck out. The ruffian who was covering the groom with his pistol called out to his friend to get on with the job and cease with the games. Lydia, issuing what could only be termed a battle cry, urged Miss Darcy to flee.

"Georgiana, go! Ride away!"

She could not understand that the girl was too afraid even to think; she just saw that she did not listen. Frustrated beyond measure, Lydia knew she needed Mibbs's help. Instinctively, she directed her mare toward the man with the pistol and brought her crop down as hard as she could on the flank of his horse. It kicked out, and, caught by surprise, its rider was unseated. Mibbs was free.

Pulling her mare about, she saw that Miss Darcy was under assault again, but Mibbs was rushing to her aid. The man she had unhorsed reached for his pistol and levelled it at her.

"Halt ye!" he called in a rough voice, expecting to be obeyed. "Everyone stops or I shoot the wench in the blue dress."

She saw, as though time had slowed down, the fellow take his eyes off her to check that the groom had obeyed, and at that moment she brought her crop down once again, this time on the flank of her own mount, and rode hard toward him.

He looked back to see that the wench in the blue dress was bearing down on him in a fury, her eyes narrowed with intent, clearly intending to mow him down. Seeing that she was not bluffing in the slightest, he turned and fled, squeezing himself through a gap in the iron railings and soon disappearing onto the road. His horse skittered away from the group, evidently very unsettled by the goings-on.

Turning once more and ready to perform the same office for the second ruffian, whom Mibbs had successfully punched hard enough to unseat, Lydia saw the third man on horseback and her heart sank. One she had seen off, the second might be dealt with between herself and the groom, but a third man? She had forgotten about him, the two nearer ruffians had so utterly occupied her.

The third masked horseman did not approach, however – merely watched as the young lady rode back toward her friend.

Lydia scowled and dismissed him from her mind, intending only to aid Georgiana, who had at last found her voice and was now screaming loudly.

She spared the observer one contemptuous glance when he let out two piercing whistles and, still watching her until the last moment, turned his horse about to leave the park. The man did not even look back to see the rogue, who had one hand on Georgiana and one hand fighting off the groom, abruptly cease his attempted abduction and heed the signal to abandon all.

The assailants were gone as soon as they had come. Quite pale with shock, Lydia and Georgiana looked about themselves warily, almost unbelieving that the assault should be over so abruptly.

Lydia nodded to the groom and said slowly, "I think they are gone. We had best go home immediately. On the road, Mibbs, and always within sight of houses. Georgiana, are you hurt? Do cease crying – there is not the time for it."

In halting sobs, Georgiana replied that she had been struck across the face and that it stung. Lydia, feeling her own face throbbing, did not offer sympathy, but nodded briskly.

"Yes, the wretch hit me too. Bring your veil over your hat, Georgiana, and I will do the same – it will cause less talk than if someone sees us with great red marks on our faces. No, don't start crying again; there will be time for that once we are safely home. Mibbs?"

"Very good, Miss Bennet. I will follow on, closer like, out through this entrance, through the street and down across the Elms. Quickest way but best keep the horses to a walk."

"All right. Come on, Miss Darcy; stay close to me."

Georgiana, still trying bravely to cease crying and having managed to let down her veil, shook her head and said that her hands would not obey her – she was too frightened.

Lydia scowled, desperate to get to safety. "I suggest that you find some pride, Georgiana, for if you do not come with us we shall leave you here, all alone in the park. We must go – now!"

Her brusque orders and lack of sympathy did the trick. Fear prompted Georgiana to try again, and eventually the mare responded.

They made their way, seemingly taking forever, out of the park and along the route suggested by Mibbs.

When they got to Darcy House, Mibbs handed the reins of the horses to the waiting stable boys and, for the first time in his life, entered with the young ladies through the front door of the house. The butler raised his brows at him, but nodded quickly when he saw the state of Miss Darcy and the white, pinched face of Miss Bennet.

"I need to speak to the master immediately, Mr. Danks – he needs to be informed of the goings-on of this morning, without any delay. I suggest you don't let Mrs. Darcy leave the house until the master has given his say-so either, not but what that's for him to decide."

Mr. Danks, seeing that there was some great commotion underway, escorted the groom across the polished floor to the door of the master's study and knocked firmly.

Lydia, seeing that they were indeed safe indoors, felt her stomach churning miserably, with a hot feeling prickling her neck that signified that she was going to immediately be unwell. The maid, when she saw Lydia retch, pointed to a little room hidden behind the staircase and watched as Miss Bennet dashed into it, not even having time to close the door before she cast up her accounts.

Trembling, Lydia emerged just in time to see Mr. Darcy come through the door of his study and catch his sister as she fainted.

"Fetch Miss Darcy's maid, if you please, Danks. You there," this to the maid, "find Mrs. Priddy and tell her I want her immediately. Mibbs, I desire you to remain in the hallway until Mr. Danks returns to watch the door; no one is to leave the house."

Here Danks volunteered the information that Mrs. Darcy had left Darcy House not five minutes previously to call on Mrs. St. John.

Mr. Darcy then, for the first time in Lydia's acquaintance with him, raised his voice, calling out orders to servants as he hoisted his sister into his arms and carried her up the stairs.

Lydia was left in the hallway with only Mibbs to bear her company. Her heart had ceased to beat so loudly in her chest, but her fingers still trembled uncontrollably. She desperately wanted Lizzy, and fumbled as she drew off her gloves and removed the pin from her hat.

Mibbs, watching her carefully lest she too should faint, offered her a delicate little chair that was kept by the door.

She was attempting to rearrange the folds of the veil on her hat and shook her head impatiently.

"No, don't worry, I shan't faint. Where is the bell in here?"

However, it was quite unnecessary for her to pull it for assistance, for, alerted by the housekeeper, a maid and two footmen appeared through three different doors in quick succession. Lydia handed over her hat and gloves to the maid.

"Thank you. I fear a scullery maid will need to be sent for to clean that little room behind the stairs. Have you two been set to guard the front door?"

One of the burly footmen bowed and said that yes, he had been.

"Well then. Mibbs, do you know where Mrs. St. John lives? I don't, you see – I haven't the least head for remembering things like that."

"Yes, Miss Bennet. I have escorted Mrs. Darcy there a number of times."

"Good. If I write you a note to deliver to her, will you bring her home immediately? I do not know that she should be out. I mean...we cannot know if there is any danger...."

Mr. Darcy came swiftly down the stairs then, his expression very grave.

"Thomas, I have asked that the doctor be sent for. He should be here within half an hour. Mibbs, you must come with me to retrieve my wife. It will cause talk but there is little avoiding that."

Lydia volunteered her idea, "I had thought that a note might work, or you could tell her that her sister has been taken ill – she will worry, of course, but...."

Mr. Darcy gave a nod. "Yes, it might answer. I shall want your account of the matter shortly, Lydia. When I have brought Elizabeth home safely, that is."

"Oh yes, very well, go!"

He did go, looking very worried but determined. Lydia went to a little salon overlooking the garden where the light was good, and collapsed in a heap. If only Mr. Darcy brought her sister home, all might be well. There was much that she could not understand about the happenings of the morning, but if anyone could make her feel easy again, and make the horrid feeling of fear leave her again, it would be Lizzy. Elizabeth would hold her, make her laugh, and then promise that all would be well, just as she did with her infant son when he cried.

After she had sat there for a while, Lydia supposed that she ought to find out how Georgiana was faring, and rose from her reverie, deciding that she would not cry now, she would cry later. Miss Darcy had, according to the doctor, awakened from her faint and gone into hysterics. Dr. Mackintosh was of the opinion that the poor delicate young woman (said in a very approving fashion) had suffered a very great deal and needed much rest.

His straight brows furrowed, the doctor told Miss Bennet that he had administered laudanum to Miss Darcy to soothe her and to assist her recovery from the dreadful ordeal. For Lydia, he recommended cold compresses to soothe the now purpling bruise on her cheek. Lydia, having forgotten it, suddenly felt the hot stinging and raised her hand to her cheek in surprise. She heard noise in the hallway below and, forgetting her discomfort, rushed to the stairs to see if her sister had returned.

She had.

Looking up to see her youngest sister dashing down the stairs in a most unseemly fashion, Elizabeth pulled away from her husband's grip and met her partway, her arms opened to receive her. It was only then that Lydia cried – when Lizzy was petting her hair, not even having removed her bonnet and gloves, and murmuring lovely words in her ear. Awkwardly fishing in her reticule for a handkerchief– a darling concoction of silk and white lace, Lydia noted absently – Lizzy wiped away her sister's tears and led her into the study, leaving Mr. Darcy to bid farewell to the doctor.

When Mr. Darcy entered, it was with his secretary, Mr. Hart, and Mibbs. Elizabeth had managed to remove her hat and gloves by now, had sent for shawls for herself and Miss Lydia (for Lydia had not been able to cease trembling), and was just pouring out hot tea into dainty china cups.

Mrs. Darcy handed round the tea to all present and they waited for Mr. Darcy to take charge.

"I have asked Mr. Hart to join us because I want a clear account of what happened this morning to be written down for later perusal. Miss Darcy is currently resting, and I will ask her for her account later on when she is well enough. For now, if you, Miss Bennet, and you, Mibbs, could say, as clearly as possible what has occurred. Mr. Hart will write it down."

Mibbs and Lydia looked at each other, neither quite sure how to begin. "It is difficult to remember, Mr. Darcy; it all happened so fast. One minute we were skirting about the park, near Holland Street, and the next we were set upon by men," said Mibbs, apologetically.

"How many men?" Mrs. Darcy asked, "In what manner did they approach you? What were they wearing?"

Mr. Mibbs thought, and spoke slowly. "Two men, ma'am – they came from the side of us and went straight for Miss Darcy; well, one of them did, the other pointed his gun at me. I could not say what they were wearing – dark garb, I suppose."

Lydia sipped her tea and shook her head. "It did happen quickly. Three men, although one was farther away and did not come close, I don't know why – I only really noticed him when he whistled to call the men off. He was watching us. They were wearing dark coats, with brimmed hats that were pulled low and scarves wrapped about their faces. I could not tell you if they were dark or fair or…or anything. There is nothing of note by which I could describe them."

"What of their horses? Were any of them noteworthy?" this question was posed by Mr. Darcy and met with an impatient shake of Lydia's head.

"Oh, I don't notice horses, Mr. Darcy; your sister might have."

The groom, looking apologetic again, shook his head. "I had my eyes on the one with the gun, sir. I think the horses were mostly chestnuts, not blood horses but not heavyset neither. Dark, again. Seems to have been deliberate, that. I'd have remarked a bay."

"Well, what next, then? One man pointing a pistol, one man near Miss Darcy, and another man at a distance…" prompted Lizzy, taking hold of Lydia's hand.

"Well, that man, the second one, he tried to pull Georgiana from her horse. I think…I think that may have been their aim. They did not seem concerned with me, just Mibbs and Georgiana."

Mr. Darcy's mouth set in a grim line and looked to the groom. "Mibbs, do you agree with this assessment? That their purpose was to abduct Miss Darcy."

"Aye, sir," said Mibbs, after a moment's thought. "They went straight for her; reckon they knew which she was."

Mr. Hart continued to write steadily as Mr. Darcy composed himself.

"Well, what foiled them then? If you had the pistol levelled at you, how is it that you are all safely returned home? An outcome for which I am deeply grateful."

"And I!" interjected his wife, still holding fast to Lydia's hand.

"Reckon it was Miss Bennet, sir, that brought us about. Started lashing out with her whip and got a few good blows in, from the sounds of the fellows cursing. I only really noticed that when the rogue with the gun trained on me turned to look – think he told him to hurry or something."

Lydia nodded to confirm this. "I am afraid that that is when the other one struck me across the face. I did not know what to do – I thought that if I stopped hitting him then all would be lost, so I carried on. He raised his hands to defend himself, I think and – oh yes! I called out to Georgiana to ride away, but I think she was in a panic and could not, and then I turned my horse nearer to the man with the pistol and brought my crop down on the flank of his horse. It reared up and unseated him."

Mibbs jumped in to continue the tale. "He turned the gun on Miss Bennet then and shouted that if everyone did not stop, he would shoot her. Miss Bennet, sir, I think surprised him, for she rode at him hard and he dropped his gun and turned and ran. Miss Darcy began screaming then, sir."

It was at this point that the steady scratching of Mr. Hart's pen ceased and Mr. Darcy pinched the bridge of his nose with his thumb and forefinger as though greatly troubled. Lizzy released Lydia's hand and covered her mouth with her hands in profound shock.

Silence, for the space of a minute, went unbroken in the study. Lydia was lost in thought, trying to remember what had happened next and Mibbs was looking worriedly at his master.

"Go on," said Mr. Darcy, in a voice quite unlike his own. "Miss Bennet rode towards a man in possession of a loaded pistol, and, having frightened him off...what next?"

"Oh! That was when the third man gave a whistle and they all rode off. I suppose it was because Georgiana started screaming then, and perhaps they thought it might attract a great deal of attention," said Lydia.

Mr. Hart began writing again with great concentration.

"I didn't see which way they went, sir; I'm sorry. Miss Darcy was clearly greatly distressed and I was mostly worrying about the fastest and safest route home. Miss Bennet was the one who persuaded Miss Darcy to get moving with us, sir. She must have been fearful frightened to be grabbed like that."

Having the full story, Mr. Darcy sat back in his chair and steepled his fingers, looking over the tips them at his young sister-in-law.

"Lydia, it seems that I owe you a great debt of gratitude – your extraordinary actions today have saved my sister from disaster. I thank you."

Elizabeth, uncaring of the audience, flung her arms about Lydia and squeezed her tight. "Indeed, Lydia, although I think I may never recover from the shock of hearing that you risked yourself so – you are so very brave, dearest. I am prodigiously proud."

Lydia did not feel very brave, but feeling Lizzy's arms about her and hearing such a declaration went a long way to quieting the dreadful feeling in her stomach, and for the first time her shoulders relaxed.

Mr. Darcy spoke again. "I do not know what manner of men sought to do harm to my family, whether it was a deliberate targeting or if it was merely footpads having chanced upon what seemed an easy quarry. I will do my utmost to find out. I will give orders that will mean an increase in the protection for the household. For the present, Mrs. Darcy, you, your sister, and mine must not stir out of doors without an appropriately armed escort. I hope such measures will not be necessary for long, but for now I require it. My son must not be taken out of doors with his nursemaid without suitable protection either. Hart, Mibbs, I should like you to relate my orders to the relevant parties, if you please. You may go now. We shall get no more work done today, I fear, Hart."

Elizabeth, upon hearing her husband mention protection for her baby, had sat up straighter in her chair and had gone very pale. Lydia, seeking to comfort her, stroked her back lightly.

"Lydia, I think perhaps you might like to rest in your rooms for a while – you have had a very trying morning. Your maid will wish to find you a compress for the bruise on your cheek."

It was a clear dismissal and Lydia had not the will left in her to argue with him. She quietly moved to the door, and turned to look back just as she opened it. She had thought that her brother might be wishing to comfort Elizabeth, and was glad of it for her sister's sake. To her surprise, when she looked back over her shoulder she saw that it was Elizabeth who had risen from her chair and wound her arms about her husband. Mr. Darcy, evidently in much need of her love, buried his head in her shoulder with a great shuddering sigh.

Quietly, feeling as though she had seen something intensely private, Lydia slipped through the doorway and very softly closed the heavy door behind her.

Chapter Four

Mr. Kentmire, hearing within a few days of Miss Darcy's near abduction, came to call upon her and was clearly greatly agitated to see her white face and tear-stained cheeks. She had refused all other callers, but when Lydia skipped up the stairs to tell her that she had been looking out at the street and had seen him alight from his carriage, Georgiana brightened and came down.

He held out his hand, hardly noticing that it was not correct for him to do so. Mrs. Darcy, a twinkle in her eye, took advantage of her husband's absence from the room and ignored it. Lydia raised her brows and retreated to the window again, looking out at the passers-by below.

Miss Darcy did not seem to mind Mr. Kentmire's forwardness, and permitted him to lead her to a little pair of chairs by the fireplace. There was a pronounced air of fragility about her that day, even more so than usual, and her suitor could not help but respond to it.

"I was concerned, Miss Darcy, to hear from Sir Anthony Alberhey of the goings-on in the park. I am very glad to see you are not injured but I do not like that you have been made to feel unsafe. I assume your brother has engaged adequate protection for you in the future?"

Mrs. Darcy, taking exception to this, took her share in the conversation. "My husband, Mr. Kentmire, is the most conscientious of brothers. He, being such a decent-minded man, could not have foreseen the incident but, having been made aware of the danger, has taken every precaution for the safety of his family."

Mr. Kentmire, bowing in his seat, begged Mrs. Darcy's pardon. "Forgive me, madam; I misspoke. I did not intend to criticise your husband's arrangements. I was merely thinking that I have brought with me, from India I mean, several native men who were trained to protect the ladies of the sultan's court. Might I send one or two of them to you? To assist in the protection of the household? I should rest much easier if I knew they were here."

Miss Darcy smiled on him and softly thanked him for such thoughtfulness. Mrs. Darcy tilted her head consideringly.

"I do not know that my husband would think it proper to accept such assistance from anyone outside of the family, sir, however dear a friend you have become to us. Perhaps you might ask him?"

Mr. Kentmire blushed slightly and looked at Miss Darcy. She was looking at him with soft eyes. "Ah yes, of course. Forgive me – I had not intended to overstep the bounds of what is acceptable. I am still acclimating to English customs again – it seems I was in India too long."

Finding her courage, Miss Darcy exclaimed that she was not in the least bit offended by such a friendly offer of assistance, and thanked him as effusively as she was able. She managed so well that Mr. Kentmire felt encouraged enough to request a private interview with her, subject to Mrs. Darcy's permission.

Feeling very matronly, Mrs. Darcy rose from her seat and shook out her silk skirts. "Lydia dearest, perchance you will find the view of the road more satisfactory from the yellow salon. Shall we go and see?" She smiled at Georgiana, who now seemed more cheerful and hopeful than she had since that day in the park, for all that her delicate hands were clenched tightly together in her lap.

The two sisters left the room together and made their way to Mr. Darcy's study.

"I do not mean to stay for long, Fitzwilliam. Mr. Kentmire has requested a private interview with Georgiana; doubtless he will wish to speak to you afterward. He seems gravely concerned for her wellbeing, my love."

Mr. Darcy nodded in response. "Very well, Elizabeth. I will see him."

His wife dimpled at him. "You had best begin rehearsing a very grand speech about her ancestry and accomplishments. He will grovel appropriately if you do."

Mr. Darcy sent her a stern glare that sent her off into a trill of delighted laughter. Lydia sometimes did not understand her sister one little bit – she seemed to love her husband best of all when he was excessively grumpy. To his credit, he did not seem to mind being teased by her sister, so perhaps it was that they had an understanding that was beyond her.

They went to the yellow salon and Lydia looked out to the street again, studying the passers-by. Elizabeth rearranged a vase of flowers that had been sent by Sir Daniel James, one of Lydia's circle of suitors. They were pretty enough in their way, Lydia had thought, and it was pleasant to receive them, especially with the polite note of concern that accompanied the blooms. She could have wished that he had not selected such a cacophony of colour, but owned that they did not look so bad with the pale yellow walls.

It was not long before the door opened and Georgiana came eagerly in.

Elizabeth held out her hands to her sister-in-law. "Well?"

"Oh, Elizabeth! He has asked me to marry him!" exclaimed Georgiana, expecting to find her brother's wife quite brimming over with surprise.

"Given that he asked for a private interview with you, I should hope that he did!" laughed Mrs. Darcy. "Dare we hope that you have accepted him?"

"Oh, did I not say? I am sorry – yes, of course I did. He has gone to see my brother now. He said that he would not have troubled me so soon after I had had such a great upset but that he could not tolerate being unable to assist by sending his servants. Is that not so very kind of him?"

"Very kind, my dear. Do you know, I cannot at all fathom why our Mama used to be in such a fret that we get husbands, Lydia. It seems to happen with very little interference from me – perhaps I have the knack of it. I had better write a letter to Lady Catherine, boasting of my great success as a matchmaker. She will enjoy scolding me for my vulgarity of mind, I do not doubt."

So it was that Miss Georgiana of Pemberley became engaged. Her betrothed, being a very wealthy man and inclined to indulge her, promised her that should she desire it, he would build or buy her a house in whatever county she wished. Unsurprisingly, she very quickly answered that she would not wish to be very far from her dear brother, and if he could arrange a home for her within half a day's travel from Pemberley, she should be very well pleased to live wherever he liked.

Some two days after the engagement became a settled thing, Mr. Warwick came to call. He rode up the street, and Lydia, stationed by the window once more, called out to Georgiana that she had a visitor. Thinking it to be Mr. Kentmire, Georgiana came to the window and then stiffened.

Lydia looked at her.

"I think it is only Mr. Warwick, Georgiana. He has probably heard of your engagement to Mr. Kentmire and is come to congratulate you – or to persuade you that you ought to marry him instead. I should laugh at him if he did."

"It is not that. I do not fear that, despite the awkwardness, it is just that...Lydia, do you not recognise that horse?"

"Now why should I recognise a horse? Do speak plainly – you are making no sense."

"I think that I have seen it before, that morning in the park. The other horses were mere job horses but that one...at least I think it was that one...it is clearly of superior stock – do not you agree?"

Lydia, looking out interestedly now, frowned. "I could not say for certain either way. It is a black horse; that is all."

"But what if Mr. Warwick has bought it from someone recently? Perhaps he might be able to help my brother find the men who set on us."

Her mind in a whirl, Lydia nodded. "Oh yes, I suppose he might be able to help. I have been wondering, you know, if your brother is in the right of it – perhaps they were footpads after all. They may never be caught."

Georgiana shuddered. "I wish they might be. It is not pleasant to feel so vulnerable."

Lydia, thinking of the fear she had felt once the danger had passed, agreed. "At least Mr. Kentmire has sent additional men for your protection. Just think! You will be as well-defended as a king's wife."

"Mr. Kentmire said they are called sultans in India," Georgiana informed her.

This interested Lydia not at all and she waved it off. Mr. Warwick entered the room and made his bow. Lydia found it very vexing that there was nothing amiss with his clothing or manners. There was no reason whatsoever for the prickle of irritation that shot up her neck when he entered. She braced herself to graciously accept being ignored by him, and, hoping to see him make a fool of himself to Georgiana, schooled her face into bored indifference.

To her surprise, after offering Miss Darcy perfunctory congratulations on her betrothal, he turned to her and addressed her directly for perhaps the second time in their acquaintance.

"Miss Bennet, might I persuade you to come out riding with me as far as Hyde Park? The ground has dried up now and we might have a pleasant canter if you liked."

Lydia, quite shocked at such unusual civility from him, did not like, but she was prevented from saying so by her elder sister entering the room.

Mr. Warwick bowed again, his green eyes assessing and cold. "Mrs. Darcy, good morning, madam. I can see that you are well. I was hoping to persuade your sister, Miss Bennet, to come riding with me this morning, if you do not object."

"'Tis a charming thought, Mr. Warwick, and if my sister does not mind a morning of exercise I cannot see any objection."

Lydia, having thought of a reasonable excuse, piped up. "I did not think Mr. Darcy was wishful for us to go out without asking him first, sister."

"Very proper of you, dearest, but I think that between Mr. Warwick and a groom you ought to be well enough protected." She paused and looked concerned, "If you are feeling frightened to go out, I am sure Mr. Warwick would understand it. I do not know if you have heard, sir, but my dear sisters were set upon by ruffians at the beginning of the week."

He was watching Lydia still, with that careful green gaze, and she felt a chill. "I did indeed hear of it, madam. Of course I would understand if Miss Bennet was frightened."

It was almost indiscernible, the slightest touch of contempt that coloured his last word, but Lydia picked up on it and the chill disappeared, to be replaced with the heat of hurt pride.

"Frightened? I am not in the least bit afraid."

It had not been entirely true, she thought, as she scrambled into her riding habit with the harrassed assistance of Cason, her maid. Her hands were trembling as she did up her gloves and clutched her crop. A quick glance in the mirror assured her that she looked very well; the blue of the habit and the flowing lines of the skirt suited her height. If one ignored the restless, worried eyes that looked back at her in the mirror, one might be thoroughly convinced that she was just like any other young lady going out for a ride with a suitor.

Except he was not her suitor. He was Georgiana's. Lydia wondered what he was about, when he had ignored her so completely for nigh on a month and she did not even like him enough to have felt slighted by it.

The groom helped to throw her up into the saddle, and once Mr. Warwick had mounted, they set off. Lydia felt her courage returning with every pace her mare took.

Mr. Warwick, still looking at her in that horrid, assessing fashion, had maintained his silence. The groom rode some eight yards behind them.

Lydia, very quickly made impatient by silence, broke it with an opening volley.

"I do hope, Mr. Warwick, that you are not too crushingly disappointed to hear of Miss Darcy's engagement to Mr. Kentmire. I did warn you, you know."

It was not in her nature to dance around a topic, but far from taking offence, Mr. Warwick looked a little amused. "You are very direct, Miss Bennet. No, I am not in the least bit crushingly disappointed. As you correctly surmised, it was not so much Miss Darcy that interested me as her fortune. You need not worry on that head."

He did not seem embarrassed by the confession, and Lydia frowned. "Oh, I was not. I am glad, of course, that you are not nursing a broken heart – Miss Darcy is very sweet and has never wished to injure anyone."

He looked bored by the subject and Lydia was nettled.

"Do tell me, Mr. Warwick, if you find my company tedious. I should be quite content to return home, you know."

"It is not your company, Miss Bennet, but I have no interest in discussing Miss Darcy with you." They rounded a corner and crossed over the road to pass through the gates of Hyde Park. Lydia spotted a few of her acquaintances and waved to them. "I do hope you did not take any serious injury during the unpleasantness of your encounter in the park the other morning, Miss Bennet."

He sounded almost sincere when he said that, and Lydia could very nearly understand why he had such a reputation for being too charming with ladies.

"Oh, I am well enough. I gained for myself a bruise or two, but it is of little matter. "

"From what I heard, you dealt out a few also."

"Where can you have heard that?" exclaimed she.

Mr. Warwick looked mysterious, his pale eyes taunting her. "Ah, I cannot reveal my source to you, Miss Bennet, but it is a reliable one."

Lydia frowned, deeply unsettled by this man.

"Why did you wish to ride out with me?" she demanded. "Have you an odd curiosity about young ladies being set upon that you wish to satisfy?"

"No, Miss Bennet, I don't wish to bleed you for information. Do come down out of the rafters, my pet. We shall be friendly now, I promise. I will not seek to expose any mysteries you want hidden."

She maneuvered her mare between a cart and an irritated carriage driver in silence. When she had accomplished this, she responded.

"I do not in the least bit understand you, Mr. Warwick. I have nothing to hide. I am exactly as I seem to be. I just thought your excessive interest to be distasteful, that is all."

"Like the baying mob that crowds about a public hanging?" he quietly asked, a smile hovering in the corners of his mouth.

She nodded hesitantly, surprised that he had summed up her discomfort so well when she herself could not have done.

He changed the subject then, and became very nearly engaging for the rest of their ride. She was not in the least bit pleased by him, but allowed that he could be entertaining when he exerted himself.

When they arrived back at the house, Lydia realised that although she had not been easy in his company, she had not given more than two thoughts to the possibility of being attacked again. At least Mr. Warwick had proved useful in that regard.

He dismounted smoothly from his horse and tossed the reins to the waiting boy. "I shall assist you down, Miss Bennet, if you will permit."

Lydia, being no stranger to depressing presumption, lifted her eyebrows at him, glad to have the upper hand. "It hardly signifies, sir; the groom will help me." Nodding to the man in question, she reached her hands down and thanked him carelessly.

Duly snubbed, Mr. Warwick offered his arm up the steps but Lydia was occupied with the train of her habit and carried her crop in the other hand, so declined once again.

"In short, Miss Bennet, you need no assistance from me. I am very neatly put in my place, I see."

Lydia impatiently put back her veil and noted that his eyes looked immediately to her right cheek. She covered it with her gloved hand, wondering why she disliked him knowing of it. It had been a much uglier bruise the day before, but had now faded to yellow and was easily covered by a little powder. He noticed her wary look and his mouth twisted.

"I see it is not so very bad after all. I am glad of it." She could see then why he had such a reputation for charm, even if she had seen little of it. He sounded absolutely truthful but something like mistrust danced along her nerves.

Coolly, she waved off his concern. "No, it is not so bad; just a little thing. Are you coming inside? My sister will have tea soon, I should think – but you must not let me keep you from your other commitments, Mr. Warwick. I am sure you are a very busy man."

"I am a gentleman, my dear. It is a point of pride for me to never be too busy to wait upon a beautiful lady."

Lydia took a glance back at the horses as they were being led away to the stable, and the reason for her mistrust clicked into place like the latch on a very heavy door.

"How long have you had your horse, Mr. Warwick?" she asked accusingly.

He looked back at it and barely hesitated before replying, "No, Miss Bennet, I will not sell you my horse. He would be far too strong for you to manage."

Lydia stared at him. "My only interest in your horse is that I fancy I have seen it before, very recently."

He smirked. "I daresay it was too much to hope that you would have noticed its owner."

Clearly, this man thought that she would not call him on his bluff. Did he think her so constrained by polite society that she would not declare him to be a villain based on her suspicions?

She led him into Lizzy's favourite room, where she often served tea. It was empty and she rounded on him.

"I did not tell you that I was struck on the cheek, Mr. Warwick," said Lydia, seriously, her heart beating at a rapid pace. "In fact, I think that you are more hopeful that I did not recognise your horse's owner."

Something like admiration crossed his face and she knew for certain that she had found him out.

"It would have been simpler if you had not," he admitted, and Lydia drew back a pace from him in surprise. "No, don't cower from me. What precisely do you think I would do in your brother's home? Come and sit down like a civilised person and we will talk."

"How can we sit down like civilised people when one of us is not?" said she, rudely. "I do not know what you are about, Mr. Warwick, but you will not harm Miss Darcy. She will be married very soon. I will encourage her to hurry up with it. Whatever scheme you have planned will fail and...and I am not afraid of you."

"I hope it will not," he replied, ignoring her bluntness, "Miss Darcy may marry Mr. Kentmire with my blessing, not that she needs it. I told you earlier, I believe, that I had no interest in discussing her with you."

Lydia shook her head. "I do not believe you. Why try to abduct her and then give up so swiftly? She is still a wealthy heiress and you are still a dreadful knave, so why give up?"

His eyes rested on her face for a moment before he decided to speak honestly. "Because I witnessed what I had never thought to see. An extraordinary young woman showed all the courage of a man and fought off two attackers." His eyes almost glowed, so pale they looked in the light airy room. "I do not think I have ever been more surprised in my life. I compliment you, my dear – having freed yourself, you turned your horse about again to aid the others. I covet that sort of loyalty."

The blood thrummed in Lydia's ears and she felt sick.

"Why tell me this? I do not understand. You admit that you are a villain and then tell me...what exactly? I do hope you do not think you are in love with me or any such horrid notion."

"Why not?" said he, seriously.

"I think you are a madman." she spat at him. "How dare you? Do you think I want anything to do with a man like you? I do not. I have more sense than that, for all people think me an empty-headed, frippery girl. If you come near this house again, I shall tell Mr. Darcy all you have admitted and he will very likely have you hanged or some such thing."

Mr. Warwick laughed. "I do not think so – I am still the next earl, after all. There is not a court in the land that would hang a powerful man on such dubious evidence as your say-so."

"Well, he will probably challenge you to a duel then." she ground out, now beyond furious.

Mr. Warwick took a seat. "It is possible, if he believed you," he said, considering the matter.

"No, do not sit down, you are not staying. You are...oh! I cannot think of anything bad enough to call you but you are not staying. I do not want you here."

It was unfortunate for Lydia that her sister chose that moment to walk in, carrying her son in her arms.

"Lydia!" she exclaimed, looking at Mr. Warwick for any signs of offence. "I beg your pardon, Mr. Warwick – my sister is not ordinarily guilty of such bad manners. I can only suppose that she is overwrought by the events earlier this week. Will you stay for tea? I hope you had a pleasant ride? Miss Darcy has gone out with Mr. Kentmire, so I am afraid she is not in. Lydia, will you ring the bell, please? Theodore is in need of his nurse, I think."

Lydia looked at Elizabeth, lost for words, and went to ring the bell. She looked at her nephew, then at her sister, and then at the odious Mr. Warwick, who was entirely unruffled and murmuring that he was not in the least bit offended by Miss Bennet's high-spirited manner. Lydia yanked the cord that hung in the corner of the room.

Elizabeth looked at her smilingly and then tilted her head in question. This was her moment – she had only to tell her sister, to openly accuse Mr. Warwick of his crime, and Lizzy would believe her and tell Mr. Darcy. The baby waved a tiny-fingered hand in the air, patting his mama on the cheek.

Lydia hesitated.

Only it would be a pity if Mr. Darcy were injured or killed. Lizzy would be very upset and their son would never know his papa.

Lydia shook her head in response to her sister's silent question, angry at the unfairness of life that Mr. Warwick might get away with it.

Her nephew wailed angrily, and Lydia was inclined to agree with him.

"Oh, my dear, do excuse me for a moment. I had better take him upstairs myself. Lydia, pour for Mr. Warwick, will you, dearest?"

Then she left the room in a flutter of primrose silk and an armful of increasingly cross baby.

"Having second thoughts about getting me hanged, Lydia? Do you know, I rather like that name – it suits you."

Offended, Lydia hissed at him. "I don't care if you like it, you hateful man – you mayn't use it. I would very cheerfully see you hanged. Oh, I wish you would go!"

"I can't go," he said reasonably. "Mrs. Darcy has promised me a cup of tea, poured by your own fair hand, and I want to ask Mr. Darcy's permission to marry you."

Lydia snarled at him then, and stamped her foot. "Are you so stupid that you cannot tell when a woman hates you? If I give you any tea at all, I will throw it at you. I shan't marry you, so you can save yourself the humiliation of being rejected. Do get out, Mr. Warwick – whatever games you are entertaining yourself with are not amusing me."

"I want to know why you did not reveal your suspicions to your sister, and then I will take myself off for now."

"Why should I tell you that? Who are you to demand any answers of me?"

"Very well. I hope the maid will come in soon. I shall enjoy a cup or two of tea."

"I cannot for the life of me imagine why you would remain when you are so clearly not wanted. If I tell you," demanded Lydia, "will you leave?"

He nodded once and she huffed an irritated sigh.

"My nephew does not deserve to grow up fatherless and my sister is too happy with her husband to be widowed. I do not doubt that you are precisely the kind of horrid creature that would shoot to kill in a duel, and so I have remained silent. If...if ...if you will leave Miss Darcy alone and not try to interfere with her and not try to abduct her again, I will keep quiet, but if you try anything I will tell all."

He rose then, and Lydia did not trouble to hide her relief. He crossed over to where she stood and she retreated a step. Her hand went to a little side table upon which rested a heavy silver statue of a Grecian lady bearing an urn. Curling her fingers around its neck, Lydia was entirely prepared to hurl it. Mr. Warwick stopped where he was.

"There is no need for your fear, Lydia. I was merely going to kiss your hand."

"I do not want you to kiss my hand. I do not want you to come anywhere near this house again and do not dare to call me by my Christian name ever again, Mr. Warwick. I do not know how many times I must repeat this to you but I am not afraid of you. If I retreated, it is because I think you are utterly repugnant and I have never known such a wicked cur as you."

"I wonder," said Mr. Warwick pleasantly, "if you can be aware of the things I have done to men for such insults as you have thrown at me." He bowed deeply and turned to depart. "I shall call upon you tomorrow, Miss Bennet."

Chapter Five

Lydia Bennet was no coward. She knew this for certain fact. She might not have given a great deal of thought as to the origin of her courage but she was aware of its existence. The next time she saw the Dreadful Mr. Warwick, he had marched up to her as she stood beside Jane Bingley, as bold as brass, and requested her hand for the first dance.

Miss Bennet, entirely unwilling to sit out the dancing for an entire evening on his low account, accepted with little grace. In fact, she quite made up her mind, as he led her out to the floor, that she would be as uncivil as she could possibly get away with in public. She hoped that the horrid man would not manage to get her alone, but if he did she would drop all veneer of politeness and show him how little she thought of him.

"I like your dress," he said, before he bowed deeply.

"I do not care," she retorted, as she barely curtseyed, elegantly sweeping her light green skirts out of the way, before smiling sunnily at the man further down the set who was to take a turn with her.

"You were out yesterday when I called," he remarked.

"Yes," said Lydia, shortly, "for that very reason."

Mr. Warwick had a skin like shoe leather, she decided. Disdain all but poured from her as they danced and he did not heed it one little bit. It was quite exhausting, really, to think of impolite things to say to him in return for his compliments. If she did not know what a cad he was, it would have made her feel quite churlish. What was worse was that Mr.

Warwick seemed to realise that she wished him gone and was amused by her efforts.

"Are you coming to my cousin's rout party tomorrow evening?" he asked.

"Yes," she bit out, knowing there was no getting out of it.

"May I reserve a dance?"

"No," she said, very irritated.

"Do you not intend to dance tomorrow, Miss Bennet?" He sounded surprised.

"I am afraid I will have the headache for that dance. Doubtless I will recover once it is over."

"Very well," he replied, seeming to accept the rebuff. The dance at this point called for them to link arms above their heads as they turned slowly in place. Lydia, obliged to look up in order to glower at him, decided that this was her least favourite dance figure and elected to look away instead.

He looked down at her consideringly and his thin lips formed a smile. "You had best accept it, Lydia. I am very persistent."

Her eyes shot to his.

"Don't call me Lydia, nodcock – someone might hear you! If you are attempting to force my hand, know that I shan't marry you. Even if you abducted me and made me, I should stab you in your sleep, depend upon it."

He laughed. A few other dancers noted it and murmured amongst themselves that Miss Bennet must truly be a sparkling wit if she had succeeded in amusing the toplofty gentleman.

"Do you know," he said, "I really think you would."

"I would," confirmed Lydia. "I really wish you would desist. It is not as though you could afford me at any rate."

"I wonder where you can have gotten the impression that I am impoverished, my pet. Things are not so bad as all that, for all I thought

Miss Darcy's fortune might suit me nicely for a year or two. You will soon see, Lydia, how it is not in my nature to give up when there is something I want."

Sourly, Lydia took his hand to promenade, releasing it as soon as they had moved down the dance. "I do not think you are so persistent as you believe. You called off your hounds pretty swiftly as soon as you met with any resistance the other day."

"I was not myself at that moment, I confess. Falling headlong into love with a young woman I have barely spoken to is not an experience I have encountered before. I promise you, my pet, that you will know me better soon enough.

"I do not think it," was all Lydia would say, and refused to speak to him any further. He returned her to Mrs. Darcy in silence.

In the wake of this party, word spread around the ton like wildfire that Mr. Warwick had clearly abandoned his suit of Miss Darcy and was pursuing Miss Bennet of Hertfordshire, Mrs. Darcy's nearly penniless sister.

Beau Brummell heard the story at White's, and strolled over to call on her and congratulate her on her conquest.

Lydia ordinarily found him a very amusing man, but on this occasion laughed bitterly and shook her head. She would be glad when notice of Georgiana's engagement appeared in the papers.

"I hope you've not wagered on it, Mr. Brummell – I would hate to see you lose money based on gossip."

"My dear Miss Bennet!" exclaimed he, "there have been many caps set at Mr. Warwick and all have failed to make any headway. Do you mean to tell me that you don't want the fellow? How extraordinary."

"Well, you see, Mr. Brummell, he inflicted the most dreadful waistcoat on us last evening. I shall spare you a description but I could not be interested in a man who was badly dressed, after all."

"Beautifully delivered, Miss Bennet," he said, with that charming smile hovering about his lips. "I shall be certain to quote you verbatim. I almost wish I had thought of it myself."

He went away smiling and was true to his word. Miss Bennet, whispered the ton, who must be held to be a Judge of such matters, did not like Mr. Warwick's waistcoats and so would have none of him. Naturally, this reached the ears of her suitor, and the next time he saw her, he approached while she was amongst a crowd of eager young gentlemen. They parted, waiting to see if she would send him on his way.

"I have heard, Miss Bennet, that you did not care for the waistcoat I wore last time we danced. I am relieved to hear it, for my fault is so easily amended. I had worried that there was a more pressing reason that you did not seem pleased by me. Have you any objection to the one I am currently wearing?"

Lydia sipped at her drink. One of her admirers had run to fetch it after she had complained of thirst, and she had been delighted to be waited on so well. She regarded the waistcoat seriously. Here was a grand opportunity to snub the man publicly and be well rid of him.

"I adore the pattern, Mr. Warwick," she said, grinning wickedly. "I have a nostalgia for such floral patterns as that. My grandmama had such a print hanging at the windows of her music room."

A shout of laughter went up amongst the gentlemen, but was silenced when Mr. Warwick, instead of looking wounded, smiled in such a way that gave Lydia to understand that she had played into his hands, and her eyes widened.

He bowed to her and turned to depart.

"Warwick, where are you going, man?" called Mr. Spillings.

"To change my waistcoat, of course. Then Miss Bennet will have no reason to refuse to dance with me."

He said it loudly enough to attract the attention of Mrs. Darcy and several of the matrons present.

If rumour had been rife before, it was now rampant. Miss Bennet was clearly destined to become Mrs. Warwick. Surely she would not have been so bold as to tell him to change his clothing if she did not mean to accept him.

He returned within the hour, wearing a green affair with a gold thread running throughout it. It was not a bad effort, but it was the wrong shade of green for him. She suspected that he knew it.

Elizabeth, having listened with increasing dismay to Mrs. St. John's report of the matter, saw him enter, saw Lydia's tense expression, and leaned in to whisper in her sister's ear while walking with her away from Mr. Warwick.

"Lydia, dearest, take care. Everyone in this room will be watching you. Refuse to dance with him and you will be labelled a dreadful flirt; dance with him and they will all think you and he are a settled thing."

Beginning to feel a little alarmed, Lydia whispered back, "Should I feign a headache?"

"On no account! If you run away now, people will talk even more."

"Lizzy, what should I do then?" Her voice neared a whine.

"What can he be about, I wonder. I was so sure that he was angling for Georgiana! Are all of your dances taken?"

"All but the last."

"Well then, you had better dance with Fitzwilliam and we will carry things off. Don't fret, little sister – we will manage very well. Go to the ladies' retiring room and write in Mr. Darcy's name on your card. I will find Fitzwilliam. If Mr. Warwick approaches you, you had better say that you would, of course, have obliged him after such efforts as he has made but sadly all your dances are taken."

"Oh, that is very good," said Lydia, rather enjoying the thought of foiling any of Mr. Warwick's schemes. "I will do that – thank you, Lizzy."

Mrs. Darcy glided off to find her husband and charm him into aiding her youngest sister, while Lydia made her way to the little room reserved for the ladies who needed to pin up their dresses or repair their coiffures.

Mr. Warwick wandered over after she had reentered the ballroom. Lydia, seeing him coming, stepped a little closer to Mrs. Colchester and her matronly friends, bidding them a polite good evening.

"Will you dance with me now, Miss Bennet?" asked he, a gleam of mockery in his eyes.

Lydia fluttered her painted fan and tried to speak as carelessly as she could. She could not manage Lizzy's arch lightness and so careless it must be.

"La! Mr. Warwick, how amusing you are, sir. I would have been only too pleased to dance with you, but your condescension has persuaded all the other young men at the ball that I am so delightful a companion that I fear there are no more dances left. I am so dreadfully sorry."

She heard the starched-up Mrs. Colchester mutter a low "Good gel!" behind her and felt glad of the approval.

Mr. Warwick, his aim achieved, regardless of the outcome in terms of dancing, looked sardonic and said, "It is my loss, Miss Bennet, I am sure. I shall be certain to wear this waistcoat next time I see you, and seek your approval on others ahead of time to avoid such disappointment."

Taking advantage of the public setting, he reached for her gloved hand, noticing the slight flinch she made, and kissed it, muttering quietly as he did so, so that only she could hear, "I guarantee you, Miss Bennet, you will not have half so many young men desirous of a dance with you by the time the week is out," before he said more audibly, "Enjoy your dances, madam. Good evening."

Lydia could not entirely work out how he had done it, but within two weeks she was obliged to own that he had been correct. The number of young men that had flocked to dance with Beau Brummell's favourite dwindled considerably in the face of Mr. Warwick's determined pursuit.

Never one to be cast down quickly, she tossed her head and made a glib remark to Lady Beatrice that she could not care for cowardly men, so the decline in admiring gentlemen at parties did not trouble her in the slightest.

With Lady Beatrice, Lydia was happily browsing the selection of fabrics Waddington's had available. Mr. Darcy had permitted her to go out with her ladyship but only if Mibbs might accompany her, armed with a gun. Her brother-in-law had not smiled when she had suggested that he might like to further bolster her safety by providing her with a weapon also. She had been only half-joking when she said it. Indeed, she thought, as she ran a hand across a gold damask that would be delightful for a ballgown, if she could find out where to purchase a gun, she would do so.

Lady Beatrice, having a very indulgent father, bought three different bolts of cloth that afternoon with little thought as to whether or not she might actually wear them. Lydia was not jealous, precisely, but wished she might do the same. Instead, she selected only a length of blue ribbon for Georgiana and a pretty Chinese silk reticule for herself. Lydia might frequently find herself with little money available at the end of a quarter but she was not selfish. If she wanted to wed a rich man, it was not solely for the purposes of living in luxury herself. She spent her money freely if she had it, largely because if she saw something pretty that might please her sisters or a good friend, she bought it without a second thought.

She had given the matter some consideration, over the years, since Lizzy had first suggested that not marrying well meant harder work for a wife. It had taken her a good while to realise that although she wanted a charming, handsome husband, she also wanted a generous one who would not quibble with her if she wished to spend her money on pretty things. Surely such a man must exist in London?

"Look, Justin! It is Lady Beatrice and Miss Bennet. Good afternoon."

The young ladies curtseyed to the Countess of Warwick, who was on the arm of her husband's cousin. Lydia's lips tightened when Mr. Warwick caught her eye with a smile.

The countess, unaware that Miss Bennet had quickly turned her head to ascertain the whereabouts of Mibbs, struck up a conversation with Lady Beatrice about her purchases that day. Mr. Warwick drew beside Lydia and ran his hand over the gold cloth that she had previously been admiring.

"This would look well on you, I think. There is something about the warmth of it, although I cannot tell what it should be."

Lydia, for all she detested the man, could not resist educating him.

"A ballgown, obviously. It would look garish in full daylight but candlelight would make it shimmer delightfully." Lest he think that she was being friendly, she frowned at him when he looked triumphant.

"This is your favourite place?" he asked, unwilling to let her be.

"I cannot see that it is any of your business where my favourite place is, Mr. Warwick," snapped Lydia.

"You looked happy," he mused, "when I spied you through the window, I mean. I had thought that you were at your most cheerful at a ball, but I do not think that is right."

"Mr. Warwick..." said Lydia, annoyed.

"I know, I know – you hate me and I am a contemptible swine – but what is the harm in speaking with me?"

"I speak with you only because the talk will be quite dreadful if I don't. Why can you not see that I do not want to know a man such as you?"

"Because you don't know me, Lydia. You have naively painted me as a villain for one questionable act."

"*Questionable!*" she cried and then winced, for it drew the attention of Lady Warwick and Lady Beatrice.

Mr. Warwick smiled widely at the other ladies and lied through his teeth without a blush.

"Miss Bennet does not think I ought to have this beautiful gold fabric for a greatcoat, cousin – what think you of that?"

Lady Warwick looked at the gold cloth and her delicate grey eyebrows spasmed.

"I think it is a very good thing that you asked me for my advice, Justin. A coat, absolutely not. You need a darker, heavier fabric – you'd be a laughingstock if you wore that, not that any reputable tailor would do it for you. Miss Bennet is quite correct. Lady Beatrice is going to show me where the silver net is, Justin. Do not on any account let him buy anything without my aid, Miss Bennet!"

The other two ladies went to the far corner of the shop and Lydia scowled at the man she was left with.

"It wasn't only *questionable* to try to steal Miss Darcy and you know it!" she hissed at him.

"I will admit that I was wrong, Miss Bennet. Will that suffice?"

Lydia was flummoxed, and shook her head at him, entirely devoid of speech.

"Are you going to buy it, then?" he asked, seeing that she would not answer his earlier question.

"What?"

"The cloth, Lydia. Are you going to buy that gold cloth and wear it as a ballgown?" he said, very patiently as though speaking to a child.

"No," she replied reluctantly. "I want to go and find Lady Beatrice now. We should be returning home soon or my sister will worry."

"Why not?" he continued, as though she had not just dismissed him again, casually leaning his elbow on the bolt where it rested on the shelf.

Impatiently, Lydia half-turned to face him, having started to walk away. "Because I want to buy a gun instead."

Mr. Warwick was surprised into genuine laughter and took a moment to compose himself. He walked with her across the shop to find their companions.

"That is more my area of expertise, my pet. You should take my advice on the matter, just as I will take yours regarding my waistcoats. You might buy a pretty little weapon that is entirely useless at firing with any accuracy."

"I don't care what it looks like," said Lydia pertly, "I just want one that will put a hole through the next rogue who tries to take what doesn't belong to him." She spied the two ladies by the array of silver and gold net, being assisted by a very obliging shop boy, and waved. "Oh, Lady Beatrice, shall you mind if Mibbs returns us to Darcy House now? My sister is still on edge if I am out for too long."

Her ladyship did not mind in the least, and after bidding Mr. Warwick and the Countess a far more civil farewell than Lydia did, she and Lydia left the shop with their purchases.

Some ten days after her shopping trip, after she had finished dressing for the day, Lydia was presented with a small, neatly wrapped box by her maid.

"Thank you, Cason. I do not remember ordering anything but perhaps Mama has sent me the old ribbons that I said I should like. I thought Master Theodore might like to play with them. I shall open it in a little while. You may go now."

After Cason had left, Lydia tossed the box onto the bed and turned to leave the room. Having nearly reached the door, she hesitated. The box had been far too heavy to contain merely ribbons, and, her curiosity being piqued, she decided to open it immediately. The clock informed her that she had a mere few minutes to do so, or she would risk being late for breakfast again and her brother-in-law would frown, Georgiana would look shocked, and worst of all, Lizzy would be disappointed.

The box did not contain her old ribbons. Inside the wrapping lay a little gun, just the right size for a young lady to conceal in a muff or reticule.

Lydia sat down heavily on the bed. It was not arduous to realise who had sent it – what was difficult to comprehend was why had he sent it. The clock chimed, and Lydia hastily thrust the little weapon under her pillow and sped from the room.

She spent much of breakfast in silence, troubled by the gift that was upstairs in her bed and very unsettled in her mind as to what she ought to do with it. She could not return it directly to his hands for fear of someone seeing and gossiping about it. Neither could she tell anyone of it for fear of Mr. Darcy's finding out and making a fuss. Lydia spread butter and jam onto her slice of bread and ate it without even registering that she had done so. Georgiana noticed her reverie.

"Is aught amiss, Lydia? Are you unwell?" she asked quietly when the others at the table had risen to serve themselves more food.

"Oh, I am never ill," said Lydia. "I am in a quandary over something, that is all. Nothing very significant, really. I shall come about."

"That is good, then. I do not wish to impose on you, Lydia, but would you mind accompanying Elizabeth and me to the dressmaker this afternoon? If I am to be wed in less than a month, I want to be sure that I am well outfitted, and would be grateful for your guidance. I cannot decide upon the length of sleeve, you know. Will you come?"

Lydia nodded agreeably. It sounded like the very thing she needed to distract her from Mr. Warwick's perplexing behaviour.

Chapter Six

On a bright afternoon, Lydia was promenading in the park with Sir Daniel James at the fashionable hour. Her maid followed at a slight distance with Mibbs, who nearly always carried a gun with him ever since Mr. Darcy had given him orders to be armed. If she were to describe Sir Daniel to her Mama in one of her short and infrequent letters, Lydia had little doubt that Mrs. Bennet would encourage her towards him. He was an older gentleman, nearing forty years, and a widower. His wife having passed away in childbirth some twelve months before, he found it once again necessary to find a wife, his family lands being in need of an heir. For some reason, he had decided that Miss Bennet was an adequate candidate, and set out to woo her. He spoke of his estate, which was not a large affair, he said, but quite comfortable enough. His late wife, he hinted, had done a great deal to it when they were first married so it had been fairly recently decorated. He also remarked that he had known the late Lady James since he was a boy, and had pointedly remarked that between the ages of twenty and twenty-five, a young woman did much growing up. Lydia wrinkled her nose at that but remained silent and listened.

She found that around Sir Daniel she could not speak a lot. She often felt that he was evaluating her when she spoke – he never said so directly, but he would ever so politely censure her if she said anything that he deemed unsuitable. Lydia did not especially like the feeling of being judged and wondered if she ought to send him on his way. She did not, however, for of all the gentlemen that had paid her attention since the beginning of the season, he was perhaps the most likely to come up to scratch and actually propose. The question was, did she want him? She turned it over in her mind as they walked along, arm in arm.

She saw Mr. Warwick out riding some little way off and watched him as he skillfully directed his mount nearer to them. Mr. Warwick certainly looked well on a horse, Lydia noted. He bowed to her from his seat and nodded very coolly to Sir Daniel.

"Miss Bennet, how do you do. I hope that you are not out unprotected? Oh no, I see that you have your groom and your maid with you."

Sir Daniel did not rise to the insult, much to Lydia's disappointment.

"Mr. Warwick, I have been wanting to speak to you," she said, trying to sound convincing about it. "Shall you be at the theatre tonight? Grimaldi is playing the clown again."

Sir Daniel patiently interjected that he rather thought Miss Bennet might have preferred Mr. Kean for his edifying Shakespearean performances.

"La! Sir Daniel, I am sure he is a very good actor in his way, but I favour Grimaldi, especially if it is an amusing piece. Half of the fun of the theatre is dressing for it, after all."

The creases between Sir Daniel James's eyebrows deepened at the dismissal. Well, she was sure she did not care in the least if he thought her a silly girl – Shakespeare was more often than not odiously dull.

Mr. Warwick laughed. "I shall be there, Miss Bennet. I shall find you in the interval, no doubt."

He did so, and if he had thought by her earlier civility that she had quite changed her opinion of him, he was soon disabused of the notion when Lydia lost no time in ripping up at him as soon as they were in relative privacy.

"What are you about, Mr. Warwick? A gun arrived addressed to me, and I certainly did not order it, and as you are the only other man apart from Mr. Darcy to whom I have said anything about one, I can only assume you are out to ruin me."

"Oh, has it come already? Yes, I can see why Mr. Darcy is cleared of suspicion – a very serious fellow, isn't he? It fires beautifully, my pet. You ought to point it in the direction of that prosy bore I saw you walking with this morning. Don't you like it? You said you wanted one and I am only too happy to oblige. Women are usually so boring in their wants; I haven't ever been asked for a gun before."

"You weren't asked this time," said Lydia, now very familiar with the feeling of vexation that this man provoked. "I was merely reminding you that you would be the most likely target if I had one."

"Well, now you do, so you will doubtless be much more at ease around me." Mr. Warwick said carelessly. "If you marry me soon, I will show you how to shoot the thing straight. I daresay you'd be the rare female who might manage to do so quite well."

Repressing any pleasure she might have felt at the compliment, she replied with some spirit, "You think I will forget that incident in the park merely because you have bought me a gift that I cannot possibly accept? It was not merely me that was fri...annoyed, simpleton!"

A gleam crept into his eyes. They were a warmer shade of green in the candlelit theatre foyer. Lydia acknowledged to herself that for all his faults, his eyes were uniquely beautiful.

"Shall I buy one for the future Mrs. Kentmire, Lydia? I will if you desire me to."

A gurgle of laughter escaped her and was hastily suppressed when he looked triumphant. She ought not to be laughing with such a villainous wretch, but the image of poor Georgiana attempting to explain such a gift to her husband or brother struck her as wickedly amusing.

She sounded a little friendlier when she said, "I wish you would not – I should probably be blamed for it. Send her a little white kitten instead. She has wanted one forever but Mr. Darcy quite detests them."

"They would blame you? That seems unfair, unless of course it is the sort of thing you might do for a lark."

Lydia considered the matter. Honesty compelled her to admit to herself that she and Mr. Warwick were not entirely dissimilar in that respect. It was an uncomfortable realisation, and she frowned.

He saw instantly that she was back to despising him again and spoke urgently. "Lydia, it is not so great a thing, is it? I wanted to buy you a pretty gift and so I did. If keeping it in your reticule will make you realise that you need not be so afraid of – I beg your pardon, I meant annoyed by – me, then surely it is a good thing."

Lydia looked up at him, feeling vulnerable, and angry because of it. She felt even crosser when she realised her own hypocrisy in her response.

"A lady can't accept expensive gifts, Mr. Warwick. It isn't done. If anyone found out, I'd be ruined."

Mr. Warwick clicked his tongue in disappointment. "Conventions are so very wearisome, are they not? I suppose," he added carefully, "you will accept only flowers from me, then?"

Having frequently expressed her impatience regarding the some of the more ridiculous rules surrounding her, Lydia could only nod, and then bit her lip when he grinned. He kissed her hand before he walked away, having delivered her to the door of Mr. Darcy's box.

"Then I shall send you flowers, my pet," he laughed, before sauntering away.

He called one morning, bearing a bouquet in his hand, when Sir Daniel James was taking his leave. Sir Daniel was returning to his estate near Bath for a few days and came to bid Lydia a very punctilious farewell.

Mr. Warwick watched him bow over Lydia's hand and sneered slightly. Georgiana was sat with Mrs. Darcy and Mr. Kentmire, discussing the upcoming nuptials, and Mr. Warwick asked Mrs. Darcy if he might escort her sister to Bond Street. Leave was granted reluctantly by a wary Mrs. Darcy. She had not approved of the position he had put her sister in the last time she saw him.

"How can you have known that I needed to go shopping?" Lydia demanded of him, once he had handed her up into his open carriage with Cason settled beside the driver on the box, her eyes trained primly forward. She attempted to keep her tone vaguely civil for Cason's benefit, and was dimly aware that she had failed when the woman stifled a gasp.

Mr. Warwick stretched his legs out in front of him. "Do not all ladies always need to purchase something or another, Miss Bennet? I suppose the household is all wedding talk these days. I shall attend, I think. I should like to see a grand affair from a family that is not famed for excess."

The noise of the wheels on the cobbled road covered some of their talk and he brought the conversation round to Sir Daniel James.

"Sir Daniel would be the same, you know; depend upon it. You would not be happy with such a stuffed shirt, my pet. You had better forget about him, I think – I simply cannot see that he would suit you at all."

Lydia wished she might stick out her tongue at him, but alas, the risk of doing so in an open carriage was too great. "Not," she said loftily, "that I think it is any of your business, but Sir Daniel James is a very ri...respectable man."

"But is a mere fifteen thousand a year worth enduring such boredom, I wonder?" asked the infuriating man beside her. "He would probably need to be revived with smelling salts if he found out the contents of that charming little reticule you are carrying, Lydia. Whereas if you would like to marry me instead, I'd teach you how to actually use the thing. We could scandalise the servants by setting up targets on the front lawn.

"I detest black," said Lydia. "My sister Mrs. Darcy is the only female I have ever encountered who wears it well, and even the thought of making myself your widow cannot tempt me into marrying you first."

"But you need not fire it at me, my dear. I am known to be very charming when I set my mind to it, and it may be that you decide you like me very well as a husband. Did you like your flowers?" he asked, smiling gently, a provocative gleam in his eye.

Lydia was instantly suspicious. His bouquet that morning had been an unexceptional but beautiful arrangement of red roses. "Why? What have you done?"

"Nothing desperately wicked." Seeing her look wary, he laughed shortly and then sighed. "I despise the rules that society imposes on courtship – most of them are entirely useless. If I wished to buy something pretty for a young lady to wear, merely for the pleasure of her enjoyment, why may I not?"

"You are not so bound up by useless rules as we women are, Mr. Warwick." said Lydia, her interest quite caught by the fact there was another human being on earth who took her view of things, "'Tis monstrously unfair. If you knew the number of silly edicts that I had to commit to memory, just to protect my reputation, you would be vastly shocked."

"There now," he nodded, satisfied, "you see that we are of a like mind in this; now we are making good progress."

Lydia sighed. "Mr. Warwick, I do not know what to make of you." She sounded quite petulant, even to her own ears.

Mr. Warwick lifted a placating hand and spoke soothingly. "You need only ask me what you wish to know, Lydia."

"You make no sense! Nothing you do adds up – it is very trying. I can see why…" she lowered her voice, "I can see why you tried to take Georgiana – her money, that is clear as day – but I cannot make out why, having been bested, you have transferred your irritating attention to me. Men hate being beaten."

"All men, Lydia?" he teased, "Such a young lady to have established such a thing with such certainty."

"Well, I have not ever met a man who loses very graciously."

"I shall not argue with you on that score. Have I not already told you what changed my mind that day? Having spent my life very certain that I understood women, and being utterly sure that they could not surprise me, you did just that." He paused and observed her wide eyes. "I spent some time fighting in Spain, you know. Believe me when I say that your courage is a rare thing, even amongst men."

When Lydia had been returned back to Darcy House, having bought what she needed from the haberdashers' while Mr. Warwick watched her every perusal with unnerving attentiveness, she slipped up to her bedchamber to take off her pelisse and outdoor shoes. The roses had been laid on her dressing table, still in their cream paper. She pulled at it idly, thinking to free the flowers and have a maid put them in water. They were pretty, after all, and why should she not enjoy them, even if it had been Mr. Warwick who sent them? She could always tell him that she had tossed them away, if he needed his pretensions depressing. Lydia could not help but smile at that. Mr. Warwick would always need cutting down to size. He was not a timid man, after all.

His voice echoed in her head as she thought on what he had said in the carriage. It was not the words that she could not shake from her mind, but the caressing tone of voice with which he said them. Gentlemen had flirted with her before, and often; some of them had even dared to whisper in her ear that they adored her and such pretty things as that, but she had never before been spoken to by a man with that degree of tenderness. It was very flattering, but she was not quite sure how she felt about it.

She separated the blooms and reached for a small pair of scissors with which to trim them. Picking them up, she gasped loudly. Cason poked her head around the door to the dressing room.

"Did you call me, miss?"

Lydia, her eyes fixed on the flowers in front of her, did not turn to face the door. In a slightly weak voice, she responded. "What? Oh. No, Cason, I did not call you. I...I almost pricked my finger on these roses; that is all. It gave me a fright. Carry on with what you were doing."

"Very good, Miss Bennet."

Wound about the stems, gleaming with milky white purity, was a pearl necklace of some considerable length.

Lydia swallowed and set to disentangling it from the roses. Once she was done, she lifted it up and stretched it out. It was the length of her arm, stretching from shoulder to fingertip. Each pearl was beautifully matched with its mates on the thread. It was a very fine, very expensive necklace.

Quickly, before she could think twice about it, Lydia wound it about her neck three times and looked in the mirror. She bit her lip and something an awful lot like glee filled her.

She had tried on her Mama's pearls before and admired them immensely. They would go to Jane, of course, when Mrs. Bennet no longer lived, and as a younger girl, Lydia had been quite sick with envy over them.

Such a dreadful torment it was, to now have a necklace ten times as beautiful in her possession and know that she really ought not to keep it. She could hardly wear it in any case. Someone would be bound to ask her where it came from and she could hardly tell them the truth, could she? Lydia pondered the matter seriously, running a fingertip over the smooth surface of the pearls and enjoying the cool weight of them against her skin.

Quickly, she took the necklace off and slipped it into the box that had held her gun, then hid the box in a drawer and quit the room before she could be further tempted, resolving that she would not think of the pearls or their giver any longer.

The day of Miss Georgiana Darcy's wedding dawned. The bride came down to breakfast looking as though she had not slept well. To Lydia, it was difficult to tell if she was excited or terrified, but judging by Elizabeth's soothing remarks, it might well have been a healthy dose of both.

Mr. Darcy, who was not usually a talkative man, barely spoke a word at breakfast – he did not appear to view the events of the day with any joy. Elizabeth did her best to cheer him and managed to elicit a smile, but he soon relapsed into the doldrums.

Lydia rather thought that on the day that she married, she would wish everyone to be happy and cheerful, just as she would be, and she struggled to comprehend the mournful looks on the faces of Mr. Darcy and Georgiana on what ought to surely be a day of joy. She knew better by now than to point out the things that she herself would like about getting married – she had learnt fairly early on that Georgiana did not seem to find the enjoyment that she did in being the centre of everybody's attention. Darcys, she decided, were decidedly baffling people.

Mrs. Darcy entered Lydia's bedchamber later that morning, just as Cason was putting the finishing touches to her hair.

"Ah! Lydia dearest, you are nearly ready. I am so glad. Would you go to Georgiana's room and assure her that she is in every way a radiant bride, please? Theodore has been wailing for me. I think my poor darling may be suffering from teething pain and I would take him with me, of course, but I do not think that it would aid his aunt's nerves."

Nodding, Lydia did so, and spent above a quarter of an hour attempting to cheer up the bride, who seemed to vacillate wildly between feeling very well pleased for herself and happy to be getting married to feeling quite overwhelmed with guilt in leaving her brother's house.

By the time they had reached the church, Lydia was almost certain that she would have preferred to have spent the time with Master Theodore, for all the success she seemed to have in soothing his other aunt.

After her duties as bridesmaid were accomplished and the deed was done – mysteriously restoring both Georgiana and her brother back to cheer – Lydia took her seat in a pew and looked about her as the bishop delegated the task of delivering a sermon to a vicar. Twisting her neck to the left, she spied Mr. Warwick looking as bored as she felt, and almost felt disposed to smile at him. He caught her eye and pretended to look stern, gesturing with a wagging gloved finger that she ought to be facing the front and paying heed to what was being said. Tossing her head a little, she did so, and did not give him the satisfaction of looking in his direction again, even if he had looked so very droll.

He found her afterwards, as she stood on the steps of the church in lively conversation with the bishop, and exchanged a few polite words with the splendidly robed man before the Right Reverend went to speak with the Countess of Warwick.

"I like his dress," said Mr. Warwick, eyeing the back of the richly embroidered robe with disfavour. "I do hope it will not become the fashion, though."

Miss Bennet could not repress a grin. "You ought to speak more quietly, Mr. Warwick – if you insult a bishop, they will likely speed along your execution when that day inevitably comes." There was no heat in her words, however, and recognising this, the corner of his mouth curled up in a roguish grin.

"I sent the bride a darling little pistol in the good bishop's name, you know," he said to her in a low, provocative voice, and then watched with great pleasure as she stifled a snort and struggled to contain herself by biting her lip. Avoiding his eye, Lydia turned her attention to the wedding party and seeing the blushing Mrs. Kentmire being warmly congratulated by the officiant, she quite lost her composure and her giggles rang out as clearly as the peal of bells that were clanging loudly from above them.

Chapter Seven

Mrs. Darcy, having expressed a mild interest to her husband some weeks beforehand, was one morning presented with tickets of admission to the museum in which Lord Elgin had elected to display the various artifacts that had been brought back from Greece. Elizabeth in return had rewarded her husband with an admiring glance and an expressive smile.

"How can you have accomplished such a thing so quickly, Fitzwilliam? I was entirely certain that I should have to drop gentle hints for several weeks more at the very least."

Lydia watched as Mr. Darcy rested a hand on his wife's shoulder and kissed her offered hand. He was by no means an expressive man, but Lizzy seemed able to coax him out of his dour habits merely by being so delighted with him.

"On the contrary, Mrs. Darcy, I think you were very aware that I should arrange it as soon as I could, once you casually raised the matter. Shall you like to go later today? I must spend an hour or so with Mr. Hart – Kentmire asked for my opinion on some land in Staffordshire, and I shall need to write a few letters."

It was decided, therefore, that the three of them should have an afternoon outing to that dullest of buildings – a museum. There was no question that Lydia might be left at home, or that she should be permitted to go off and enjoy some other form of amusement more suited to her. Fitzwilliam Darcy had not forgotten that both of the sisters currently under his protection had narrowly escaped disaster in the park, even if he was by now fairly sure that the situation had been an isolated one.

He soon repressed thoughts of danger, and enjoyed wandering the exhibits with his pretty wife on his arm. He even managed to rein in any irritation he might have felt at Lydia's poorly disguised boredom.

Lydia was not so uninterested as her brother-in-law supposed her to be; the friezes did not please her in the slightest, but the cunningly wrought statues, with the graceful folds of stone dresses, she thought very fine. But admiration of the long-dead sculptor's skill did not absorb her for very long, and in a short time she had separated herself a little from the Darcys and gone in search of further interest.

She found it in the adjoining room, wherein she found more statues, and to her vague dismay, the Earl of Warwick and his wife. She was greeted very civilly by them.

"Ho! It is Miss Bennet, my lady. Have you come to admire my friend Lord Elgin's acquisitions, madam?" began the earl.

Rising from her curtsey, Lydia replied in the negative. "I think the dresses are very cleverly done, my lord, but I am here because my sister wished to come. Mrs. Darcy has always been fascinated by historical things."

"Excellent – is Darcy in the other room? I have been wanting a word with him, and I daresay you will be wishful to speak to his wife, Lady Warwick. Come along. Miss Bennet, if you see my young scamp of a cousin lurking about, tell him we have not gone off and abandoned him, would you?"

Lydia wondered if Mr. Warwick, with his practiced charm and decided air of town polish, would like to be described in such terms, and smiled at the earl in acquiescence. She wandered the quiet room, occasionally reaching out to feel the cold smooth marble as she passed by. Her reticule hung from her gloved wrist, the perfect shade of green to match the ribbons on her hat. She felt the weight of her little gun as it occasionally knocked against her leg. A stray curl had sprung loose from her elegant coiffure and she lightly brushed it away from her cheek, careful not to crush Cason's work.

"'See how she leans her cheek upon her hand! O, that I were a glove upon that hand, That I might touch that cheek,'" quoted Mr. Warwick in deep soulful tones as he emerged from behind a statue.

He would doubtless have been pleased to learn that Lydia was hard-pressed to refrain from turning to look at him, but resisted on the grounds that she could not quite decide whether she wished to smile or scowl in his direction.

"So that is how you attained such a reputation with young ladies, Mr. Warwick. I could not account for it before, but I do admit that you spout nonsense very prettily." She did not give him time to answer, but continued, "Lord Warwick wished me to direct the 'young scamp' to the other room if you were looking for him."

Mr. Warwick looked rueful, and she nearly laughed. "There is nothing so lowering as one's relatives, I find. However dashing and debonair I think myself, my cousin can be relied upon to make me feel like a scrubby schoolboy in an instant."

Lydia smirked unsympathetically and then relented. "My father is the same. I had just put up my hair on my fifteenth birthday and was feeling quite the young lady, but he soon ended that notion."

"I cannot suppose that he called you a 'young scamp,' Lydia," exclaimed Mr. Warwick, leaning casually on a pedestal that displayed a tarnished bronze helmet. Lydia thought it an ugly old thing.

"No, a 'silly miss.' I suppose it is the equivalent. I imagine he will think of me as such even when I am married with a half-dozen children in tow."

Mr. Warwick cocked his head, his light green eyes considering her.

"What?" she said, irritated again.

"I am trying to imagine it and failing. I cannot see you as anything other than how you are now."

Lydia softened at that, but said, "I cannot either, really, but I suppose the inevitable must come eventually. It is a pity; I cannot imagine having anything near so much fun when I am a proper grown-up as I do now."

"Oh, I don't see that – I should think you would like the liberty that being married will give you."

"Depends on the husband, I suppose," she said, a little glumly, thinking of Mr. Collins and Mr. Darcy. Her other brothers-in-law seemed to be a little more liberal.

Mr. Warwick ceased to lounge against the pillar and blinked. "Ah yes, I was forgetting that. You can't be still considering Sir Daniel? I was rather under the impression that he had fled."

An inkling of suspicion crept up the base of Lydia's neck and into her brain. "Did you have something to with that?" she accused.

"I, my pet? What influence do you suppose I have? If your fair charms aren't enough to bring him up to the mark, must it necessarily be my fault?"

"My charms are quite sufficient, Mr. Warwick," said Lydia with some tartness, "if I am permitted to wield them without interference. I notice that you did not say 'no.'"

"Lydia, my dear, I am wholly delighted to think that you would believe me if I had protested my innocence." He grinned rakishly and Lydia bit her lip.

"You haven't any innocence to protest," she responded, and was quite pleased with her own wit.

He laughed. "That is true enough, but I think you are converting me a little more each time you see me. Imagine what a gift I shall be to society if you consented to see me every day ever after."

Lydia felt her face go hot, and swallowed, turning to look at the same dull group of statues she had been pretending to admire for the past five minutes. A horse's head, a pair of seated women, their hands elegantly raised, and a female standing beside them, her dress billowing in the wind.

"Do you know who they are?" she asked, not from any particular interest but in a bid to change the subject.

He looked at the figures. "Elgin supposes them to be Demeter and Persephone, but I should think it's anyone's guess, given that it is difficult to identify headless people." Seeing that she looked blankly at him, he knit his brow. "I had a tedious professor at Cambridge who was very thorough in our lessons. Demeter is the mother and Persephone the daughter. Legend has it that she was abducted by her uncle who wanted to take her to wife in the Underworld."

Lydia stared at him pointedly and he swallowed.

"It is hardly the same!"

A window in the room had been left open and a breeze wafted in, rippling the ribbons of her bonnet. Still she stared at him until he could not meet her gaze. Something like shame crept into his eyes when she said, with far more seriousness than was her wont, "Mr. Warwick, it is exactly the same."

Mr. Warwick looked blindly at the seated statues and twisted the gloves he carried in his hand before turning his face back to her.

Cold, marble-like silence descended between them, and somehow Lydia knew that it must not be broken just yet.

"You make me seem a beastly fellow, Miss Bennet," he said at length, somberly. "No, that is not right; you don't. You have merely pointed out what is already there, have you not? Honest Lydia, brave and unflinching! Does nothing frighten you? No, never mind that. You have found me out and you are quite right. I behaved very badly and I am sorry for it. Mrs. Kentmire...I rather thought that her brother would force the issue out of propriety and so I would not need to. It amounts to the same thing, does it not? Or at least it would have done for her."

Having finished his incoherent speech, he stepped nearer to her but did not reach out his hand. When he spoke next, he spoke quietly and with every semblance of sincerity.

"You do not trust me; I am not such a conceited fool as to not see it. I would have you know, Lydia, that I mean what I say at present. I do think that I might become...that I am already becoming a better man for love of you. Think on that before you accept some dowdy bore to live beside every day and before you assign me a lifetime of madness brought on by jealousy."

There was something about his expression as he spoke that made Lydia feel both pity and triumph over him in the self-same moment. She knew what to do with a man she had conquered – that was easy enough; but when coupled with compassion rather than contempt – that demanded rather more thought. What was she to do with a man who was remorseful? Her breath hitched and she was utterly at a loss for words, just like the silly little miss her father supposed her to be.

She nodded once and the moment was gone.

"Let us talk of something else now, Mr. Warwick," she begged. "My head is all a-whirl."

He bowed a little and smoothly changed the subject. "Have you frightened any of your sister's servants by aiming that pretty little gun at them yet, my pet?" he asked softly, offering her his arm.

She accepted it without giving the matter much thought; perhaps she was beginning to trust him more than she had previously supposed. Imagining Cason shrieking at the sight of a loaded gun made her lips quiver with amusement.

"Not yet, although if my maid tries to offer me a Chinese blue stole to wear with an emerald green dress again, I shan't be responsible for my actions."

He laughed, and they viewed the statues from a little distance away. Lydia remarked that she should have been more impressed if the horse had been complete, not that she had any interest in any of them.

"By the by, Mr. Warwick, since you have made me a present of it, I should like to know how to unload a pistol. I managed to load the thing well enough with the little tamper and some gunpowder – it is very hard to buy gunpowder if you are a single young lady, you know; shopkeepers ask the nosiest questions – but I cannot seem to work out the mechanics of emptying the thing...why, what is the matter?"

Mr. Warwick had glanced down at the little silken reticule that rested between them, and had sprung away from her with great alarm.

"Do you mean to tell me, Lydia, that the thing is loaded?" he asked, greatly agitated.

"Well, what would be the point of having one if I cannot shoot someone with it?" she said reasonably, not understanding in the least why he should be looking at her so.

"The point? Lydia, it could kill either of us at any moment if you knocked the trigger!"

"Could it? Oh," she said, digesting this information and then infuriating her companion by shrugging. "Well, it hasn't done so far, so it may not be worth worrying over."

"Give it to me," he demanded, apparently unaware that Lydia did not respond well to such tones.

"I shall not. It is mine and I want to keep it."

He seized her reticule and tried to undo the string. She grasped it back and pulled.

"No! Don't do that – you'll set the thing off. I shall hand it back to you the very next time I see you; only let me take it away and discharge it and I will...."

Having broken the string tying the reticule at the top, he fished the little gun out and held it aloft. Lydia, beginning to feel very angry, for she did not much like to give up her things, stood on her tiptoes and reached for the pistol.

It went off with a very loud retort. The arm of one of the seated female figures behind them cracked and fell to the ground with an echoing clatter.

The two of them looked at each other in dismay until Lydia broke their shocked speechlessness by giggling, and Mr. Warwick, his eyes alight with tender amusement, choked out, "Lydia, *you*...."

He did not have time to complete his thought, because there was a shout and the museum officials came running, with Mr. Darcy and the Earl of Warwick in hot pursuit.

"We heard gunfire!" gasped a plump, balding little man with a badly tied cravat.

Lydia, no longer laughing, looked to Mr. Warwick for rescue.

"Yes, that was me." he said. "A little foreign fellow came in through that open window there and, not realising we were here, attempted to make off with some of the delightful treasures here. I very politely asked him what he was about and he waved a gun at me. Fortunately, since Miss Bennet and Mrs. Kentmire's having been frigh...annoyed in the park, I have gone about armed and I opened fire. He ran off shouting in...in Greek, I think it was. Possibly French; I cannot say. I am only sorry that the shot went wide, but Miss Bennet was upset and clutched at my arm at quite the wrong moment, I fear. Ah...yes, I see that the arm has quite come off that lady. I am sorry for it."

The curator of the museum rushed to the window and looked out. The courtyard was deserted. Mr. Darcy looked at Lydia, frowning.

"Miss Bennet? Can you corroborate this extraordinary story?"

Lydia, having no idea what he meant, nodded vigorously and clutched her reticule. She was not very much concerned with the immorality of this man being such a smooth liar, but was instead quite immensely relieved that he had covered things up so tidily.

"Can you describe him?"

"Describe him?" she repeated, blankly.

"Yes," said Mr. Darcy with great patience, "the foreign fellow who ran off – can you tell me what he looked like?"

"Ah...yes. Well, no." She stuttered a little, "It happened so quickly, you see and I hardly...I suppose he looked just like anyone really."

Elizabeth, looking very pale and very ill, came near then and put her arms about her. Her fingers were shaking badly and Lydia felt wretchedly guilty. What had seemed a fine lark only a few moments ago was not so very amusing now. She looked anxiously up at Mr. Warwick and met his eyes. His expression warmed when she did so, and she felt a little better. Only hold your nerve, his eyes seemed to say, and we will carry this off together.

Mr. Darcy looked as though he was far from satisfied, but the balding man came back from the window and said, "Courtyard's deserted. I don't suppose anyone would have seen the man get away; all the rooms with facing windows have been shut up for the present. Shouldn't really surprise me if it was a French spy." He shook his head over the matter. "You are to be thanked, Mr. Warwick, for frightening him off as you did. Awful cowards these Frenchies, I believe; why, when I think what might have happened – Lord Elgin would have been distraught at such artifacts having been removed from their rightful places."

Mr. Warwick modestly disclaimed the accolade in such humble tones that Lydia wanted to laugh madly. Elizabeth swayed on her feet while holding her sister's hand with white fingers.

Mr. Warwick, seeing that she was about to faint, caught her before she could fall and called out. "Mr. Darcy, sir! I do think your wife is not quite feeling well."

Mr. Darcy, his attention now quite diverted from the unlikelihood of Mr. Warwick's story, came forward with haste and took Mrs. Darcy into his arms.

"My Lord Warwick, might I trouble you to find a servant to call our carriage? I should like to take the ladies home. Mr. Warwick, thank you for your quick action; Mrs. Darcy is...well, let us say that a fall might have been disastrous to her health at present. Lady Warwick, have you any smelling salts? Thank you, madam. Let us go to that little chair in the corner, away from the draft."

Thus he carried his wife over, and spoke to her in low tones, trying to rouse her from her unconscious state. She came to and shook her head quickly to clear it.

"Oh, did I faint? I am dreadfully sorry for alarming you, my dear."

Mr. Darcy dismissed this. "There is no need for apologies; only sit still for a while and I shall have you home soon. The carriage has been sent for."

Elizabeth smiled, if a little weakly. "Yes, that is well. I shall do that. Might I have a drink, do you suppose? I am very thirsty."

Lydia stepped forward. "I will go and fetch one for you, Lizzy."

Mr. Darcy shook his head. "No, Miss Bennet; I should like you to remain where I can see you, please. This is the second time in quite a short period that you have been subjected to guns and an unpleasant shock – the man responsible might be anywhere about. I am sure this gentleman here," with a nod in the direction of the curator, "can find something for your sister to drink."

Eager to please and quite relieved that the precious marbles had not been stolen on his watch, the man nodded and scurried off.

Lydia met Mr. Warwick's eyes again, and once again felt an urge to laugh. What a pity it was that she couldn't share with anyone but him why her brother's words had made her wish to giggle.

When Lord Warwick came back in, bringing word that the Darcy carriage had pulled up, Mr. Darcy lifted his wife up and was followed by a small entourage of people out into the bright sunshine.

Mr. Warwick offered his arm to Lydia once again. They walked on together, at a steady pace.

Before they descended the steps, Mr. Warwick's hand came up and covered hers. "Lydia, can you not see how like we are to each other? We are kin. There is no other woman in England that would have giggled at precisely that moment, and...Lydia, no, don't go just yet. I will only be a moment. Can you not see...surely, surely you cannot contemplate marriage to anyone else but me. I shan't stop, Lydia. I cannot stop trying to persuade you that it would be a waste to marry anyone but me. I know I have done wrong. There is no other man who can appreciate the whole of you as I do...wonderful Lydia. Yes, I see that you must go. I will call tomorrow. Think on it, will you? Think on it."

Chapter Eight

Lydia, having spent the night tossing and turning and getting very little rest, arrived at breakfast late that next morning. Mr. Darcy, however, appeared to be in an unusually mellow mood and elected not to send his flighty young sister a steely glance. Having piled as much on her plate as she could politely carry off without remark being passed, Lydia went to sit near her sister at the foot of the table and asked her how she was feeling.

"Hmm? Oh yes, of course," said Lizzy absently. "Yes, thank you dearest; I am very well this morning."

Lydia looked at her in the morning light and raised her eyebrows. Mrs. Darcy might have been pale and trembling yesterday, before she fainted at the museum, but was now the very picture of glowing good health. Elizabeth was smiling a good deal and would not divulge the cause of her good mood.

Quickly growing tired of her sister's determination to be a mystery, Lydia was relieved when, having finished her raspberry conserve and bread, a servant came in bearing a silver platter and presented it to Mr. Darcy.

He reached for it just as Elizabeth was elaborating upon her plans for the day.

"I must write to Mrs. Reynolds this morning, dearest, but after we have eaten our noonday meal, I thought that we might take Theodore out to the park. He does so love the ducks and I thought that...Fitzwilliam?"

Mr. Darcy had neatly broken the seal of his paper and was reading it with a troubled brow. Lydia supposed that Elizabeth must have some secret way of distinguishing it from his usual expressions, seeing as whatever she saw there had caused her sufficient concern to break off speaking so abruptly.

Mr. Darcy looked at his wife and hesitated before addressing the servants who waited on them at breakfast.

"Thank you; you may go." In the time that the servants had moved in stately fashion across the room and closed the door behind them, Mr. Darcy had scanned the note again and gravely set it down beside him.

"I have received an express from Longbourn, Elizabeth – from your mother."

Elizabeth, grasping instantly what was to come, sat very still and watched her husband with bated breath, waiting for the axe to fall.

A little behind her sister in speed, Lydia wondered aloud what her Mama could have to say that would be so urgent as to need to be sent by express.

"It seems that the housekeeper found your father in his book room when she went in to lay the fire this morning, and being unable to rouse him, raised the alarm. I am afraid he could not be wakened. I am sorry."

Elizabeth swallowed slowly and stiffly rose from her chair. She stared blankly ahead of her, clearly greatly shocked.

Lydia, not quite believing her own ears, voiced her question.

"Does that mean that Papa is *dead*?"

Mr. Darcy, who had been carefully watching Elizabeth as she rounded the table toward him, took his eyes off his wife at this point and nodded to his sister-in-law.

His voice was gentle when he replied, "Yes, I am afraid it does, Lydia." With that, Lizzy reached his side and made an agitated gesture and a half-sob caught in her throat. Her husband rose instantly from his chair and folded her in his arms.

Whatever it was that he whispered tenderly into her hair broke the dam within her and the choked sob became a keening wail that was terrible to Lydia's ears. She herself remained seated at the table, unable to move and trying to absorb the information, wondering what was wrong with her that she was not distraught as her sister was.

Lydia waited. For some long minutes the room was filled with Lizzy's cries, and then at last she spoke. "Tell me what to do, brother," she said, in a small voice. "I am sure I ought to do something but I cannot think what."

He was stroking Elizabeth's hair and regarded Lydia from over her head.

"I understand," he said, raising his voice a little so as to be heard over Elizabeth's weeping. "It took me three days together to comprehend that my mother had passed away and I threw myself into any occupation I could find."

"Give me something to do, please," Lydia begged, fixated, for the first time in her life, upon doing something that might usefully distract her.

Mr. Darcy drew in a deep, steady breath. "I must take Elizabeth upstairs. Will you see the housekeeper and give orders for the knocker to be taken off the door? We have but an hour before callers might come. If black crepe can be found, that ought to be put up too. Tell your maid to pack all your things; we must leave for Longbourn as soon as we are ready. If you are able, a note to your sister, Mrs. Bingley, may be helpful; Bingley informed me last week that they were not removing to Netherfield for above a month, and Mrs. Bennet may not have sent word to them. We must make ready to leave. I do not wish your mother to be left alone without family any longer than is necessary."

Relieved beyond measure to be given such a list, Lydia attempted to smile in gratitude. The effort of upturning her lips felt stiff and foreign to her face.

"She will have Lady Lucas nearby, and my aunt Phillips will come, no doubt. *Thank you.*"

With that, she pushed away the plate of food that she had been so hungry for but moments ago, and with steady steps went to the doors that led into the airy hallway.

When Mr. Darcy led his wife out five minutes later, her face buried in his shoulder, he saw Lydia sensibly and concisely giving orders to Mrs. Priddy as though she had been doing so all her life.

"...and I should think Mr. Darcy's valet and Mrs. Darcy's maid ought to be informed also – they will need to pack. Oh! and Master Darcy's nurse, too. Have someone bring the trunks and portmanteaus up to the family rooms. Tell the footmen that no callers may be admitted unless they are direct family. I shall need a boy to take a note over to Mrs. Bingley in a half-hour or so. Do send my maid up to me, will you please. Thank you; that will be all."

With that, she turned and ascended the stairs.

"That was well done of you, Lydia," said Mr. Darcy quietly, the faintest inflexion of surprised respect in his voice.

"*Black*," replied Lydia, already thinking of the next task to be done, "I do so detest black."

Nevertheless, when her maid had scurried up to her dressing room, she found that Miss Bennet had arrayed most of her clothes on the bed and was promptly handed three dresses that must be dyed black or altered with black crepe.

"All of these other dresses will need to be packed away, Cason, but that may be done after we have left. I shall wear my grey coat and bonnet for the journey, which will suffice if an armband can be sewn on in time. Those three dresses in your arms must be placed near the top of my trunk so that Hill can dye them when we return home. Send a man out to Waddington's for crepe and material for armbands – we must have sufficient to go on the door in a wreath. I daresay the housekeeper will oversee that."

With that, she sent the maid off to do her bidding and was alone in the room.

Crossing over to the drawer beside her bed and opening the little box in which her pistol had been kept, Lydia took out the string of pearls that lay at the bottom, gleaming milky white upon the red velvet lining of the box. She wound them about her hand and brought them up to her cheek, and thought of her sister, held so tightly in Mr. Darcy's embrace. The pearls felt cool against her skin. A moment later, and they had been deposited in her pocket, well out of sight. Lydia seated herself at the seldom-used little desk to write a note to Mrs. Bingley. How did one write such news as she had to tell? She thought, with some little pity, of Mr. Darcy and how he had related it simply, without any fuss or flowery words, and directly began to write.

> Dearest Jane,
> We must all travel to Hertfordshire as soon as may be. Even now the household is making ready. We heard by express only this morning that Papa is dead and Mr. Darcy says he does not wish to leave Mama without family to comfort her. I do not know any of the details save that Hill found him in his book room and could not wake him.
>
> Elizabeth is quite distraught and would doubtless be glad of you to bear her company. No doubt we will see you in Hertfordshire soon.
>
> Lydia.

With remarkable efficiency, all was made ready within a few hours, and thus the largest of the Darcy carriages pulled away from the town house but an hour or so after luncheon, arriving at Longbourn just as daylight was beginning to fade.

Mrs. Phillips came out to greet them, for, as Lydia had predicted, Mrs. Bennet was reclined upon her bed, having been given a draught by the apothecary to calm her hysterical sobbing.

"Oh! Dear Mrs. Darcy, I told your Mama that Mr. Darcy should likely bring you today or tomorrow, as soon as could be done. Lydia! How grown up you look – I should hardly have known you, save that I knew you must be coming. Is this dear Master Theodore? How sweet he is! Oh, you must not be shy of me, you know – I am your Great-Aunt Phillips and I have known your Mama since she came out screaming from your Grandmama and would only settle for her Papa."

Even Lydia was impressed by the silliness of such a speech. Seeing Lizzy's face crumple, and Mr. Darcy retreat to icy hauteur, she interrupted before her aunt could rattle on any more.

"Yes, Aunt, but is it true? Is Papa indeed gone? We had no details, save that Hill could not wake him."

"Yes, child, it is quite true, I fear. Poor Fanny, she has been quite undone, you know; I could not persuade her to take anything at all to calm her until after Lady Lucas had left. She is asleep upstairs now – Mr. Bennet has been laid out in the music room; the back of the house is not so warm, you see, and I thought it might prevent any...."

Seeing that the well-meaning lady was unlikely to cease her tactless babbling without being interrupted, Mr. Darcy coolly suggested that they all go inside.

"For the evening is growing colder and I do not wish my wife and son to take ill."

Mrs. Phillips was a simple woman, and easily overawed by such an air of command. She curtseyed slightly and incoherently remarked on such husbandly thoughtfulness. If Mr. Darcy thought her ridiculous, he refrained from saying so, only turned to Lydia, and with solicitude urged her also to step inside.

"Come in, Miss Bennet; I should not like you to become ill either."

Feeling quite unlike herself, Lydia found herself far fonder of her sister's husband than she ever had before. There was something very nice about being taken care of so well; she could not recollect that Papa had ever concerned himself with such minor details as how long she was kept standing in the cold.

This thought, coupled with crossing over the threshold of home, caused a hard lump to rise in her throat, and her eyes prickled with tears.

Why now? Of all times, why only *now* did she wish to cry? There was still too much to be done. She unbuttoned her coat and handed it to Hill, who welcomed them back to Longbourn with a curtsey and condolences. Lydia thrust her hand into her pocket and wound her pearls about her fingers while Mr. Darcy tenderly assisted his wife and son.

Elizabeth had barely spoken for the entire journey, save to speak of necessities as concerned Theodore, who had contentedly sat on his Mama's lap. It was evident that she was deeply affected and that grief had its hard grip upon her.

Taking her hand out of her pocket with renewed strength, Lydia instructed Hill to set up a large pot of black dye, first thing in the morning.

"For we must have something to wear until mourning clothes can be made. I shall come up and pick out a half a dozen dresses for Mrs. Bennet. She may not need them immediately, though; doubtless she will keep to her bed for a while. No, I don't need to go into the music room, thank you. I will go upstairs. Are you staying the night, Aunt? It might be best if you would stay with Mama. Where shall we put Theodore and his nurse, Hill?"

Mrs. Hill, taking Miss Bennet's assumption of the household arrangements in her stride, gave a slight bob and suggested that Mr. and

Mrs. Darcy might prefer Mrs. Bingley's old room and that Miss Bennet might go in Mrs. Darcy's room, thus leaving space for Master Darcy and his nurse to go in the room that she herself had once shared with Mrs. Osmond-Price.

"Oh, yes, Kitty! Do you know if anyone has written to Fletchley Grange, Hill? It will need to be done, but that may wait until tomorrow; there is little point in doing it tonight. Yes, I should think those arrangements will suit. Mary will need to be written to also, I suppose."

Here Mr. Darcy, smiling slightly at her natural air of command, offered up his own services in that regard.

"Thank you, Mr. Darcy – I dislike letter-writing immensely. I suppose I inherited that from P...well, never mind. Will the room arrangements suit you, Lizzy? We had best eat, too – we haven't all day."

"Harding will carry up a tray to Mrs. Darcy in her room," said Mr. Darcy firmly, when Lizzy disclaimed any feeling of hunger. "We are all quite tired so I see no need for us all to dine formally. The rooms suggested sound perfectly adequate. When the Bingleys arrive, we might remove to Netherfield; doubtless the Collinses will arrive within a day or so of receiving a note."

Lydia nodded, glad that he was able to think of such practical things. It was comforting to know that with Lizzy so affected and her Mama lying above stairs in a drugged sleep, they had his quiet strength to help them through it. He might not be amusing or flamboyant in the way that she liked in Mr. War...in the way that she liked a young man to be, but there was no denying that he was reliable and steady. Such a person was needed sometimes. Perhaps Lizzy's choice was not so incomprehensible after all.

She reached once again into her pocket. "Right, then. Hill, give orders to cook that we shall all have trays in our rooms; something simple will suffice – you will not mind that, Aunt? Good. I shall find some dresses for Mama and then go to bed myself. Goodnight, sister," she said, kissing Lizzy fondly and smoothing a hand over her nephew's hair. She hesitated briefly before standing on her tiptoes to kiss the intimidating Mr. Darcy lightly on the cheek. He caught her eye and smiled, not displeased. "Goodnight, brother."

She climbed into her bed an hour and a half later, having found numerous other little things to arrange with the servants, and orders to give regarding armbands and black crepe. Mrs. Hill reminded her that the funeral biscuits ought to be made as soon as might be so that they could be sent out once the funeral date was known. Lydia had gone belowstairs and asked cook to start them immediately after breakfast was finished in the morning.

She had to undress herself, for Cason had been left in London, there being no real need for her at Longbourn, and found herself lonely that evening for perhaps the first time in her life. Lydia thought, dolefully, as she tied on her nightcap, that everyone else in the household had someone with them to bear them up. Lizzy had Mr. Darcy, Mama had Aunt Phillips, Theodore did not precisely count but he had his nurse, and even Papa, who did not need it in the least, was being borne company this night by the faithful old butler, who had offered to keep a vigil. It was only Lydia Bennet, who had never felt the want of company ever before, who was left entirely alone.

Having climbed into her bed and blown out the candle, she slid out of it again and crossed to the chest of drawers. Longbourn was cold at night, even in the summer months. She fumbled in the darkness for a pair of thick stockings and put them on.

She could not lie to herself for long. She did not really want the warmth – she wanted the strand of pearls that she had hidden in the drawer, and, not caring to examine the reason too closely, brought them back to bed with her.

Lydia lay awake playing with them, winding them about her fingers and sliding them across her palms. She thought of Mr. Warwick at length then, for the first time that day.

What must he have felt when arriving at Darcy House that day, finding the knocker taken off and black crepe hung in a wreath at the door?

Had he been mounting the steps, she wondered, as she had been hurrying about and making ready to leave? What was wrong with her? He was a grown man, after all, and certainly she did not need to be lying awake worrying that he might be worrying too.

As she began to drift off to sleep, she spared a thought for her father and heaved a shuddering sigh. Her face was wet now and she was not quite sure which man she had wept for in the beginning, but now was certain that she cried for her Papa.

He might have thought her a silly creature, and she knew that she was not his favourite, but she would miss his presence sorely. He had sat quietly in his place at the table for nearly every meal at home since she had left the nursery, and if she suspected that his occasional wry smiles were not always quite kind, well, they had never been *un*kind, either.

For Lydia, home meant Longbourn and Longbourn meant Father and Mother and all of her sisters. The sisters had left one by one and only Papa and Mama had remained, but somehow Longbourn had remained home. She supposed that Mr. Collins would inherit now and that she and Mama should have to live elsewhere once the six months of deep mourning had passed.

She would not think about that tonight, though; for now, all that needed to be done was to sleep. Everything else might wait until morning.

Her pearls lay clutched in her fist and she was sure that if she did not release them soon, her hand would bear the imprints of them – yet she did not move to put them down.

Her last thoughts before sleep overtook her were of two pairs of eyes, one pair pale green and alight with tender laughter, the other pair grey and hooded, with wrinkled lids that were now sewn closed.

They would not open again.

Chapter Nine

The next few weeks passed by in a blur of boredom and loneliness for Lydia. Mr. Bennet was buried within the space of a week, and the Collinses had returned to Hunsford Parsonage to arrange their affairs there before settling at Longbourn. The Darcys had relocated to Netherfield once the Bingleys had come, and thus it was not long before the only people left at Longbourn were Lydia and her mother.

Mrs. Bennet had been a great deal shocked by her husband's sudden death; the doctor had told them, in the vaguest possible way, that he could only suppose that Mr. Bennet's heart had given out and that they should be grateful that he had neither lingered nor felt any pain. Mrs. Bennet, once the men had returned from the churchyard, had risen from her bed, dressed from head to toe in sober black, and received the condolences of the entire neighborhood with sufficient dignity. Then, having done so, she had retired to her rooms again.

At first Lydia had not minded this so much, although she was fond of her mother. In the past she had been very glad of the additional license that was given her on account of being a favourite, but, as each evening closed with her sadly eating alone, quite worn out from the day-to-day running of the household, she found that she should have been glad of anybody's company, even if the resultant conversation was as tearful as Mrs. Bennet's had been when that lady had joined her for the space of ten minutes. She was robbed even of Kitty's comfort during the ordeal; the Osmond-Prices wrote in reply to Mr. Darcy's letter that although they were deeply sorry and grieved at the news, Kitty's delicate condition meant that she could not currently travel such a great distance alone and that, it being so far, Mr. Osmond-Price chose to remain with Kitty and not attend the burial. It was disappointing of course, Lydia thought, that she would not see her closest sister, but how odd to think of Kitty becoming a Mama. Kitty was only two years ahead of her and Lydia could hardly imagine her sister so.

She rode over to Netherfield one morning, on old Nelly, after she had received an awkward letter from Mary regarding the arrangements for the house.

Mrs. Bingley greeted her affectionately, for all that the good lady was deeply grieved by her father's passing.

"Good morning, Lydia. How lovely it is to see you."

Lydia kissed her sister's cheek and embraced her swiftly. "Jane, I have had a letter from Mary and I am come for advice from you and Lizzy on what I ought to do. She wants to...oh, good morning, Lizzy."

Elizabeth kissed her sister. Gradually, under her husband's tender care and her son's need of his Mama, she was emerging from the fog of grief that had so afflicted her. It was not quite fair, thought Lydia, that she should look so elegant in mourning clothes; even the black lace cap that was pinned to her hair did not look so haggish as it did on the rest of the married women. She herself had barely been able to face her reflection in the mirror of a morning recently.

"What is the difficulty, dearest? Have you left Mama alone or does our aunt sit with her this morning?"

"Yes, Aunt Phillips has come; don't worry over that. Mary has written that it would be better if Mama vacated her rooms before she arrives, because it will be easier that way. She seemed to indicate that Lady Catherine had advised as much – that Mary should be able to take her rightful place in the mistress's rooms. Is it not very soon, Lizzy? I know of course that Mr. Collins has inherited now, but I do not think

Mama will precisely understand...she has not come downstairs above twice since Papa was buried."

Elizabeth sighed. "We had all better come over to Longbourn to persuade Mama that it is the best course of action. There may be some way of hinting to her so that it is she that suggests it. Shall we go tomorrow, dearest?" This said to Jane. "Perhaps if I bring Theodore it will entice her out."

"Poor Mama!" said Mrs. Bingley sweetly, "and poor Mary too; they will neither of them adjust very easily, I shouldn't think. I cannot think of any other solution, though; I cannot see that she would wish to leave her home permanently, for all that dear Charles and Mr. Darcy have offered her a house in Meryton."

A gleam stole into Elizabeth's eyes, and she looked thoughtful. "I wonder if I might have thought of a Very Clever Idea, sisters. No! Do not ask me," she said, with a fair imitation of some of her old liveliness. "I shall see if I may write a letter and bring it about first. It may be just the thing. When are the Collinses to arrive, Lydia?"

Mystified, Lydia replied that they were not to come for another ten days at the very least, and Elizabeth nodded, satisfied. "We shall not say a word to Mama for now, then; let her enjoy her rooms undisturbed. If I cannot manage things to my satisfaction, I shall come myself and persuade her to give place to Mary."

Lydia spent a few hours at Netherfield, enjoying her sisters' company; for all that they were more subdued than they had been in the past. Well, so too was she, and it was good to be with them.

Mr. Darcy encountered his sister-in-law in the hall as she was putting on her gloves, and stopped to have a quiet word with her.

"Good morning, Lydia. Are you riding back to Longbourn alone?"

"Yes, for I had to leave the male servants behind. Mama was anxious, you see, that she should not be left unprotected."

Mr. Darcy frowned, and Lydia, out of habit, looked away and pretended to study the stained glass in the hallway window. It was pretty, with the sun shining through it and casting patches of coloured light onto the polished floor.

"I shall send Carter home with you, then," he said shortly. "Have you been enjoying a visit with your sisters?"

"Yes; I was asking how I ought to manage Mama and Mary when they come. I do think Lizzy may be plotting something, Mr. Darcy," she warned him, feeling generous.

His eyes crinkled ever so slightly at the corners and he nodded. "I am pleased to hear it. She took the news of your father quite hard. I have been concerned, and at quite a loss as to what to do for her, but if she is back to managing people again, I daresay she will eventually mend."

"Mr. Darcy," said Lydia impulsively, "have you heard any news from our friends in town?"

"Only from the Kentmires," he said slowly, watching her carefully. "I believe Georgiana has been writing to you; doubtless you will receive her letter soon."

"Oh," said Lydia, disappointed. "Well, I shall be glad to hear from her, it...it is so very dull at Longbourn, you know."

Mr. Darcy nodded, seeming to understand what it was she meant. "I will send a man to fetch Carter," was all he said.

Three days after that, Lydia received a letter from Mrs. Kentmire, which she read as she sat at breakfast. Her Mama had attempted to get up that day, but having walked into the breakfast room and seen Mr. Bennet's empty chair, had immediately turned around again and been taken back up by Hill, weeping.

Lydia sipped at her tea and spread open the thick paper before her.

Dear Miss Bennet,

I was very sorry to hear of your Father having passed away so suddenly. I remember very clearly how difficult it was when my own Papa died; I was younger then, of course, but some things do not leave you. I shall not dwell on such things, as I do not know that you would wish me to; but I would have you know that the grief you feel now becomes gradually easier to bear over time and happiness will one day come again.

My primary reason for writing to you, aside from wishing to offer you my sincerest condolences, was to tell you of a strange letter I received last week. I cannot yet tell if I found it alarming or comforting, but I shall relate it to you regardless, particularly as the reason for the note concerns you.

Mr. Kentmire and I returned from our honeymoon on Tuesday morning. We did not go out into society until Thursday evening when we attended a musical evening at Mrs. Colchester's home, but when we returned from there, an anonymous note had been delivered by a link boy, addressed to me. I have copied it out, word for word, below, because I do think you ought to be aware of it. If it can be trusted, then I would not have you uneasy any longer than is necessary.

I do hope that you might consent to visit us, once we have moved into the house that Mr. Kentmire is going to build. For now, we remain in London, but I do so long to return north again and settle in.

Yours,
Georgiana Kentmire.

Immensely curious, Lydia reached for the second sheet of paper that had been enclosed and read:

Dear Madam,

I have for some time now been the victim of a guilty conscience regarding yourself and the other young lady who was set upon in the park some weeks ago. I wish for you to now be made aware that you need not fear a recurrence of such an event. Suffice it to say that you were the victim of an error of judgment and as such may go about your life hereafter with every reassurance of your safety.

I deeply regret, madam, any unhappiness that you have experienced at my hand.

Lydia looked at the note for some time, reading it over thrice before folding it carefully and putting it beside her plate. The clock chimed the hour and Hill entered the breakfast room.

"I beg your pardon, Miss Bennet; I had thought you might be finished. Mrs. Bennet has lain down in her room again."

Lydia thrust away her half-eaten roll.

"Yes, I am quite finished, Hill. I will go up and sit with Mama when she has her tea. I think I may go for a walk, only so far as the church. Send a servant for me if anyone calls and I am wanted."

Lydia did not walk for her enjoyment as a general rule. In her youth, she had often walked into Meryton with Kitty, but that walking had been done with purpose. How long ago those days seemed, when a mile or so of quiet road passed by with little effort because the pair of them were so full of laughter and high spirits – or more often petty squabbles – that they did not notice the distance.

Lydia wandered into the churchyard. A blackbird looked at her quizzically as she closed the gate behind her, and she looked about her for her father's grave.

No headstone had been put in yet, but it was the only plot that was freshly dug, and flowers had been laid there.

Lydia stood silently, staring down at the red clay soil. She was not so silly as to suppose that her father would have advised her; far more likely he would have waved her away and told her to take such girlish troubles to her Mama.

"Except, I cannot do that, Papa," she whispered bitterly, feeling a surge of hot anger at him for having disrupted her life so completely. "Mama has barely spoken three sentences together to me since I have returned, and my sisters are all married, and I have no one. I wonder if I am a fool, Papa, for believing him – why else would he write a note that he did not need to? If he did not mean it, he might have gone his whole life and not written a single word of comfort. No, I am sure that I believe him. I know him, Papa. He may be a rogue, and awfully sure of himself, and he may be the smoothest liar I have ever encountered, but he is strangely honest for all that."

She leant down to rearrange to her satisfaction the white roses that someone else had left. Lydia could not fathom why someone would have left them not looking as pretty as possible, but she often did not understand other people.

"Mr. Collins and Mary are to come soon. I am sure you would find my predicament ever so amusing if you were alive, but I cannot think how to get Mama out of her rooms. Lizzy has said she will manage it, but I cannot see how she will do any such thing. How could you have done something so odiously selfish as dying, Father? If you had just waited another month...oh! I don't know; perhaps I would have known better what to do."

Glumly, she turned and trudged her way home. She did not feel like herself; she knew she did not even look like herself, nothing like the pretty, bouncing, fearless girl she had always been. The mirror in her bedchamber reflected a pale-faced and frightened young woman now, quite crushed by a solitude not of her own choosing.

One full week after Mrs. Darcy had promised to arrange matters in some mysterious fashion, that same lady arrived at Longbourn to breakfast with her sister.

"Why, Lydia! Do you eat alone, dearest?"

"Mama still keeps to her room," was all the reply Lydia ventured.

Elizabeth looked sympathetic. "And you have been quite shamefully neglected by Jane and me – I know it and I am sorry. I...I am afraid that I quite forgot myself these last weeks."

Elizabeth sat beside her sister and helped herself to a muffin.

"I have missed company, it is true, but you need not be sorry – I know how you loved Papa."

"Yes," said Lizzy, reaching for the jam, "but I also love you, Lydia, and I have not been present anywhere near enough. Fret not, though, dearest; I have come bearing the solution. It is in my reticule at present and very soon we shall take it up to Mama and emerge victorious from the battlefield."

"Elizabeth," said Lydia, bewildered, "you are not...you are not *foxed*, are you?"

Mrs. Darcy set down her knife and laughed for the first time in what felt like an age. Her husband would have been glad to hear that sweet sound, for all he would have disapproved of the question that caused it.

"No, Lydia, you scandalous child, I am of perfectly sound mind and entirely sober. I shall reveal all once we have gone up to Mama. Is the tea in that pot still hot?

Having fortified themselves, the ladies went up to Mrs. Bennet's chamber and knocked on the door. Upon being bidden to come in, they entered to see Mrs. Bennet in her dressing gown and shawl, reclining on the chaise longue. She looked up when they greeted her, and surveyed them.

"Well, Lizzy, you are looking well. Lydia, my love, ring the bell for Hill to remove my tray, would you?"

Lydia did so as Elizabeth arranged herself in a little chair beside her mother. Mrs. Bennet's bed-chamber was a light and airy room, full of knick-knacks and pretty things. The mantel over her fireplace was laden with china figurines and delicate little vases. She herself was arrayed in her dressing gown, a frothy creation in white that suited her and her room very well. Both Elizabeth and Lydia looked odd in such a room, clad as they were in unadorned black. Lydia made a small grimace of distaste as she caught sight of herself in the large mirror beside her Mama.

"Mama, I have much news. We have good reason to suppose that Theodore will become a brother next May. Mr. Darcy is very pleased, I think."

Mrs. Bennet fluttered her handkerchief, "Oh, how fortunate that is – you have done well, my dear. Of course he is pleased with you, and why on earth should he not be?"

Lydia, curious about her sister's schemes, offered Lizzy her congratulations. "But I had no idea, Lizzy!"

Mrs. Darcy smiled. "No, dearest; I asked Fitzwilliam if I might pass the news along to Mama first, you see."

Mrs. Bennet preened. "That is very proper of you, Lizzy. Naturally you would want your mother to know before anyone else."

"I will write to my other sisters with the news in a few days, I think, although Mary will be arriving here herself soon enough."

Mrs. Bennet nodded at this. "Aye, very true, in but a few days in fact, and Kitty will be brought to bed herself come the winter."

"Mary did not have an easy time of it with Catherine-Elizabeth, from what I hear," responded Mrs. Darcy, directing the conversation where she wanted it to go.

"No. Lady Catherine apparently said herself that had she not been in Bath at the time, she should have instructed the women how best to go about things."

Lydia rather thought that Mary should have disliked such interference; she knew that she would have, but Elizabeth seemed to think differently. Lydia slipped her hand into her pocket and fiddled with her pearls as Elizabeth answered their mother.

"I was glad of her ladyship during my lying-in with Theodore. I hope that she will come to Pemberley again when this little one is ready. I have had a letter from her this morning, Mama, and she has extended a very gracious invitation to you and to Lydia."

"To stay at Rosings?!" exclaimed the two women, concerned.

"No-o, to bear her company in Bath and partake of the society there once your six months of deep mourning has passed. She writes – and you will forgive her lack of delicacy; she is very much used to ordering things how she likes –" Lizzy extracted her letter and read, heroically refraining from any impersonation of Lady Catherine de Bourgh's intonation or manner in her reading, "I remember very clearly the way in which my own mother-in-law, Lady Susannah, vacated Rosings when I arrived as a new bride. I was most anxious to take charge of the household in my own way, and the old mistress, having removed herself to the town house in Bath, cleared the way quite satisfactorily. I am aware that your family has no such townhouse, of course, and I would be glad of the change of scenery myself for the season there, should your mother and sister join me. Your Mama could not attend many society events at present, of course, but I daresay Miss Bennet might find me a sufficient chaperone in her stead, once she comes out of full mourning."

Lydia's mouth gaped slightly, and she shut it rapidly once she saw her reflection in the mirror.

Mrs. Bennet pursed her lips and Elizabeth closed her letter.

"I do hope that you will consider it, Mama. Lydia's season has been necessarily cut short and...and I rather think that it would be just what Lady Catherine needs after having lost Cousin Anne; she does so love to be of use. Mr. Darcy was very pleased to see that she is paying due deference to the relationship between us all since our marriage." Mrs. Darcy paused here to see the effect of her words and pressed home her advantage. "I do think, Mama, that it would be very...very *daunting* for Mary to return here as the heir's wife, knowing how effortlessly you have run Longbourn and wishing to find her own two feet. Fitzwilliam's mother has long passed away, you know, but I cannot help but think it might have been very awkward."

Mrs. Bennet was looking about her room as she listened to her daughter speak. Lydia wisely remained silent, quite impressed by Elizabeth's capabilities.

"Lydia, ring that bell again; I cannot think why Hill shall have tarried so long. Our things must be packed and made ready! This room will need to be cleared and aired for Mary – I would not have anyone say that I made life harder for my own daughter. Her ladyship speaks admirable sense – why, I remember when I arrived at Longbourn, your Grandmother Bennet – but one must not speak ill of the dead. Come! There is so much to be done. Might Mr. Bingley lend me one or two footmen, do you suppose, Lizzy?"

Elizabeth answered readily that if Mr. Bingley could not do so, she was certain that her husband would.

Mrs. Bennet nodded absently to this, and, now having an aim and an occupation to busy herself with, rose from her reclined position as Hill entered.

"Hill! Where can you have been? There is much to be done. Your new mistress is arriving in but a few days and this room will need to be cleared out. I will want my clothes and such packed away for now and my mourning attire to be moved to Mrs. Bingley's old room. There will be extra hands sent over from Netherfield soon to help you. Oh, Hill! Such a to-do! Miss Bennet and I have been invited to Bath by Lady Catherine de Bourgh herself – is that not good news?"

Hill, blinking at such lively spirits from her mistress, replied that she hoped Mrs. Bennet might find some comfort in the change of scenery.

Belatedly remembering that she was a widow, Mrs. Bennet wrinkled her brow at that.

"Oh, it is not for my *enjoyment*, Hill. Miss Bennet must have the opportunity to be Seen and Mrs. Collins must be allowed to work out for herself how best to run Longbourn. She was always a studious girl so I have no doubt she will do a fine job of it."

Mrs. Darcy rose, smiling. "She was taught very well, Mama, so I am certain that she will. I must return to Netherfield; Mr. Darcy is most anxious that I do not overexert myself. I will ask about the footmen. Lydia, in six weeks or so, you might put off your blacks and wear some colours again, but I should, if I were you, keep to black gloves. Her ladyship is a stickler for propriety."

With that, she left the room and made her way out from her childhood home to the waiting carriage. If she felt a sharp stab of sorrow as she passed her father's book room, it was not readily apparent by the time Carter assisted her up the step. It had been a most satisfactory morning's work.

Ushered out from Mrs. Bennet's chamber with the motherly advice, "But you must look over your own clothes, Lydia – to think we shall go to Bath! Your father never cared for the place or you may be sure that he would have taken me," Lydia wandered to her own room and began to consider her dresses.

She held up a plain white gown that might easily be turned to lavender for an afternoon dress. Lizzy was a marvel! She had resolved any issue between Mama and Mary before it had even arisen, and she had ensured that they would be away from Meryton, somewhere that, although not so exciting as London, might do very well for the pair of them once they went into society again. What had her sister written to Lady Catherine to precipitate such an offer?

She thought, as she held up a green silk shawl that she had often worn in London to great effect, that the only problem that she could see with the scheme was that there was no possibility of Mr. Warwick finding her in Bath and she might never see him again.

The shawl was tossed on the bed and she turned to face the mirror. That was an unpleasant thought; she would not like to go through the world, to live the rest of her life, and never again be the focus of that pale gaze or see his handsome face, or be made to giggle by him – even when she was sure she ought to be annoyed.

Lydia blinked at her reflection and shook her head. There was little point in thinking of it now. If he loved her, as he had said he did, he would come, and when he did….

The butler knocked upon the door with a sharp rap, having brought up the first of her trunks as per Mrs. Bennet's orders.

She stared at it for a full minute, once he had gone. Her whole life was to be packed away in these chests, not for a short exciting jaunt but perhaps for the last time. Lydia would have to bid farewell to this house as she had known it; she knew for certain that she did not want to be dependent on Mr. Collins or Mary. Odious thought!

Thus it was, that by the time Mr. and Mrs. Collins arrived at Longbourn, Mrs. Bennet and Miss Bennet were ready to leave it within two days and to travel in Mr. Darcy's coach to meet Lady Catherine de Bourgh in Bath. There would be some weeks in which they would not be permitted to go out much in society, but, Lady Catherine had written, once Miss Bennet was in black gloves, she should be glad of the favour of her company to the Pump Room.

Lydia had stifled a giggle when Mrs. Bennet read that particular passage to her.

Clever Lizzy!

Chapter Ten

Bath was a pleasant enough place, in Lydia's opinion, and Lady Catherine's house was suitably large and well situated for the three ladies who dwelt in it not to be forever in each other's way. Her bedchamber overlooked the park, and the sandstone houses made a sufficiently interesting picture to study when they were kept indoors by the persistent rain that seemed to plague the city.

Her ladyship, after having declared that Lydia's education had been shockingly lacking, had decided, a week after her arrival with her mother, that she liked the girl for all that. This was in part on account of Lydia having returned with a delightfully fashioned fan for her, on her very first shopping trip out. The ebony sticks were made interesting by the delicate feather patterns that had been etched onto them and the silk had been painstakingly painted to resemble a peacock's tail. With the careless generosity which she showed to everyone, Lydia had instantly thought that Lady Catherine might carry the fan with one of the dark green velvet and black lace evening gowns that she so favoured.

Lady Catherine, having previously considered that Miss Bennet was shamefully ignorant, decided, upon being so prettily presented with the fan, that she was a good sort of young lady, really. After all, a mind could be educated, but a bad nature would have been far more disastrous.

It was indeed fortunate for Miss Bennet that Lady Catherine was there to aid her; there was nothing she relished more than a challenging project and, upon consideration, it would not be so very impossible to get a good-humoured, attractive, and elegantly dressed girl well settled.

Lady Catherine looked forward to writing to Mrs. Darcy of her triumph in the matter; her niece deserved some sort of riposte to the crowing notes she had sent to Rosings after her successes with Mrs. Osmond-Price and Mrs. Kentmire.

In a similar fashion, Lady Catherine was pleased with Mrs. Bennet. There was a sort of dignity about her guest that she recognised well; she liked to mention her late husband often, but was not forever weeping and wailing over that which could not be altered. Part of this must surely be on account of her own condescension toward a fellow widow. Her ladyship did not at all mind that Mrs. Bennet was a little silly – she was clearly willing to be guided. Lady Catherine herself had instructed Mrs. Bennet that she must not be idle, and, upon discovering that she had something of a knack for menu planning, delegated the task to her to their mutual satisfaction.

Mrs. Bennet treated their hostess with a faintly awed respect. She had never before met a woman of rank who spoke her mind in such forthright tones. If Lady Catherine declared that it was perfectly acceptable for Miss Bennet to attend a party in lavender, well then, it must be so – she even accepted with meekness the implied order that Mrs. Bennet must remain at home. Such high-handedness both annoyed and amused Lydia, who had never before encountered anyone who managed her Mama half so well. She said to Lady Catherine, one evening in the carriage, that she reminded her very much of Lizzy.

Her ladyship nodded graciously, pleased to see a glimmer of intelligence in her protégée.

"I have said it myself, Miss Bennet, when I first met your sister at Rosings. Quality is instantly recognisable when one has it oneself. Now, you must first be introduced to Beau Nash this evening, before anyone else. You may not dance, of course, but you will like to make new acquaintances."

For Lydia, Bath did not hold a candle to the delights and joys of London. Perhaps this was why she did not view it in the same-starry eyed manner as she had in her imaginings as a young girl. She acquitted herself well enough in company, but at home she very easily became subdued, and spent long afternoons lost in thought, her hand in her pocket.

Mrs. Bennet confided to Lady Catherine that she thought the poor child was still grieving the loss of her father. Her ladyship, unable to fathom that anyone could be unhappy in her household, accepted this explanation, and, with an interfering sort of kindness, attempted to distract Miss Bennet from her grief by telling her about her own father, the late Earl of Matlock.

The months passed and very soon Mrs. Bennet went into half-mourning. Lydia was very glad of this, for her Mama did not look so pretty as she was used to, and she put her energies into suggesting various colours that might suit her mother. It was decided that a gentle dove grey would become Mrs. Bennet very well, and when paired with black gloves and black lace cap, her Mama looked decidedly elegant.

Mrs. Bennet tittered a little when Lydia offered the suggestion that no one would think her old enough to be anyone's widow. Lady Catherine, who was not more than a decade ahead of Mrs. Bennet, took exception to this tactlessness and pointed out that she herself was often mistaken for a much younger woman.

It so happened that one evening, at a card party, Sir Daniel James sought her out from across the room. Seeing her sitting at that moment sitting docilely beside her ladyship, he smiled and walked toward her. Bowing, he said, "Miss Bennet! I had not expected to see you in Bath. How do you do?"

Lydia rose and curtseyed to him, glad to see any of her old friends from London and quite forgetting that she had been a little relieved when he left without making a declaration.

"Sir Daniel! What do you do here? Oh! I beg your pardon, madam. Lady Catherine, may I present Sir Daniel James; he was used to call at Darcy House when I was still in London. Sir Daniel, this is Lady Catherine de Bourgh. Mama and I are staying with her in Bath for the present."

Sir Daniel bowed, and Lady Catherine, quirking an eyebrow at him, was so gracious as to nod.

"How do you do, Sir Daniel. Am I correct in thinking that your late father was Sir Nathaniel James?" This being confirmed, Lady Catherine almost smiled. "I had thought so – there are few people with a better memory than I for names. Sir Lewis de Bourgh was used to attend house parties hosted by your parents, you know – before he married me, that is."

Sir Daniel made light, if vaguely dull, conversation with Lady Catherine whilst Lydia played with the ribbon she had tied about her wrist that evening. She watched enviously as a young blonde woman floated by in a cream satin and blue jacquard gown. How she missed proper colours!

"...and Miss Bennet will confirm that, I am sure," she heard Sir Daniel murmur. Blinking, she nodded, despite having little notion what he had been talking of. She had quite forgotten how easily she lost track of his conversation; it was his voice that did it. He took such an age to select his words that she quite lost interest in hearing the remainder of the sentence.

Lady Catherine, pleased by something, cordially invited Sir Daniel to call upon them one morning, and gave him the address.

Once he had gone, she turned to her charge and, looking her over critically, said that Lydia had the unusual knack of knowing which men did not like to hear young ladies forever talking.

"It is a rare gift of discernment, Miss Bennet; depend upon it, you might do very well indeed."

Lydia did not think that Lady Catherine would be amused to hear that her mind had simply wandered, and so smiled in thanks for the compliment. She hoped that Sir Daniel did not come to call very soon.

Alas for poor Lydia, he did.

On the third morning after having been introduced to Lady Catherine, he presented himself at the front door and handed Evans his card. Lydia was sat in the drawing room, tearing apart a bonnet of her Mama's. She had bought some grey silk with which she thought to re-cover it in neat little pleats. Her mother was sat beside the fire, opposite Lady Catherine. They had both received letters that morning and were exchanging news.

"The Darcys have returned to Pemberley, Mrs. Bennet. I gather that Mrs. Darcy will be requiring my assistance in the near future."

"Oh yes, *indeed*, Lady Catherine; I recall her saying that she was very grateful for your help when Theodore…."

"Certainly I could do no less, Mrs. Bennet. My own dear sister would have wished it, I am sure."

"Truly, you were very good and…."

"Ah! Young Theodore has taken his first steps; Mrs. Darcy is very properly enquiring of me if Darcy did so at a similar age. I remember it well, for Miss de Bourgh took her very first steps within a few days of my receiving that letter. How does Mrs. Collins get on, Mrs. Bennet?"

"Oh, marvellously, Lady Catherine. She says that she has encouraged Mr. Collins to hire a steward; he has taken her counsel in the matter and she says that…."

"Very wise of her, Mrs. Bennet. I have often said that a good steward is really essential to the smooth running of an estate. Mrs. Collins must have remembered my having mentioned it while they were yet at Hunsford Parsonage. I will write to her, I think; it is good for a new mistress of an estate to have the advice of those more experienced."

"Oh yes, I am sure…."

"Sir Daniel James is below, my lady, and desires me to request an audience with your ladyship," intoned Evans in his deep voice. Lydia did not think she had ever met a man with a lower octave of speech than this butler. She reluctantly set aside the bonnet with the pleat that she was carefully aligning, and laid down her pins.

"You must not interrupt Mrs. Bennet, Evans!" Lady Catherine reprimanded.

Evans bowed to Mrs. Bennet. "I beg your pardon, madam."

"It is of no matter, Evans; I cannot recall that I was saying anything very…."

"Well, you must show him up, Evans – do not keep Sir Daniel standing in the hallway."

Evans left and returned with Sir Daniel in tow.

"Lady Catherine, Miss Bennet. Good morning to you. It is a very fine morning, is it not?"

"Good morning, Sir Daniel. We have not yet been out thus far, but thought we might take a trip to Lady Metcalf's musicale this evening. You are not known to Miss Bennet's mother, I do not think. Mrs. Bennet, this is Sir Daniel James. Doubtless Miss Bennet will have written to you of him when they became acquainted in London. Sir Daniel, Mrs. Bennet."

"It is a pleasure to meet you, Mrs. Bennet. I was sorry to hear from her ladyship that you are recently widowed. My condolences, madam. I myself am painfully familiar with the grief one feels for a departed spouse. My wife died less than two years ago now.

Mrs. Bennet, quite struck by the tragedy of bereavement, thanked him in disjointed words. He was quite charmed by what he saw as timidity, a trait he admired in ladies, and exerted himself to please.

Lydia, ordinarily disliking to be left out of any conversation, was quite relieved and mentally began trimming the grey silk bonnet with black velvet ribbon. Tied with a simple bow, it would be really quite delightful. Her Mama would doubtless look very well in it. It could be made even prettier with the addition of a veil. Lady Catherine favoured veils on a bonnet and Lydia really thought that she might be onto something with them. They lent a decided air of mystery, and one was obliged to study the rest of the hat carefully as there were fewer distractions in terms of a person's face to contend with. Upon consideration, veils ought to be compulsory.

"Lydia!" hissed Mrs. Bennet. Lydia noted that all the occupants of the room were looking at her, waiting for her attention.

"La! I am sorry, I was thinking of..." She caught sight of Lady Catherine's brows rising high upon her forehead and improvised, "...my father. Do forgive me."

Her ladyship nodded her absolution, Mrs. Bennet looked affected, and Sir Daniel James offered his sympathies.

"I beg your pardon, Miss Bennet. I was quite caught up with offering my condolences to your mother, having been widowed myself, and quite forgot a daughter's grief. Do not give your lapse in manners another thought, Miss Bennet. Under the circumstances it is quite understandable."

Lydia rather thought that a lapse in manners was quite understandable in any circumstances surrounding him, but did not say so. Instead she fiddled with the pearls in her pocket, imagining for a moment what Mr. Warwick might have said to Sir Daniel.

This brought a smile and she directed it at the gentleman in question. "Would you mind repeating yourself, sir?"

"I thought you might like to visit the park, Miss Bennet. The flowerbeds there are looking quite pleasing at present. I have some thought of having something similar put into the garden at my estate."

Lydia looked at the bonnet on the table. She did not particularly wish to leave it half done, but suspected that it would be a little too rude to state her wishes. She nodded. "Very well. I will just dash upstairs and change into my walking clothes."

Twenty-five minutes later, Miss Bennet and Sir Daniel exited the house and strolled toward the park. Midden, an elderly servant of Lady Catherine's, followed them at a distance.

"You must not permit your earlier rudeness to cast you down, Miss Bennet," began Sir Daniel, thinking that her silence was shame. "You are yet young and have not the same resilience to bereavement that a more experienced woman might have."

Lydia, quite unaware that she was doing so, took the wind out of his sails by assuring him that she was not in the least cast down.

"I have been wondering, Sir Daniel, if perhaps your gold tassels might suit a rather better-fitted boot – but of course I am no expert in men's footwear. Is it very far to the park? I have been re-covering a bonnet for Mama, you know, and I do think she would like to wear it soon."

Struggling for a moment, Sir Daniel supposed that Miss Bennet was a very devoted daughter and complimented her for it. "However flighty the means of expression, Miss Bennet, I commend you for your regard for your widowed mother. I have occasionally thought that if my late wife had been able to leave me with a child, I should have drawn great comfort from it."

Lydia wondered if the late Lady James had perished merely to add some interest to her life.

Sir Daniel did not leave pause for her to comment, however, so she remained silent.

"I should still very much value a child, Miss Bennet. The entailment upon my estate leaves me in something of a predicament. There is not even a distant male cousin who can inherit once I am gone. My family name will die out, and my lands will revert to the crown. Given that I cannot approve of the conduct of the royal family at present, I wish to avoid this. I have settled upon it that you ought to be the next Lady James. I had an inkling of it in London and seeing you in Bath quite confirms it. I know that you are young and have moments of...well, perhaps it is better not to dwell on such things, but you will certainly learn dignity when you are in a respected position in society. I will guide you myself."

Lydia wrinkled her nose. How did one refuse a request that had not actually been requested?

"Hmmm...." said Lydia.

"Miss Bennet?"

"You see, Sir Daniel, I don't think I want to."

He was perplexed. "I do not comprehend your meaning, Miss Bennet. You do not want to *what*?"

"Be the next Lady James, produce you a child, learn dignity, be guided by you. Any of it, really."

Sir Daniel missed his step on the pavement and stopped stock still where they stood. Disbelief was apparent in every line of his expression.

"I do not think you quite know what you are saying, Miss Bennet," he said at last, "I do not think I am being immodest when I suggest that it would be a very advantageous match for you."

"Yes, I had thought of that already, Sir Daniel, and I still do not think we should suit."

"I am worth fifteen thousand pounds a year," he said, clearly intending to rebuke her.

Lydia was swiftly becoming wearied by now. "No, I am sure that you are not." Mr. Warwick had been right about that – fifteen thousand pounds was simply not worth enduring such a boring husband for the rest of his life. She half smiled then, and had to look away. Mr. Warwick would have enjoyed this moment; no doubt his eyes would have smiled at her, crinkling at the corners even as his mouth remained straight.

"...can see you intend to insult me, madam. I have clearly misread your character very badly. To think I had meant to honour you so – I have been very badly misled."

Riled, Lydia replied with some spirit, "Misled! Sir Daniel, if you fooled yourself into thinking that my character was any different from the one I present to everyone, then it is not my fault. How am I to know what silly fancies you will take into your head?"

Angrily he cast off her hand which until now had been resting on his arm, and turned to the servant that stood a little behind them. "You there! You had best escort this young person home, for I shall not do it."

Midden raised his eyebrows. It was not right, to his way of thinking, to refer to a young lady in such terms, and Miss Bennet was a pretty, lively thing after all. Her eyes were blazing fire at the rude gentleman with her.

"Don't think y'should be callin' Miss Bennet a young person, sir. Correct term is 'young lady.'" Midden was an elderly servant, but was very clear on his responsibilities. If an ill-bred fellow insulted a guest in his mistress's house, or anywhere else for that matter, he knew what to do with him.

"I could call her much worse!" retorted Sir Daniel, straightening his coat with a sharp tug. Lydia surveyed it, critically.

"I do think you ought to have refrained from adding those last few capes, Sir Daniel. I am not convinced that you have the height to do them justice."

"I see that you have naught but flightiness and vanity in your head, madam. I have had a very lucky escape indeed. I am thankful that I have not allied myself with one who is so frivolously minded."

"Want me to put him in a heap for you, Miss Bennet?" asked Midden, quite willing to teach Sir Daniel some manners.

"Give me a gun, Midden, and I will do it myself! You are talking a good deal of nonsense, Sir Daniel. Escape? How have you escaped? You were rejected! I shall tell you this for nothing, sir – you have spoken to me as though I should fall over myself with gratitude at your proposal, but I cannot see that any amount of money or any size of estate is worth the dullness of *you* being part of the bargain. I know of only one woman who might be desperate enough to consider you – Charlotte Lucas – and she has been a confirmed spinster for these last ten years at least!"

Having had these last words hurled at his head, Sir Daniel, his face set in a sneer of disgust, turned and stalked off without so much as a bow.

"'Twasn't how it was done in my day, miss," said Midden, evidently feeling the need to speak. "In my day the gentlemen that was *called* gentlemen, was all a spot pleasanter about taking a lady's rejection. Lady Catherine got shot of a fair few herself, miss, if you'll forgive the liberty of my saying so."

Chapter Eleven

To Lydia's surprise, Lady Catherine de Bourgh did not direct any anger toward her when she returned from her walk alone. Beau Nash had called upon them and was sat making conversation with Mrs. Bennet beside the window when she re-entered the room.

"Are you returned so soon, Lydia, my love? I had expected you to be much longer. Did Sir Daniel not wish to come up and take his leave? Look, here is Mr. Nash come to call upon us. You are acquainted already, are you not?"

Lydia dropped a curtsey to the bewigged gentleman. "Good day to you, sir. Mama, you will be vastly shocked by this, but Sir Daniel quite abandoned me in the park! If Midden had not been with me, I should have been quite unprotected!" Seeing that she had drawn the unblinking attention of her hostess, Lydia continued, "Your ability to select your servants is to be congratulated, dear Lady Catherine, for I was never more glad of anyone than when he offered to teach Sir Daniel some manners – Sir Daniel was so very rude, you know."

Her ladyship, nodding decisively, said, "Midden has been with me since before I was married, Miss Bennet. I was celebrated for my judgment even then, and I specifically told the late earl that I wished him to come with me. I am appalled at such a lack of good manners from Sir Daniel and I shall ensure that the other chaperones in Bath are made aware of such a lapse. It is insupportable that a gentleman should comport himself so; depend upon it, there can be no excuse. I am seriously displeased."

Beau Nash, seeing the distress on Mrs. Bennet's face, said in a comforting tone, "I too shall make sure it is known, Mrs. Bennet – I am not little known in this town, I do believe, and I will certainly use what influence I have to see that the fellow is suitably punished by good society. You need not fear, madam, that your dear daughter will have to meet him again."

Her dear daughter felt a little disappointed by this, as on the walk back she had thought of half a dozen things that she would like to say to Sir Daniel. It seemed she would be denied the opportunity. Lady Catherine appeared to agree with her defender, for she said, "Mr. Nash, Miss Bennet need have no fear of such a thing, for if I see him again, I shall tell him precisely what I think of his conduct and publicly censure him for it."

Lydia looked hopefully toward Mr. Nash, who shook his head. "I am sure that any young man facing your ladyship's wrath ought to quake in his boots, but Mrs. Bennet here would likely wish to avoid such a scene – it might cause some talk, you know."

Mrs. Bennet looked at the established leader of Bath society and fluttered her lace-edged handkerchief a little. "Oh sir! So very kind and thoughtful – I do not know that I have ever come across such gentlemanly manners; I am altogether quite…."

"That is all very well, Mr. Nash," said Lady Catherine, her mouth twisting slightly in amusement at the admiring look that he was casting toward the widow. Why gentlemen had such a preference for weak females was a thing she could never comprehend. "But I am adamant that the fellow be brought to realise his error – that he should insult a young woman under my protection is beyond the bounds of anything – I am deeply, yes, *deeply*, offended by it!"

Her ladyship eventually calmed down, once she had visited all her friends in Bath and written to many of her acquaintances in Kent. Within the space of a week, it was widely established that Sir Daniel James was quite unfit for the title of gentleman and thus he was suddenly and comprehensively excluded from the strict society that Bath was so famed for.

Midden, already greatly favoured by the former Catherine Fitzwilliam, found himself even more so once he related the entirety of his overhearings into her ear that very afternoon. He knew full well that she was not so very severe as she made herself out to be; she had been a lively sort of girl in her youth, after all, and he rather suspected that in spite of her tuttings and shaken head, she had enjoyed hearing of Miss Bennet's spirited rejection of her suitor. Certainly her ladyship had smiled at him when he had, with greatly offended dignity, rejected the guinea she had offered him in thanks for supporting Miss Bennet.

"Accept money for doing my duty to your ladyship? I should say not, ma'am. I do not think, my lady, that I have ever been of a grasping sort o' disposition, and beggin' your ladyship's pardon, but you been around just as long as I have to well know it. Given how I performed that same duty to your ladyship often enough."

Lady Catherine de Bourgh, feeling for all the world as if she were eighteen years old again and whisked back to the time when she had eviscerated Mr. Peregrine Malmsbury, who had dared to squeeze her hand during a carriage ride, quirked an eyebrow and returned the guinea to her purse. She informed Midden, with a wry glint in her eye, that there was nothing so revolting as misplaced pride, and sent him off on his way. Loyal servants were so very hard to come by, after all.

Lydia found pity to be quite intolerable; she never wasted it on other people herself, and so rather resented it when she knew that it was directed towards her. She was almost relieved when, having endured three successive evenings of comforting words and gentle support from the matrons of Bath, her throat became quite sore and her head ached enough so that, upon returning home, she was sent directly to bed by her Mama and told not to emerge until she felt better.

She was a very healthy girl in general, and to be so confined and fussed over was a dreadful ordeal. Having further endured the foul potions that the apothecary supplied, Lydia recovered quickly enough, but was greatly annoyed to be forbidden to go out until a full week had passed. Lydia rather suspected that Lady Catherine had informed the doddering old apothecary of her opinions on the matter, and so the wretched coward had not dared to argue. She once again found herself biting her tongue, and bitterly regretted the necessity of it.

On the last morning of her imprisonment, another day of rain, Lydia was sat listlessly by the window, watching the droplets of water collect on the pane of glass and run down in miniature rivers toward the sill.

Had she been in, Lady Catherine would have given her something useful to do, and Mrs. Bennet would have clucked over her. The two widows had gone out that morning, however, to the Pump Room, where Beau Nash would undoubtedly flirt outrageously with the pretty Mrs. Bennet. Lydia felt little by way of loyalty to her dead father, but found it unsettling to be constantly hearing from her Mama of another gentleman's virtues. Perhaps it was the change of it that bothered her so. It would be just her ill luck if all of her sisters and her own Mama married before she did.

She detested feeling maudlin, and did not quite know what to do. Everything had altered in her life so awfully fast. Her sisters all married, her home gone (for it did not matter what Mary said in her letters – she did not belong there any more), and her mother moving on with such horrid ease. She did not wish to live at Longbourn, neither did she want to go to Pemberley again, she didn't especially want to live in the same house as Caroline Bingley, and she certainly had no desire to journey all the way to Norfolk to be bored silly by endless boating expeditions such as poor Kitty was subjected to.

Lydia closed her eyes and rested her hot forehead against the cool glass. A teardrop gathered and traced its way down her cheek. Lydia felt a longing for the years gone by, when they were none of them married but all happily and noisily living under one roof. She had never felt lonely then, never worried herself about good manners or not saying things she ought not; the Bennet girls were her sisters – she could say to them whatever first popped into her head and know that they would either tolerate it or object and reply just as honestly.

There was now only one other in the world to whom she could speak so, and he must not even enter her head. How could it be, that she missed him of all people? That when she thought of London, she thought of him and those green eyes and that smile hovering about his mouth whenever she said something a little shocking?

She had bought two ribbons at the haberdashers', each of them green, and brought them home, tacking them together so that they might not be separated. The one side reminded her of Mr. Warwick's pale eyes in the bright sunshine, and the other, the slightly richer tint brought about by candlelight. The paired green ribbons lived in her pocket with her pearls, and her hand visited them often.

The tears fell hot and fast from her eyes, and she did not care. Lydia felt utterly miserable and wished she had never met him. That thought brought a lump to her throat and the tears fell yet faster. She heard the sound of the door from below and sighed; her solitude was at an end. Lady Catherine and her mother were already returned. They would likely go to their rooms to change into their slippers before coming into this ugly striped parlour (Lady Catherine had not thought it worth changing the paper).

She turned at the door opening, and the butler stepped in.

"Begging your pardon, Miss Bennet, but the Earl of Warwick is desirous of a few minutes of your time." He looked at her blotched face and said delicately, "But perhaps miss is not yet feeling quite well enough to receive callers."

Lydia fished about for her handkerchief and dabbed her eyes. She did not know what the earl was doing in Bath but perhaps he had news from her London friends. Maybe she would even be able to glean from him how his cousin was and whether or not he had found a suitable heiress to marry, seeing as how his letter to Mrs. Kentmire suggested that he had changed his ways. She was sure she was not even jealous. What did she care whom he married? It is not as though she wanted him anyway. The vague hope entered her mind that he was sent by Mr. Warwick, her Mr. Warwick, as an ambassador of sorts, and she swallowed.

"It's all right, Evans; you may send his lordship in. Doubtless he will wish to pass on a message to me or some such thing." Lydia sniffed and Evans concealed a wince. "Could you have tea sent up, please? I do not think the earl copes with the damp so very well, and he may wish to be warmed."

The stately butler bowed and retreated.

Lydia went to the little round gilt-edged mirror that rested on a table, looking to see if the tear stains were obvious, and was dismayed to see that they were. Worse than that, her nose was quite red. Perhaps the earl would attribute it to grief for her father and overlook it.

His lordship, entering the room with a quick step, checked on the threshold and saw at once that Miss Bennet had been sobbing her pretty eyes out.

"Well, my pet, it is a good thing I came when I did. Shall I take you out shopping, Lydia?"

Lydia's heart dropped to her feet and then bounced back up to her mouth.

"Mr. Warwick!" she gasped, "Evans did not announce you – that is, he did, but he said…."

"Ah, you've not heard. My cousin, the late earl, passed away a month ago. I am only just out of mourning clothes and the immediate business concerning the estate was done with yesterday."

He crossed the room to her and held her face in both his hands, tipping it towards the light. Joy flooded her, and then immediately after realising it, she was cross with herself for feeling so. She looked into his eyes, trying to lose herself in them, so that when he was gone again she would remember them forever. Neither ribbon had been quite right – the shade was so very light that it would be hard to replicate, and even if she could find the correct colour, there would not be that laughing tenderness in it that made her feel so light and free. Her heart hammered in her chest and she wondered if he could hear it.

"What on earth are you doing here?" she asked, closing her eyes and leaning her face further into his warm palms.

"I came to convince you to marry me for my money, Lydia. I am come armed with bribery and blackmail, and I shan't be sent away without your promise." He sounded serious enough, for all that his eyes were crinkled in amusement.

"Oh, *don't*. I have been very unhappy. Papa died, you know, and since then everything has been awfully dull and sombre."

"Yes, I had heard," he said soberly. "I was frantic, to call that morning at Darcy House and discover you had gone. It took me a week of misery to discover what had happened, but just as I was about to mount my horse to come to Longbourn, my cousin fell quite dreadfully ill and the countess needed me. I wished so much to be with you, Lydia, but…my conscience would not permit me to ignore it any longer and I felt I must do my duty to my family. He hung on for nigh on three months; each day we thought that he could not possibly manage another day, but…."

"Mama sent an express in the morning and we were gone as soon as we were ready. There was no way of leaving you a message or anything."

"Did you want to, Lydia?"

She nodded.

"It was only when I did not think I would see you again that I...." she stopped, not knowing what to say.

"Lydia, my pet, if you do not complete that sentence I shall strangle you." His hands dropped down to her shoulders, but they were gentle and drew her closer to him.

Lydia wondered how it was that she felt more like herself with him near. When had it begun, that she could not feel complete without him nearby?

"I had not realised how freeing it was to have someone with whom I did not have to mind my tongue. It is the very worst thing about being a young lady, you know; you cannot say the first thing that enters your head, and it is exhausting."

Her suitor smiled tenderly and swept away a tendril of hair from her cheek.

"Is that what you were weeping over, when I came in?"

"In part, yes. I was ill this week, after the incident with Sir Daniel – no, you must not interrupt me! It was a minor thing and he is now quite cast out of society because of it – but what was I saying? Oh yes, I am a little melancholy to be so displaced. Home has always been Longbourn, but now it is not. I don't have anywhere to throw down all my ribbons and feel comfortable. This is Lady Catherine de Bourgh's house and she is very fond of order – like her nephew."

The Earl of Warwick, for the moment permitting Sir Daniel to go uninvestigated, laughed quietly at the irritation in her voice. His hands moved from her shoulders and dropped to rest on her waist. She uttered no protest and even laid a hand on his chest.

"Lydia. Marry me. You can spread your ribbons willy-nilly over each and every one of my houses if you wish to. Marry me. I am sorry I ever considered taking your sister-in-law. You are the other half of myself. If I had not spoken to you properly I should have been miserable all my life because I should not have known you – wonderful girl that you are! I was wrong, so very wrong, that day in the park...what is worse is that I think I knew it all along but I ignored my own conscience. Well – I may never be a saint, my pet, but I hope to be less dreadful than I have been."

Lydia, for the first time in an age, dimpled.

"Mr. Warwick – oh no, that is wrong – my lord...."

"I like that. It sounds almost docile, coming from you." he interrupted.

"Oh, do be quiet!" she said, and reached up to kiss him.

It was perhaps a little unfortunate that Lady Catherine de Bourgh, Mrs. Bennet, and Evans (who was bearing the tea tray) chose that moment to enter the room.

Mrs. Bennet gave a small shriek, Lady Catherine de Bourgh tutted audibly, and Evans, being a very fine butler indeed, carefully set the tray down on a little table before retreating to laugh at his leisure belowstairs.

"Miss Bennet, I insist that you desist from such behaviour immediately!" cried her ladyship in commanding tones.

Lydia smiled at her, and taking the earl by the hand, said, "Oh, Lady Catherine, I am so happy! This is the Earl of Warwick, Mama! Mama! I am to be a countess. Is that not exciting? Of course, I am a little sorry not to have had the excitement of eloping and being taken to Gretna Green, but I daresay I shall be just as content to be wed in the ordinary fashion."

My Lord Warwick, grinning at his bride-to-be, interceded at that point.

"I take it that I must apply to you, Mrs. Bennet, for permission to marry this delightful baggage."

Quite charmed by the tender care with which the earl looked at her daughter, Mrs. Bennet – with what Lady Catherine thought to be undue eagerness – replied without any noticeable hesitation or regret, "Oh, you may have her, my lord; of course."

Chapter Twelve

He took her out after that, and they walked together down the street. They set off without any firm direction in mind, and ambled along entirely absorbed in each other's presence. There seemed so much to speak of, so much that they had missed of each other in half a year, that they hardly knew where to begin.

Yet begin they did. Lord Warwick, Lydia's gloved hand tucked into the crook of his arm, told her of his failed visit to Darcy House only hours after they had left.

"The wretched butler couldn't, or wouldn't, tell me anything whatever about where you had gone or why. I tried again the next day and my heart dropped to my boots when I saw the black crepe go up and did not know for whom it was hung."

"I suppose you thought I had misfired another gun," interrupted Lydia, able, for perhaps the first time in her life, to imagine the feelings of another person. Her tone was jovial but her face was sympathetic.

He smiled, as she hoped he would, and the corners of his eyes crinkled. "The thought crossed my mind, my pet. You shall have yours back as soon as may be; I have kept it in my pocket all the while. I really must show you how to fire the thing and load it properly – perhaps we will head to Warwick when we are married and I will set up a firing range for you."

"What need have I to know how to shoot a gun, Mr. Wa...oh bother...my lord? You are the only man I ever wanted to shoot, and I don't any more."

"I told you that you would like me better by and by, did I not?" answered her future husband, with clear satisfaction. "If we continue like this, you will be in a fair way to being head over heels in love with me by Michaelmas."

It was not in Lydia's nature to be reticent with her feelings.

"Probably; I should think it very likely, since I already am."

His breath hitched and she watched him carefully. She rather thought he would be pleased but it was not very obvious if he was. She remarked on it.

"Pleased! Yes, but what are you about, Lydia – to say such a thing to me now when I can't respond as I should like?"

Lydia laughed and looked about her. It was true – they were surrounded by a large number of people, most of whom probably knew Lady Catherine.

"Kiss me, you mean? I should have liked that; I don't mind all the people if you do not."

Lord Warwick looked about him, scanning the area. His mouth twisted wryly, and then he laughed, an edge of rueful self-mockery in his voice. "No, can't be done, my pet. People might think I had to marry you to save my reputation."

Now Lydia giggled, thinking how good it was to be teased by him again. "Well, I shan't make you if you don't want to, Mr. Wa...oh, this is annoying – I am afraid you will just have to be Justin until I remember correctly. To think that earlier, this very morning, I was thinking how much I should like to be called 'Mrs. Warwick' and now I shan't be. I had no notion that your cousin was so very ill."

"'Your Ladyship' will suit you much better than a mere 'Mrs. Warwick,' my pet. Doubtless you will rule the ton with an iron fist like that Brummell fellow. How is it we have reached the shops without any error? Come; I shall find us a little tea house and feed you cake."

"Oh, dear Mr. Brummell! How grand we shall sound, Justin. May we marry very soon? I do not think I like Bath so much as London – it is a very dreary place."

The earl looked down at the young woman by his side and found it curiously hard to swallow. Happiness suited her – there was a spring in her step and a merry sparkle in her eyes. A dimple on one side of her mouth was in evidence, and although she was not an incomparable beauty, he found that he did not care in the slightest. This darling lively girl was all he had wanted for months now, and having finally won her, he found that his next aim in life was for her always to be thus. The slumped shoulders and red eyes that he had seen from the threshold of the reception room door did not please him at all. Lydia should always be happy – and she would be, if he had anything to say about it.

"Lydia."

"Hmm?" she said. She was looking at a bonnet in a shop window, and thinking it might be improved upon with the addition of a ribbon or two.

"Lydia."

She turned then, and looked at him. "What is it, Justin?"

"I am sorry, you know. For the abduction, I mean. I think it must have made you very frightened to do as you did and fight off those hired men. I can't help but feel I should give any other man a sound thrashing if he alarmed you so."

"Oh! That. Yes. Well, I mean, no. It was not very pleasant and I did cast up my accounts as soon as we returned home, but you have already said that you were wrong – at Waddington's and at the museum, remember? Let it be done with; I have learnt to love you and I do not think I am wrong in deciding to trust you. In any case, at least I have had a grand adventure that I can boast of. Not one of my friends has such a story to tell as I do."

Her betrothed looked a little rueful. "Yes, I suppose that I did," he said slowly. "In the interests of honesty, and I hope we always will be honest with each other – I did not mean that at Waddington's. I had meant that I was wrong in attempting to wed Miss Darcy – she was all wrong for me, or at least, I was wrong for her. I don't entirely know what I was thinking. It was not until after that I began to realise how far I had sunk; I do not think I knew myself until you had gone away from me."

In spite of herself, Lydia giggled. "She did not enjoy the adventure one little bit, not even afterwards. Poor thing."

He shook his head and walked onward with her. A crowd had gathered at the entrance to Milsom Street and Lydia wondered what it might mean. She spied one of Lady Catherine's many acquaintances, who had just come out of the clock-maker's shop and was watching her with disapproving surprise.

"Miss Bennet, are you quite alone? I do not think Lady Catherine would be quite pleased to see you walking with a gentleman and no footman in evidence, particularly since Sir Daniel James turned out to be less than gentlemanly."

"No, Mrs. Worthing, for you see his lordship is quite enough escort for me. We are to be married, you know; it was just decided this very day. You must be the first to congratulate us, aside from my Mama and Lady Catherine. Oh! I beg your pardon – Mrs. Worthing, this is Lord Warwick; he is only come to Bath today."

The Earl of Warwick bowed elegantly. Lydia admired the graceful bend of his neck as he did so.

Mrs. Worthing's brows rose and she peered about her for any sign of friends to whom she could carry the news. "May I offer my felicitations then, my lord, and Miss Bennet. I am so pleased. Lady Catherine was quite convinced that you would do nicely, even after Sir Daniel behaved so, and I do see that she was quite correct. I do not think you should attempt to go down Milsom Street, my dear; Mr. Nash is there and in quite a rage. There is a radical preacher come to Bath and the Beau has gone to meet him and means for him to leave. Wesley or some such name. At any rate, I am to go home – Mr. Worthing would not like me to be caught up in a mob, for that is what I am certain it will turn out to be, judging by what I have seen. You had much better go down past Bilbury's and then on to the park, if that is where you were headed. Oh! Lady Eugenia, do wait for me one moment – I have something to say to you!"

Lord Warwick's brows had reached almost comical heights by the time Mrs. Worthing had left off speaking. Lydia looked at his contemptuous expression and could not contain her laugh.

"If you had asked me yesterday what I thought of Mrs. Worthing, I should have declared her quite unbearable, but today I am feeling friendly towards everyone. Although now that I think of it, I do wish she would not tie her bonnet ribbons quite like that, for her nose is not very straight and she really ought to balance it by tying her bow on the opposite side of the twist. I cannot understand why people do not see these things, Justin. La! Do you mean to put your arm about my waist in such a crowded spot?"

"Yes," said the earl, "for if I do not, then that talkative woman will be sure to announce our engagement to all and sundry and I mean to get there first by making it very evident that I adore you, Lydia." He removed his arm some minutes later, however, when they had lost sight of the crowds of people. "Sir Daniel James," he began, with determination. "I should like to know what 'less than gentlemanly' implies, if you please."

Lydia rolled her eyes. "I do not think I need to tell *you* what it means, sir. Must we speak of him today? I sent him off without any difficulty and he was so very offended that I do not think he will wish to see me again. Really, Justin, I was very rude to him in my rejection."

Lord Warwick laughed darkly. "Oh, that I can believe without any difficulty, my pet. I have the privilege of having heard you brutally issue a well-deserved rejection before. I want to know if I ought to pay a visit to the fellow."

"No," said Lydia, shortly.

"No?" he replied, his brows lifting a little again, but the corner of his mouth had curled up, ever so slightly.

Lydia shook her head. "No."

The Earl of Warwick bowed to Miss Bennet, accepting his orders. "Very well, then; I suppose I have little enough right to object, after my behavior to you during the season. He may live," said Lord Warwick, with a shrug.

They passed a public house, and a drunkard stumbled out, having been thrust forth from within. He wore a tattered militia uniform, and almost colliding with Lydia, he lost his footing and reached for her to steady himself.

The Earl of Warwick disengaged the man from her with a sharp kick to his knee and the man fell over. Blinking blearily against the piercing brightness of daylight, he rubbed a hand across his beard and stared at the young lady.

"I know you – *I know you*," he said to himself. "Can't remember, can't remember, anything."

"Take yourself off," ordered Lord Warwick, "else I shall call the magistrate and have you dealt with. You are fortunate that I am in such a good frame of mind today. The lady does not know commoners like you. Be gone."

George Wickham looked hard at Lydia Bennet one more time, and seeing that the tall man was in earnest, shrugged his shoulders and loped off towards Milsom Street. His knee hurt from the man's boot, and he wondered if he could find another tavern in this awful city that might serve him an ale or two on credit, just to dull the pain. Something like regret rose in him at the depths to which his life had sunk, and he squashed it down quickly. What did it matter if he had once stood tall and proud, looking every bit as much of a gentleman as that arrogant rich man with the pretty girl on his arm? It wasn't his fault after all, was it? Women did not look at him like that any more, not like that young lady had looked at her companion, as though he were something quite wonderful.

Lydia spared a pitying glance for him over her shoulder as he hobbled away, and then, shrugging her shoulders, looked back to the earl. He was prodigiously handsome, and she grinned up at him, feeling pleased with her choice.

"How strange!" was all she said, after they had walked a few feet further. She considered the drunkard's behaviour with a little frown. He had seemed to think he knew her, but she would vow she had never laid eyes on the fellow.

"The man was drunk, my pet; don't think on it – you need not be troubled by anything today."

They stopped for half an hour at a little chocolate shop that catered solely to the very wealthy inhabitants of Bath. Lydia, sat near a window, enjoyed sipping at her sweet drink whilst watching the passers-by go about doing their errands.

Having finished her drink, she set her cup down on the saucer with a contented sigh and noticed her companion studying her. She smiled at him and his eyes lit up.

"I suppose that my lady wife will need to be brought a chocolate drink in bed every morning by her maid, judging by your enjoyment of that. Shall I get you another?"

Lydia beamed at him. "That sounds very charming, Justin. I had better not – I think I have had a little too much cake as it is. I shan't be able to get into above half of my dresses if I have more."

He bowed. "I had better make sure that you have new dresses in such a case, hadn't I, my pet?" he said grandly, then sobered. "You can always have anything you want, Lydia."

Lydia gave a little crow of laughter and, uncaring of the other patrons in the shop, reached for his hand. She would not consider such dull things as proper behaviour, not today. She wanted to hold his hand and so she did. His eyes were tender as he pressed her fingers.

"I do not think there is anything else I want that is not here. I shall like to be married to you. It will mean I can wear my beautiful pearls at long last, for one thing, and...Oh! Justin, will you take me to Paris, please? I want to buy some French lace. Lady Beatrice wrote to me months ago that her father travelled over the channel and brought her some back. It was a very trying letter to read when I was sat looking like a drab little blackbird in mourning crepe; I shall write one to her once we are married and see how she likes it. Well," she added, charitably, "perhaps I won't."

"Paris? Yes, we can certainly sail to France if you like. I might like to take a jaunt to Italy with you too; you will like the silk there, I am certain. We ought to avoid the museums, though, I should think." He grinned, amused by the memory. "You liked your pearls? I had rather thought you might be hopping mad at me. I was expecting you to throw them at my head and call me all manner of shocking names that I should be embarrassed to admit I knew."

He possessed himself of her other hand.

"Like them? My dear, they are the most perfect things. I hid them with my pistol. Yes, I was very cross with you, I thought you were trying to manipulate me or force my hand, and yes, I would have thrown them back at you, but...but I tried them on and then I couldn't quite bring myself to do it. I don't think I have ever owned anything so lovely."

She removed her hand and reached for her reticule when her eyes felt a little damp. Lord Warwick offered his handkerchief to her and looked grave when she dabbed at her eyes.

"You must not mind me! I am happy, I am. I was just thinking how glad I was that I kept them – my pearls, I mean. I like to buy little presents for people, you see. I am not like my sisters, they – well, Jane and Lizzy – seem to know how to make people happy only with a few kind words but I...I like to give something a little more permanent that will not be forgotten a moment later. So...so when Lizzy puts on a pretty hat, she can say to herself, 'Lydia gave me this,' and she will know that I did so because I love her. I must be making little sense to you. It is only...when Papa died and I could not see you, I wished, above anything, that the pearls were bought for me for similar reasons and it gave me hope – that is all. It isn't merely that I like pretty things. My pearls will always be my most special thing for all my life."

"Lydia," said Lord Warwick, sounding a little hoarse, "do stop, or else I will need to take my handkerchief back from you and wipe my own eyes. We will go to France and to Italy and wherever else we wish to wander, after we are married, and shall be utterly, utterly happy. Do not cry, my pet; I intend for you to laugh every day with joy. Yes, of course, of course your pearls were bought for you for such reasons as you say. I love you and I mean for you to know it fully."

Lydia considered this.

"Justin," she said, quite seriously, handing him back his fine lawn handkerchief, "is there any *good* reason why we cannot climb into a carriage this very instant and simply elope?"

THE COUNTESS

AND THE

HIGHWAYMAN

The Earl and Countess of Warwick, returning from a lengthy honeymoon on the continent, had, for the last ten miles or so, lapsed into a comfortable silence. The roads were in adequate condition, and since leaving Dover they had made excellent time. As they had spent two nights thus far on the road, the carriage had by now entered Derbyshire and was approaching Pemberley, the home of Lady Warwick's sister. There was to be a gathering of sorts there, for three out of five of the former Miss Bennets, and their respective husbands, had been invited to stay with the Darcys for some weeks. Mrs. Collins and Mrs. Bingley had travelled together from Hertfordshire and were already present. Lydia, being Lydia, was late – a circumstance that was not entirely unexpected by the hosts. The only pall on the gathering, in the eyes of the young countess, was that Miss Bingley was to be present. Lady Warwick had crossed swords with the woman in both Hertfordshire and London. She was not by any means pleased to have to remain in the same, albeit very large, house with her for a prolonged period.

Her ladyship divided her time equally between admiring the fine workmanship on her new travelling gown from Paris and appreciating the handsome man who sat opposite her, his long booted legs propped up on the seat beside her. She was enormously pleased with him: he had taken her to Italy, to Spain, and then finally to Paris for nearly a month. Lydia's French had never been particularly good, but she had discovered a great talent for remembering the essential vocabulary for lace and velvet. A staggeringly enormous wardrobe had been purchased for Lady Warwick and not one murmur of irritation had crossed her husband's lips during the ordering of it. Eventually she, although herself entirely delighted to be so surrounded by rolls of costly silks and taffetas, had thought to ask if he was not at all bored; the earl had merely smiled and softly commented that he had been correct, so long ago in Waddington's – shops were where Lydia was at her happiest, and so they were to be tolerated, and even encouraged.

Feeling his wife's eyes on him, Justin opened one eye. "I have been thinking, my pet. There is really no putting it off any longer. Once we return to London after this trip to Pemberley, you will have to be presented to the Queen. I do not know how I have forgotten it for such a long time."

"Well, I must say, Justin, I am a little glad of it, for I have been wishing to meet Her Majesty this age. I mean to advise her that the current rules on court dress are against every notion of good taste. Depend upon it, once I have spoken to her, the English court will no longer be so dreadfully old-fashioned in comparison to the rest of Europe."

Both of the earl's eyes had opened during this speech, and the faintest glimmer of alarm had crept in alongside the amusement that so frequently lurked when his wife spoke.

"You wish to correct the Queen of England as regards to her rules for dress, in her own drawing room?"

"Well, of course I do, my love. Do you see any other peers in Europe being forced to endure such a ridiculous thing as hoops and a high waist? The feathers she may keep, for I have seen them used very prettily by some French ladies when we were at the opera in Paris – you know, the ones being so very noisy in the vestibule."

"I'm not so sure they deserve the description of 'ladies,' Lydia, if I recall them correctly. Do you think you might be...be *gentle* with the Queen? You have such a pretty neck," he smiled, looking at the pearls that were wound about it. "I should be distressed if she were to order it severed."

"Could she do that?" demanded Lydia, not having thought of this. "Well, I suppose it is a risk worth taking, for I do not think we ought to be forced to...what in the world was *that*?"

The large crested carriage had slowed a little as the horses made their way along the edge of a wood, and as the trees thickened, the men on the box gave an inarticulate shout just before the blunderbuss was fired. The Earl of Warwick sat upright on his seat now, alert and intent. All languor was gone when he withdrew, from the little holder affixed to the wall of the carriage, a deadly little weapon, and swiftly moved to sit beside his wife.

"Justin, are we being held up?" asked Lydia, quite breathlessly. "I haven't ever been...mmmmffph."

Her husband had swiftly and decisively kissed her mid-sentence. "Lydia, under absolutely no circumstances are you to take any risks. If you are told to hand over your jewels, do so *without* argument. Do you understand me, my pet? Not. One. Risk." He sounded very grim and serious.

Lydia's opinions on receiving these orders went unvoiced, for a masked man, holding aloft two pistols, appeared at the door of the carriage.

"Stand an' deliver!" he said in a rough voice, a little muffled by the scarf tied over his lower face. In the gloomy shadow that was cast by the tall trees lining both sides of the road, all that Lydia could make out beneath the brimmed hat was a pair of hard, narrowed eyes that were menacingly fixed upon her husband.

The Earl of Warwick very cooly levelled his pistol at the highwayman.

"I think that I shall not," he said, and fired.

The man instantly fell back where he stood and disappeared from view. Running footsteps were heard and another of his fellows appeared at the door, wrenching it open.

"Yuh killed 'im! Get out o' this fancy carriage o' yours and see if yuh man enough t'face me." The man, also armed with two pistols, one of them obviously spent and smoking, gestured to the earl to leave the carriage. His own shot now gone, Lord Warwick stood and stepped out.

"Stay inside, my lady," he commanded over his shoulder in stern accents, not turning his head to see if Lydia had meekly nodded or not. The man with the gun flicked his eyes at the finely dressed woman within.

"An yuh. Y'empty that little bag o' yours and take off them pretties from around yer neck. If yuh behave like a good girl I might let you leave alive once I shoot yer husband."

Lydia gasped in frightened outrage and shook her head at him.

"My pearls?! I shall not. You may have my reticule, I suppose, although I'll not empty it for you, but my *pearls*? No! And do not think I shall just sit idly by and permit you to murder his lordship, either."

The two men, who had been examining each other with wary contempt, both whipped their heads toward her at this. His lordship, far from being gratified by such a spirited defence of his life, appeared to be very irritated, and set his thin mouth in a straight line. The highwayman was not used to being spoken to in such a way by one of his female victims. Ordinarily they fainted or went into hysterics – this one seemed to be furious. He was so surprised that he was unsure how to respond. He elected, after a moment of gaping, to ignore her and keep his eye on the known danger of a furious gentleman.

"His lordship, is it? Well, yer lordship, if yuh could stand by me dead mate o'er there so's I can shoot yuh, yuh 'umble servant would be most grateful. An' missy, y'can empty that there fancy bag or I'll shoot you next. Now, girl, get out o' that seat and come outside."

Dismayed, Lydia saw that he was in earnest, and watched as her husband went to stand beside the body of the man he had shot. Justin's eyes flicked quickly to the guns in the dead man's hands and as quickly slid away. There was one other man on a horse, covering three servants. She opened her reticule a little and moved to the door. Two rough-looking men with pistols to be got rid of by five unarmed people; she did not particularly care for the odds.

It occurred to her in a flash, as she unlooped her reticule, that if she could distract the brute, Justin might be able to reach one of the pistols not so far from his feet. She paused.

"I need to be handed down," she said, trying for her most commanding tone. She began well but the slight tremor at the end of her words made her sound petulant instead, and she frowned her annoyance.

The highwayman, gun still levelled at Justin, barely spared her a glance this time. "Yuh need to be whipped is what yuh need. Typical gentlefolk! *Useless* women and *useless* men, just living lives of luxury on the backs of us honest poor folk."

"Very well then, I must make do myself, but I demand that you turn your back as I do so. I cannot manage my skirts and the steps, can I?" Justin, although by now heartily agreeing that Lady Warwick deserved some sort of punishment for entirely disregarding him, took advantage of the man's distraction to step a little closer to the corpse.

"Yuh *demand*? I'll tell yuh, y'wench. If you don't get down from there without any other fussin' I'll shoot you and take everythin' off y'carcass."

The highwayman turned his attention back to Lord Warwick and, although knowing that he had the upper hand, quailed at the iciness he saw in the rich man's pale green eyes. He knew that if this man were armed, he would be as dead as Welsh Harry, his fellow robber.

Lydia put her hand into her reticule, and triumph filled her as her hand closed around the handle of her little pistol. She withdrew it swiftly, and levelled it at the man who was aiming at her husband. With a weapon in her hand, Lydia's fear was now largely replaced by hot fury that coursed through her body and made her white cheeks flush red.

"You ought to know, I have quite decided long ago that no one will harm that man apart from me. Drop your weapon or I will shoot you where you stand and then *I'll* be taking everything off *your* body."

Wheeling around, the highwayman's eyes widened in alarm and his mouth gaped. His attention divided, he waved his pistol wildly between Lydia and her husband.

"A weapon! A woman with a weapon?!" He sounded stupefied, and in his great surprise, rounded on the man responsible. "Did yuh know she had a pistol? I never seen anythin' like it in all my born days."

Lord Warwick, having swiftly stooped down and taken possession of the two guns beside the dead body at his feet, began to look a little amused in spite of his very evident annoyance. Holding one pistol aloft, in what Lydia thought a very dashing fashion, he aimed it at the man covering his servants and called out, "You will now drop your weapon and lay yourself down flat on the ground, else I will shoot you from here, and believe me, I miss my shot only when I am decidedly drunk."

The man did so without question. Having seen the lady train her weapon on the leader of their little brigade, he was quite willing to believe anything of these rich folk. Lydia thought him very poor-spirited indeed, and began to consider that she might have managed to defeat such a coward on her own, after all.

"Yes," said the earl, with an unpleasant smile, "I was quite aware of her ladyship owning a gun, for I bought it for her, you see. She is shaping up to be a very fair shot. From that range I should think she might engage to send a bullet right through you."

Lydia smiled at her husband then, quite pleased that he had refrained from mentioning the unpleasant incident that almost lost him a favourite dog.

"Yuh mad," was all the highwayman could manage to say, "*mad*!"

By this point the earl's servants had successfully tied up the man who was lying obediently on the ground, and one of them approached their master for further orders. Lord Warwick handed the driver a weapon.

"Here, aim this at him; if he moves, shoot him directly. I am quite out of patience with this entire episode and cannot summon the energy to prolong it. My Lady Warwick," this said in less forceful tones, "would you care to remove to the carriage again?"

"No," said Lydia, decisively. "I do not think I would. I think I would rather shoot him, Justin. I do think he deserves it after having given me such a fright, and...and he was going to *kill* you." She said this last part in a less steady voice as her husband came closer to her. "He was going to kill you and leave me all alone and you would be lying dead on the roadside and...*oh Justin*."

"Lydia, my pet, there is no need for these tears now," he said softly in her ear. "You have been my brave and fearless Lydia, but it is done with."

"I-I am not a-afraid," said Lydia, raising the hand not clutching her gun to dash away her tears. "I am just angry; that is all. My pearls, Justin. They w-were all I had of you for six months and he was going to take them away and y-you away too and…."

Her husband carefully removed the little pistol from her grasp and stood between her and the ruffian.

"Donaldson, tie this man up tightly and load him and his companion onto the rear of the carriage. They will need to be brought to justice. Lady Warwick," said her lord, firmly, "up into the carriage now, if you please."

Lydia obeyed her husband but not without hissing quietly back at him, "But I do *not* please – that is what I have been saying. Oh, very well, then, but I am very vexed, for he ought not be permitted to live, my lord!"

A loud echoing crack issued from behind them, just as Lord Warwick was handing Lydia up into the carriage. She stood on the step and peered around her husband just as the injured party howled in pain.

"Oh," she said, sounding a little happier. "That is well, then."

Not turning around, Lord Warwick closed his eyes for a moment, as though searching for some previously unknown reserves of patience.

"I beg your pardon, my lord – the fellow raised his gun toward you and I thought I had better fire," said Donaldson, defensively.

His master's cold green eyes rested for a moment on the writhing highwayman before he ushered her ladyship into the carriage and, once having carefully ensured that her train was properly within, closed the door.

Lord Warwick was not fool enough to request that his wife draw the shade on the window; he knew Lydia well enough, and so avoided wasting his breath. She would doubtless watch everything that occurred with her little nose pressed flat to the glass.

The highwayman was bleeding profusely, and, judging by the way he clutched at his stomach, would certainly not survive. The earl set his jaw.

"Donaldson, you will climb on the box and drive the carriage some thirty yards down the road. Inform the countess that I will be within very shortly. You are to prohibit any kind of a view of this fellow from her eyes."

The servant nodded once and scurried off. The servant who remained looked grim. "It'll be a mercy, sir." Lord Warwick flicked a single glance up to him and the servant did not dare offer any more of his opinions.

Some minutes later, the Earl of Warwick stepped up into his carriage to see his wife bent over his hat in the corner, retching.

"I'm not sorry about spoiling your hat in the least, Justin," said the countess between gasps, "for it is quite your fault. Donaldson absolutely refused to let me out of the carriage."

Her husband laid a gentle hand on her back and with the other held back her artfully arranged curls as she leant over the hat again.

"It doesn't matter," he said, relieved that she was safe.

"It does matter, Justin; I am very annoyed!"

"I suppose you will find a way to blame me for the whole, regardless of whether or not I could have helped any of it," said the earl, fishing out his handkerchief and wetting it from a bottle. "Here, Lydia, wipe your mouth with this."

"Thank you. I am a very reasonable woman, my lord, but I do think that to be confined to a carriage when one is about to be unwell is the very worst thing. Do throw the hat out of the door, please. I do not know that I can tolerate the smell."

His lordship did so. "Are you always ill in such a fashion when you have an adventure, my pet?" he asked, hauling her to his side and quite crushing her beautiful dress.

"I don't know," she said, laying her head on his shoulder. "This is only the second proper adventure I have had."

"I am sorry that you have been distressed, but I suppose I had better inform you that I am really almost cross with you. I told you quite plainly that you were not to risk yourself."

"I didn't!"

"You didn't? I suppose your insistence that you would keep your pearls was intended to *placate* the fellow, eh?"

"I could not be expected to just hand them over, Justin! I think it a very good thing that I acted as I did, for it meant that you had time to get those other weapons, and yes, I do think one almost might say that I saved your neck. Really, my lord, you ought to be *grateful* to me instead of giving me a scold."

"*Grateful!* Lydia, I had it well in hand. My only concern was that you should be kept safe, a concern, I might add, which you ran roughshod over with nary a thought. Do you think I can bear the thought of you harmed?"

"Well in hand? *Well in hand?* Doubtless your walking to stand where you were told in order to be shot was all part of it and you were, in fact, intending to save the day after coming back as a ghost?"

The earl's lips twitched.

"I was intending to jump out of the way and retrieve the dead highwayman's weapons as I did so."

"How marvellous. I am so very impressed. No, stop the carriage – I need to be ill again."

"Use your bonnet," suggested her husband, callously; he was evidently very much rattled by the entire episode.

Lydia's lip trembled. "I do not know how you can suggest such an awful thing," she said, and she burst into tears.

Lord Warwick banged on the ceiling and the carriage halted. Donaldson came to the door. "Hand her ladyship down, Donaldson; she needs to disembark."

Lydia did not look at him once, but made her way to a large oak tree, and was violently ill behind it. Feeling entirely horrid from the roiling in her stomach, she leant her forehead against the bark of the tree and gave into noisy sobs.

A heavy hand rested on her shoulder, and in one swift motion she squealed, reached into her pocket, and, turning on the spot, pointed her weapon into the face of her assailant.

"I thought you didn't want to shoot me any more, Lydia," said her husband.

Lowering her gun, she bit her lip. "I thought you might be another highwayman."

"Oh, my darling," he smiled, and pulled her to him. "As though I did not have my gun at the ready the whole time you were behind this tree. Come, you are very ill and overwrought – let us get into the carriage and we will journey on to Pemberley. You will feel better by and by."

Lydia wound her arms about his waist, beneath his coat, and mumbled something into the heavy woollen folds.

He tipped her chin up. "Say that again, my pet."

"I said, 'I won't.' I am very likely pregnant. I want to talk to Lizzy, though, to be certain."

The Countess of Warwick did not sound overjoyed by the notion.

"You are unhappy with this? I thought women liked babies."

"Well, it is just that I like things as they are, Justin. I do not think I am very maternally minded – I will get fat and you will grow bored with me and then…."

"One moment, if you please, Lydia. A man does not grow bored with a wife who saves his hide in one moment and then pulls out a pistol at him in the next. It just does not happen."

"Well, there is that, I suppose," said Lydia, feeling a little more cheerful. "If you will still love me, I do not mind so very much, but you must not expect me to coo over a child in the way that my sisters do. Theodore was so very ugly when he was born and Lizzy looked at him as though he were the most delightful thing – it was all I could do not to correct her."

"I expect nothing of you than to be my darling wife. That is all."

"Darling?" said Lydia, tilting her head at the new endearment. "Let us go on then – I want to shock Jane and her horrid sister-in-law with tales of us fighting off an army of highwaymen."

Some three hours later, Lydia was sat in a light, airy salon sipping delicately fragranced tea from a delightfully painted cup. "I am sure that there were at least a dozen of them, Jane! It was vastly shocking, you know. I cannot think how we dared to travel on."

"It is so very upsetting, Lydia. I am glad that the earl fought them off as he did. How dreadful if something should have happened to you," said Mrs. Bingley, the very picture of dismayed loveliness in a printed rose silk gown.

Miss Bingley, less lovely in red, sniffed and raised a doubtful eyebrow. There was something that did not quite ring true in Lady Warwick's tale, although if the earl did not correct her, there was little she herself could do, but she would patiently wait to catch the countess out in her ridiculous story.

Miss Bingley had not quite forgiven the penniless Lydia Bennet for ignoring her kindly meant advice. Approaching the young girl at a ball one evening during the previous season, quite filled with envy at the her popularity, the more worldly-wise lady had advised her to set her sights on a gentleman of comfortable rank and not aim too high. Miss Bennet, having just finished a set with Beau Brummell himself, had snorted and rudely asked her if she was going to take her own advice to finally find herself a husband. Miss Bingley had deliberately forgotten most of the exchange, but she was quite unable to forget having been called a "dried up, sad old spinster," in a dreadful reply to her well-intended counsel. She had been desirous ever since to knock Miss Bennet off her undeserved pedestal.

Opportunity came two evenings later at Pemberley, when she walked about the room, waiting for dear Mrs. Kentmire to give way to her on the pianoforte, and she happened to overhear the earl speaking softly to his wife on a comfortable sofa as she passed behind them.

"...quite the dashing hero, am I not, my pet? I daresay I will even cope admirably in the face of you aiming your pistol at me in the future."

Miss Bingley, quite gleefully shocked, hurried away from them.

The next morning, she sat herself beside Mrs. Kentmire at breakfast and, the Warwicks not having yet come down, related what she had overheard. The rest of the table made sufficient noise to cover her tale, Mrs. Collins being in conversation with Jane and her brother making a valiant effort with Mr. Collins.

"I am convinced that such a vulgar creature must have encouraged the earl into such an improper remark in public, but then given her less than exalted origins, one ought not to be so very surprised."

"Are you so very sure that you overheard correctly, Miss Bingley?" said Georgiana, a little doubtfully. "It is very possible that the earl was speaking in jest."

Miss Bingley considered this. "Yes, that is very true, dear Mrs. Kentmire; you are so very sensible – but I do not think that this would entirely explain his use of such a very personal endearment in company. I should be mortified if my husband were to call me such a thing as a 'pet' in public."

"Such a fate is unlikely to befall you, Miss Bingley," murmured a smooth, snide voice from behind her.

Miss Bingley, swallowing, turned her head too sharply and felt a hot pain travel up her neck. She found the earl examining her as though she were some crawling insect, ready to be squashed beneath his boot. She had never seen a snake, but being well educated, she had read about them and decided that the earl's eyes were just as she would expect a snake's to look before it struck.

Mrs. Darcy, having seen the earl enter, and electing to remain silent as he stood listening to whatever Miss Bingley was being unpleasant about, struggled to conceal her smile and bade her sister good morning as she entered the room a little behind her husband.

"You are still unable to rise early, dearest?" she asked lightly. "I am quite astonished that Lady Catherine did not cure you of your penchant for lateness when you were with her in Bath."

"The fault is mine, Mrs. Darcy," said her newest brother-in-law. "I too have always struggled of a morning. Her ladyship has graciously permitted breakfast to be set back an hour at Warwick." He turned his cold, unpleasant gaze to Miss Bingley and continued, "It is yet more evidence of her superiority as a wife – I do not think that there could have been a more perfect Countess of Warwick than the one I have chosen."

Miss Bingley, quite red-faced and feeling decidedly awkward, found herself made further uncomfortable by the warm reception that was given the Warwicks by the others who sat at table.

That night, after the activities of the day were done, Mrs. Bingley approached her husband. "Charles, I am a little concerned for Caroline. She was telling me the most unlikely of tales this afternoon. I do not wish to seem harsh, my dear, but I am afraid...I am a little afraid that her mind may not be quite *sound*."

Mr. Bingley, well aware that his sweet wife would not have mentioned such a shocking thing if she were not greatly perturbed, asked her what might have prompted her to think so.

"I shall not repeat some of the dreadful things she said about Lydia, but she said...Charles, she said that my dear sister was a hoyden and would likely bring disgrace upon our whole family. It is not merely that – she seemed to think that Lydia would own a...a pistol and would murder us all in our beds!" Mrs. Bingley straightened her husband's cravat into a neater, more pleasing arrangement, and continued. "The rest I could attribute to some unpleasant misunderstanding, but when she started speaking of weapons, my dear, I began to think that she might not be of quite sound mind. A *pistol*, Charles – and my littlest sister!"

Some six months later, the Countess of Warwick was brought to bed for the delivery of her firstborn child. A gruelling night passed, but by the time the sun rose the following morning, the eminent doctor left the house pleased with his night's work. The countess had done her duty well and had been safely delivered of a son. It was always pleasant, thought the doctor, to be able to assure an expectant father that the family line was to remain secure and unbroken by entailments. He did not mention the decidedly off-colour insults that her ladyship had screeched at him when he insisted on examining her. Doctor Perrault had never met a fishwife, but he rather suspected that Lady Warwick had – where else could she have learnt such a varied vocabulary? He stepped into the street; the air was cold on his skin. Doubtless the thick fog would hang over the river as they crossed the bridge; it was often so on the Thames, of an autumn morning. He wearily climbed into his carriage. No doubt a nurse had washed the infant by now and swaddled him. She would likely take the infant away to the nursery and the countess would not lay eyes on him for a week or two.

He might have been surprised to hear that the reality was quite different. Although the earl had indeed engaged many nurses for the care of his child, the countess, upon being handed a squalling, red-faced infant, had stared at the boy in absolute shock and wonder. The earl, having dashed up the carpeted stairs as soon as the doctor had gone, was privileged to witness the moment in which Lydia first met her son.

A trembling finger brushed away the baby's unevenly grown patch of hair. That same finger traced down the slope of his nose and softly stroked his cheek. The babe opened his eyes for a brief blinking look at his Mama, and Lydia gasped.

"Justin! His eyes are green! Oh, how...I cannot...he is so perfect – is he not *beautiful*?"

The earl leant over to examine the boy and smiled. Having a healthy sense of self-preservation, he gravely agreed, but almost laughed aloud when his wife demanded another child as soon as might be.

"I need another one, my lord."

The exhausted maid, who was currently carrying out the bundle of bedclothes, bloodied from the night's work, heard this and missed her step. The earl did not even blink but his eyes twinkled.

"Well, I did promise you whatever you wanted, my pet. Do you think you might permit me to recover from this one first? I shall have to buy you a new jewel set to mark the occasion – do you want rubies or emeralds?"

Lydia ignored him; she was busily absorbed in her son. Suddenly, a thought occurred to her and she looked at her husband in dismay.

"I have just thought. He will grow up and want to marry!"

"Not for some time yet though, my darling," reassured her husband. "He will be little for quite some time to come, and will only want his Mama for a good long while, I should think."

"Yes," said Lydia, impatiently, "but you do not understand. What shall we do? I cannot think that anything less than a princess will be good enough for him and…and they are almost *invariably* very ugly!"

NOT ROMANTIC

Chapter One

Miss Lucas, even from her girlhood, was ever aware of the temporary nature of material possessions. Her father, Sir William, had come by his knighthood through pleasing the King. Mad King George had been very easily pleased at that time, and having been informed that the delightfully fine leather gloves he had worn on a particularly chilly autumn day had been designed by a Mr. William Lucas of Hertfordshire, had immediately sent for the man.

That mere Mr. Lucas, a kind and genial fellow, had come quite willingly and was entirely overwhelmed by the finery of St. James' court. He flattered His Majesty so well that he was given a knighthood. Granted, Mr. Lucas had been at first very alarmed when the King had hastily reached for the small sword of a courtier standing by and brandished it in his direction, but, when so instructed, had obediently knelt at His Majesty's feet and bowed his head. The bewildered man returned home from his trip to London in a daze of great proportions, not wholly believing his own good fortune. He attempted to explain to his wife that she was now Lady Lucas, and, being disbelieved, applied to his then six-year-old daughter to put her faith in her dear Papa.

It was a very great change for Charlotte, to go from being a tradesman's daughter, comfortably situated on the fringes of society but certainly not of the same rank as the Bennets, for example, to being invited by pretty Mrs. Bennet to play with her daughter Jane and to inspect the little girl, as yet unnamed, in her arms. She had asked her

Papa one night, whilst perched on his knee, how such change could come about so very rapidly.

Her father, himself unsure, had fumbled his way through an unusually wise speech about the temporary nature of life and had muttered that one ought never be too surprised when the Almighty did astonishing things far more quickly than one might have thought possible.

Miss Lucas, therefore, grew up to be a sensible girl, coolly accepting whatever situation she found herself in. Her pragmatism, she believed, came partially from her Mama's side of the family, for her Grandmama was of a similar bent of mind. Her brother John, exasperated one day that he had not made her shriek by presenting a very fine toad on her dinner plate, had exclaimed whilst he was being led away in disgrace, "I do declare that a...a *tiger* might walk through Meryton and you would not even think it so very uncommon."

She had wryly assured her friend Elizabeth when relating the tale, that she rather thought the rarity of a tiger in Meryton would be of less concern than her anxiety to remove herself from its path.

"I do not see that I need worry *why* such a beast should be in the neighbourhood – the reason would make not the slightest particle of difference if it were to maul me, and I daresay that there might be a perfectly rational explanation after all."

Lizzy, bright and vivacious, had laughed at Charlotte. There was something so very charming about her friend that Charlotte did not give two straws that the girl was all of six years her junior. Elizabeth did not remember that Sir William had once kept a shop, and so there was never any of the unpleasant judgment in her eyes that Charlotte saw in the eyes of some of the older children in the neighbourhood. Theirs was a firm friendship; Charlotte watched as Lizzy grew in wit as the years went on, and, even though left behind herself, had smiled with delighted contentment when she watched her friend wed a very wealthy gentleman from Derbyshire.

By the time Elizabeth Darcy was wed three years, Charlotte was fast approaching her thirtieth year, still unmarried and ever aware that her comfortable situation in her father's home might come to an end very soon.

Mr. Bennet, some five years younger than Sir William, had passed away with great suddenness a twelvemonth ago, and although she was dreadfully sad for her friend, it starkly struck Charlotte that her own Papa might go just as suddenly, leaving her a burden on her brother, who was beginning to show a rather mercurial temperament. It was not as though she were unwilling to marry, and had any gentleman actually given her a second glance, she would have given him as much encouragement as possible. She rather liked the idea of marriage, and to have her own home, preferably with some servants to aid her, appealed to her. She was not like Lizzy or even Jane, who had decided early on in life that they wished to marry for love. Charlotte wished to marry for herself – men, her own charming father notwithstanding, were inconstant creatures, as soon to fall out of love as into it. Nonetheless, to be married would assuredly make life much pleasanter for a female.

It was thus that she accepted with eagerness Mrs. Darcy's invitation to stay at Pemberley for the summer. If no eligible men passed through Meryton, she must try a different society. Mrs. Darcy, her laughter apparent even on paper, had boasted of her excellence as a matchmaker.

"I cannot at all fathom how I manage it, dear Charlotte; it seems that I have made great matches with very little effort on my part! Lydia, who, whatever Mr. Darcy's aunt might say, is assuredly a triumph of my own and not – as she suggested – hers, has written to me of Italy and appears very well satisfied with her lot in life. Do come to Pemberley; if nothing else I can assure you of a ready welcome. Provided you admire my son and do not remark on how

enormous I am at present, I will engage to be a delightful hostess to you."

Charlotte, upon disembarking from the carriage, did not exclaim in shock at either the size of Pemberley or that of her friend, however much that friend protruded. Mr. Darcy, greeting her quietly and with great civility, thanked her for taking such a long journey so willingly.

"My wife had a longing to see her old friends some weeks ago, Miss Lucas, and was of half a mind to travel to Meryton herself to see you all if you could not come to her."

Charlotte smiled. "I could hardly turn down such an invitation, Mr. Darcy – I have had a very lively curiosity to see a county that my friend praises so highly." She watched as Elizabeth directed servants here and there before the mistress of the house turned back to her, orders given to her satisfaction.

"Now, I will take you up to your rooms myself, Charlotte. No – I will rest after I have seen our guest settled, Mr. Darcy. I am not so very large that I cannot manage the stairs, my love." Her smile took any sting out of her words and Mr. Darcy nodded in acceptance. "I have put you in the same bedchamber as I stayed in when I first ever came to Pemberley, Charlotte. You must tell me if the views do not hinder your ability to write a coherent letter as they did me."

It was a delightful room, far larger than her own chamber at Lucas Lodge, and furnished very tastefully. Charlotte walked for a little while about the room, admiring the ornaments and the wide vista from the windows, before changing from her travelling clothes and leaving the room to find Elizabeth. She was met by that same lady at the bottom of the stairs, and, as Charlotte descended, she admired the fine drape of the dark blue afternoon dress that her friend wore. The pearl necklace clasped about her throat looked decidedly elegant in its simplicity. She mused that if she did not miss her guess, those evenly matched iridescent pearls were worth a small fortune, and she marvelled at what a transformation wealth had made to her friend's appearance. Elizabeth Bennet had always been a pretty girl, and well dressed, but Elizabeth Darcy appeared to be a very fine lady indeed.

"Charlotte! I was quite forbidden to come up again to find you. How do you like your room? Will it suit you for the month, do you think?" Upon being assured that it was very comfortable, Lizzy smiled at her old friend and led her towards a set of doors at the far end of the hallway. "Now, I am eager to give you a tour. Theodore is not yet awake and I cannot introduce you to him until he is, so a tour it must therefore be. I shall be a veritable *saint*, Charlotte, and sit down in each room that I show you, and so you may assure my husband that I have not been over-exerting myself in the least. The poor man is a little anxious, you know – he does not like to see me struggling to walk about. It will not be for very much longer, if my guess is correct. I feel very much as I did with Theodore with a mere week to go. I do think perhaps that this little one will like to meet me sooner rather than later."

Chapter Two

"My love," said Mrs. Darcy, one evening after the three of them had dined, "I rather think that I should like you to have Lady Catherine fetched for me. She did promise that she might come, as she did with Theodore, and I am of the opinion that she may need to come quite soon."

Mr. Darcy, casting a piercing look toward his heavily pregnant wife, drained his coffee cup and stood up. Charlotte watched with interest – the interactions between the two of them were quite fascinating. They were not like any other married couple that she had ever observed; after three years of marriage, their pleasure in each other's company did not seem to have faded.

"Oh, I did not mean *immediately*, Fitzwilliam – in the morning will suffice; pray do not interrupt your comfort for my whims."

Mr. Darcy smiled a little. It was not a broad smile – not like Charlotte's father's smile nor even like her brother's – it was more a slight upturning of the lips and a greater warmth about the eyes.

"Elizabeth, I gave orders to the stables last week that they should be ready to ride to Rosings just as soon as their mistress was ready to acknowledge that it might be necessary. I shall not be above a moment. Would you not like another cup of tea? Do excuse me, Miss Lucas."

He quit the room and Elizabeth, laughing softly, turned to Charlotte. "Might you pour for me, Charlotte? I am willing to admit that I am feeling very lazy this evening."

Lady Catherine de Bourgh arrived at Pemberley four days later, in an enormous carriage heavily laden with luggage. Her nephew handed her down and stepped back to bow, having first kissed her proffered cheek.

She nodded graciously to Miss Lucas, and, once she had assured herself that Mrs. Darcy was not in immediate need of her assistance, made her stately way up the stairs to her rooms to rest.

Elizabeth and Charlotte returned to the music room, where they had been awaiting her ladyship's arrival. Elizabeth made her way to the pianoforte and resumed the gentle melody that she had been practising. She winced a little as she sat.

"I do think this little one hears everything, Charlotte – as soon as I cease playing lullabies, I am kicked quite viciously from within. There, I am settled now. I wonder if Fitzwilliam will have a new chair made for me should I break this one with my weight." She played a few soothing chords. "You must not mind Lady Catherine's manner, Charlotte; she is a little overbearing on occasion but I am certain that she saved both mine and Theodore's lives when he was born. I could not fathom her not being here for this birth."

Charlotte, tidying Elizabeth's sheet music into a better order, nodded. "I suspected as much. I daresay she is pleased to be asked."

"Oh yes! She would not say so directly, of course, but she seems to be at her most content when she is needed. After Miss de Bourgh passed away...well, I understand that she wandered the house aimlessly until Mary came to her with questions on how she ought to go about gathering the women of the village for charitable works. It helped her, I believe, to have a purpose."

"Mrs. Collins has more of you in her than I had previously supposed, Eliza," was all Charlotte replied, in dry tones.

Elizabeth laughed at this and looked mischievous, as she always did whenever anyone made mention of her talent for arranging matters as she liked.

It was impossible not to fall a little in love with Pemberley, Charlotte thought, two days after Lady Catherine (a domineering woman, however her friend chose to paint her) descended on the estate. It was a peaceful and elegant house. She found that she did not mind in the least if her friend was occupied elsewhere, for there was much to admire regardless of whether Eliza was there to make her smile. Elizabeth had not emerged from her rooms that morning, and Mr. Darcy had been ordered by his aunt to take his son and heir to the stables. Charlotte, ever practical, had begged for some household mending to alleviate her own impatience for news. She did not care for the worried frown present on Mr. Darcy's face as he begged her pardon that she had been quite abandoned as a guest.

She chose a sunny window seat in the gallery to situate herself. She was not, generally speaking, given to sentimentality, but she bypassed several such seats until she found herself opposite the portrait of Elizabeth as a new bride. It was a good painting, masterfully executed, and did her friend's face and figure justice, although no painter could be expected to capture the full force of her charm. It comforted her, to look up at her friend from her seat and to see that sweet face smiling down at her.

Charlotte schooled herself to concentrate on the task she had set herself, and had sat for a full hour and a half, needle in hand, before she was approached by Mrs. Reynolds.

"Mrs. Reynolds, is there news so soon?"

"Not as yet, Miss Lucas. If you will forgive me, I had hoped for some assistance. Her ladyship cannot currently leave my mistress and the master is yet still out with young Master Theodore, but there is a gentleman just arrived. He claims some slight acquaintance with the family and says his carriage has lost a wheel…."

Charlotte comprehended the difficulty, and interjected in her sensible manner.

"Will you have tea sent into us, Mrs. Reynolds, if I attempt to entertain him until Mr. Darcy can be fetched? I am certain a wheelwright might be found in Lambton readily enough. Where have you put him?"

The good housekeeper led her into one of the receiving rooms several minutes later.

"Sir Daniel, thank you for waiting. A boy has been sent to inform Mr. Darcy of your presence, but in the meantime, Miss Lucas, who is staying here as Mrs. Darcy's guest, has invited you to share her tea. If you will forgive me, I must arrange for a message to be got to the wheelwright in Lambton. Pratchet will be in shortly with the tea tray, Miss Lucas, and will sit in the corner over there."

"Thank you, Mrs. Reynolds," said Charlotte, calmly. "I apologise for the irregularity of the introduction, Sir Daniel, but my friend is currently indisposed, and Lady Catherine de Bourgh, with whom I believe you also claim acquaintance, is with her. Do sit down."

Sir Daniel James, who had started upon hearing her name, bowed and assessed the lady before him. There was little remarkable about Miss Lucas – she was neither particularly pretty nor was she notably plain. Her eyes and hair were of a fairly common brown, her complexion appeared clear enough although it could not be likened to cream or ivory or any such thing, and her mouth, although perhaps a little on the large side, was not marked by any deformity that he could see.

It surprised him that she should be so ordinary, for in his mind, since having her name hurled at him by the former Miss Bennet in an insult that had shaken him deeply, he had imagined an ill-favoured spinster, shunned by all men.

Having found that it was not so, a certain self-deprecating curiosity overtook him. It was like having a bruise that one could not help but prod. Her very name stung his pride when he remembered that dreadful scene in Bath, and yet he felt compelled to find out what was so objectionable about this serene young woman before him – so objectionable that the flighty Countess of Warwick should have matched them up in her empty head for the common bond of sheer desperation.

She bore his silent inspection without so much of a flicker of an eyelid, and seated herself on a delicately carved chair. Her voice was low for a female, not shrill in the slightest, and he found his shoulders to be less tense as she commiserated with him for his ill fortune on the roads.

"My father, Sir William, has often said that there is nothing so upsetting to him as a journey interrupted by damage to one's carriage. Were you obliged to ride far, sir, before reaching civilisation?"

"Ah no, Miss Lucas, it was a mere matter of five miles or so before I reached Pemberley Lodge – a short enough ride in fine weather, and were it not for the circumstances, might have been very pleasant. I understand that the rock formations in this part of the country are considered particularly interesting by those inclined toward the natural world. Forgive me – you are acquainted with the Countess of Warwick, are you not? I...I remember hearing her mention a Miss Lucas and thought that perhaps you might be she."

Miss Lucas raised her brows a little, "Yes, of course, although I knew her as Lydia Bennet. She is Mrs. Darcy's youngest sister, you know; her family estate is situated on the outskirts of Meryton, which is where Lucas Lodge is." The straight brows wrinkled a little, "I cannot quite see why she would have mentioned *me* – we are not of an age and have never been closely acquainted."

Sir Daniel made an expansive gesture with his hand, "Ah, it is of no matter – I cannot quite recall – it is of no matter."

Pratchet entered with the tea tray, and curtseyed once she had put it down.

"Mrs. Reynolds said I was to sit in the corner, Miss."

"Yes, very well. Thank you, Pratchet; I will pour. How do you like your tea, Sir Daniel? Mrs. Reynolds has sent us some excellent shortbread biscuits, I see – shall I serve you one, sir?"

Chapter Three

An idea, alarming in its madness, had him in its grip and would not be shaken off. Miss Lucas, having poured Sir Daniel his cup to his liking, was now intent upon her own. He took a sip of the hot liquid and swallowed it down, hardly minding that it scorched his throat.

He needed a wife and he needed an heir – the situation was as pressing now, if not more so, as when he had offered the ungrateful Miss Lydia Bennet his hand. He knew nothing about Miss Lucas except that she was considered a confirmed spinster, she was not ugly, nor was she even that old. She appeared calm, *un*-flighty, and she made good tea.

It was enough. If he could so badly mistake the character of the current Countess of Warwick – and what a blow to his pride that had been – then surely he stood as much hope of getting a good wife by chance as by his own seeking. It was almost preferable, he decided, to know less about the woman he married before actually wedding her.

Miss Lucas stirred her tea twice in precise and efficient circles, before setting down her silver spoon and looking up at him. She appeared to be assessing him.

"It is difficult, Sir Daniel, to make my own cup precisely as I wish it to be. I have not travelled overly much but I have discovered that the water in Derbyshire produces very different results from the water in Hertfordshire."

Sir Daniel nodded. "I find that my servants never make so good a cup of tea elsewhere as they make at home. I live near Bath, but have estates elsewhere also – Devon, for example."

Charlotte sipped her own tea. It was the same blend of tea leaves that she favoured at home, but the result was lacking, and she wondered how Elizabeth managed. Perhaps she was so incandescently content with her lot in life that the quality of her hot drinks did not trouble her. This reminded her of what Elizabeth was currently enduring upstairs and she frowned a little. Her friend was suffering – that seemed to be a universal truth of matrimony regardless of one's relative happiness with a husband.

She did not choose to relate the thoughts that were flitting through her mind. Instead, she aided Sir Daniel in conversation. "I have not ever been to Bath, sir. I am told that it is a fine city. Is there much of historical interest in the area?"

Sir Daniel, having finished his cup, held it up to examine. It was a delicate piece of work, painted with various flowers. Miss Lucas spoke like a sensible woman of moderate intelligence. His mind was quite made up.

"Yes, I believe the Romans had much to do in the area at one time, and my estate, Sedgley Park, is Tudor in its oldest parts. I understand that Henry VII stayed there once, although I cannot recall for what reason. I imagine it would have had something to do with making war, though."

"It sounds very interesting, sir."

"Miss Lucas. I hope you will excuse what may seem to you to be madness – but I wonder if you might consider marrying me?" He almost could not believe his own words, even as he spoke them.

Miss Lucas's steady gaze did not waver, but her eyes widened slightly at his words. There must have been a dozen thoughts flitting through her head, but whatever they were, they were not apparent to the man who had just proposed. He wondered if she would accuse him of jesting at her expense.

Instead, she set down her cup with fingers that did not tremble, and regarded him.

"Marriage proposals are not so frequently directed at me, sir, that I would disregard one out of hand, however *hastily* made it might appear to be."

"I am sincere, Miss Lucas," he said hurriedly.

She remained unruffled, and carefully turned the delicate handle of her teacup to an angle of greater aesthetic merit as the cup rested on its matching saucer. "I did not accuse you of insincerity, Sir Daniel."

"You are very good. I am sure you must be astonished, though," Sir Daniel James responded, feeling rattled in the face of her serenity. His face felt hot and his hands awkward. He did not entirely know what to do with himself and so he picked up the little sugar spoon and fiddled with it. Charlotte glanced to the corner of the room, Pratchet was sat, looking anywhere but at them. There was little possibility that she had not heard their conversation.

The lady raised her eyebrows ever so slightly at his manner, and almost smiled. "I am not often surprised, sir, but I would say that you have accomplished it today. If I may, I should like to ask you one or two frank questions – should you object to walking out with me on the front lawn?"

Sir Daniel, seeing the sense of the suggestion, rose immediately and offered her his arm, still staggered that she had not instantly said "no." She relieved him of the spoon and returned it to its proper place on the tea tray.

"I hope you do not mind, sir. Lady Catherine de Bourgh is here at present and I am certain she would somehow learn of a silver spoon being taken out to the front lawn. Pratchet, you may return to your duties now, we are stepping outside."

The maid, looking relieved, rose and curtseyed. Sir Daniel had stilled. "Lady Catherine de Bourgh is here? Is she unwell, or did she just not wish to receive me?"

"She is assisting my friend, Sir Daniel – I would imagine that she does not know of your being here as yet." She was curious as to the cause of his discomfort, but she did not inquire. There were other ways of finding such things out, after all.

They made their way to the neatly kept grassy area in front of the house and looked about them. Sir Daniel commented that it was a fine estate, although clearly a more modern building than Sedgley.

"I have no objection to old buildings." Charlotte replied, "I imagine there are benefits to be seen in both modern and ancient estates. Mrs. Darcy informed me that most of Pemberley was rebuilt some generations ago but that the Darcy family has lived in this very place for a very long time indeed."

"Aye, that is very true," was all Sir Daniel said, lost in his thoughts.

Miss Lucas stopped in her walk and turned to face him. "Sir Daniel, I shall not insult you by asking if you were in earnest just now. You appear to be a sensible enough man and you have paid me the compliment of not pretending to have fallen instantly or madly in love with me on first glance."

He had been studying a blinding ripple of sunlight dancing on the lake before them, but he started at this and looked at her, the thought of romance not having even passed through his head.

She continued on, smoothly. "I do not mind in the least. I am not romantic, you know – I never was. I ask only for a comfortable home and security. If you are as dispassionate a man as I am rational a woman, I see no reason why we ought not get on well enough. You are not, I hope, given to violence or wild behaviour?"

Sir Daniel shook his head, feeling decidedly wrong-footed now by this female that he looked set to marry. The first Lady James had blushed and stammered quite charmingly that she would be delighted to wed him. Miss Lucas was not in the least like his late wife, nor was she like the chit he had last proposed to. He wondered if his friends and acquaintances would call him a dispassionate man. The dark-haired lady looked at him directly, awaiting an answer.

"No, Miss Lucas, I am not given to either – I am a simple enough man. I like a good table set and grouse hunting when it is to be had. Are you not curious as to why I have asked you to marry me, madam?"

She lifted a shoulder slightly, in what might have been a shrug. "I daresay you require a wife and children, sir."

He huffed out a relieved breath; suddenly he did not regret the lack of blushes in the slightest. "Yes, *yes*. I haven't any heir, you see, at all. I come from a long line of only children – that is, not one of us had any siblings. Where most families have branches of cousins, all eager to take up the mantle of head of the family, I have no family to be head *of*. There is only I. Not even a second or third cousin can be found to inherit Sedgley. My man of business has been searching through my family bible and has found no provable blood relatives. I must marry. There was a child – but my late wife perished alongside the babe. I often wonder how different things might have been had either one of them lived."

Charlotte, her eyes finding their way to the window behind which Elizabeth endured that which might easily kill her, did not comment politely on the unfortunate prevalence of such instances. "A marriage of convenience seems very sensible, in such circumstances. I see that we may benefit each other by an alliance. I require a home – my father, Sir William Lucas, may not live long, I fear. I cannot see any difficulty there, although my friend Mrs. Darcy will likely be quite displeased with such haste."

"Do you mean to say that you will agree, madam?"

Again that slightly lifted shoulder and direct gaze. "Yes, I will."

Chapter Four

My dear Eliza,

You shall forgive me for my foolhardy choices eventually, I feel, if only because your curiosity will not permit you peace for long and you cannot mean to cut me off entirely, my dearest friend.

Sir Daniel rode down to see my father some two weeks ago, as he said that he would, and formally offered for my hand. It took a mere ten days to have all in order, and four days ago we walked to church and were married. I cannot make your claim, my dear, that it was the happiest day of my life and in every way perfect, but neither was I discontent with my choice. I find that I am able to face the strange adjustment to marriage far more easily when I do not have to worry about my husband's affections growing dim or transferring to another. Ours is a business arrangement, after a fashion, and so far more likely to succeed than most matches.

I must tell you about Sedgley. It is something of a hotchpotch of architecture, with the oldest parts being of Tudor design and excessively draughty, but some of the later additions to the house are rather pleasanter to live in. I have found myself a sitting room to the south of the house that I like rather well – I should like some new paper put up but that can be done once I have put everything else in order. I must tell you, Mrs. Darcy, that having glanced over the quite *awfully kept accounts, I am unsure as to whether I should dismiss the current housekeeper on the grounds of her theft or her ineptitude. I will investigate the matter more thoroughly and write to you soon of my decision.*

Charlotte looked up as her husband entered the room, and slowly put down her pen. He stood for a moment on the threshold examining her.

"Ah, Lady James, I had been looking for you."

"You have found me, Sir Daniel. I think that this may be my favourite room." There was a large bay window overlooking the green hills, and Charlotte had spent a little time considering a better arrangement of the furniture. A small round table had been placed centrally in the bay and a comfortable little seat put beside it for her convenience. It afforded her a good view of the drive that swept down through the parkland to the front of the house. The room was not overly large, thus feeling rather cosier than the enormous and rather more ornate sitting room that, according to the housekeeper, the late Lady James had favoured. Charlotte was not very sure that she liked the housekeeper.

"Good, very good."

He stood looking about him rather quizzically, as though he could not entirely place what was different about the room. Charlotte began to feel a little impatient. There were plans and letters she wished to write in solitude if only her husband could be got rid of. "What is it that you sought me out for, Sir Daniel?"

"I wished to verify that you are not put out by my having been largely absent this past week."

Charlotte smiled. Put out? Not a bit of it. The less she saw of her husband, the better, as far as she was concerned. She was quite content to remain peacefully at Sedgley and do battle with the housekeeper.

"Not in the least, Sir Daniel. I am not the type of female that requires constant company, you know. I have found plenty to occupy me – which puts me in mind of something I wished to ask you. Were you quite sincere in your wish to put me in charge of the household affairs? I have something of a knack for efficiency, you see, and I should rather like to make one or two changes that will contribute to the smooth running of Sedgley."

"I was indeed sincere, Lady James. Do as you please – I am sure I am very relieved that you don't expect me to be always dancing attendance on you. You weren't intending to economize on my table, I hope?"

Charlotte smiled inwardly. A husband who objected to her doings only if his table was affected was no great challenge to keep content. Men, she believed, were a little like children in that respect. So long as one ensured that they did not have to encounter changes too rapidly, they could easily be brought round to adjusting. "No, Sir Daniel, I am satisfied that the changes to be made are related to efficiency rather than economy. I do not imagine they will even be noticeable. Were you intending to head to Newmarket, sir?"

"The races? I had not thought of it this year – being newly married and all."

"I do wish that you would."

"Eh?"

"Oh, I don't mean it personally, Sir Daniel; rather I should not wish our arrangement to curtail any of your customary enjoyment. Go to the races by all means – I shan't sulk or complain of neglect."

His lips pursed in consideration as he looked at her. He was tempted, it was clear, but the temptation of a week's enjoyment warred with his vanity that his wife should be so evidently willing to be out of his company. Perhaps his lady wife was not so practical and unbothered as she made out, though; mayhap she was so very grateful to him for having wed her that she did not wish to put him out or make him regret it. He frowned and compromised within himself.

"Well, I shan't neglect you for the whole week, my lady. I will go to Newmarket for a few days. I do enjoy the races, after all – it was good of you to think of it." After a moment's thought, he added, "You are quite a marvellous wife, I declare!"

Lady James smiled serenely and thanked him for the compliment in that cool, unruffled voice of hers. For a moment, he doubted himself – had he indeed pleased her with his compliment? She did not look to be particularly joyous that he was glad to have wed her, rather she looked as though such a sentiment was merely her due – either that or she suspected him of empty flattery. His first wife would have blushed prettily and returned the sentiment.

"If, Sir Daniel, you decide to stay the entire week, do not hesitate to do so – I intend to rearrange the kitchens whilst you are gone and will very likely hardly notice that you are missing. I shouldn't wish you to be inconvenienced. I shall dine very simply myself for a few days, and you know that there will very likely be a deluge of morning callers from the locality very soon. Do ring the bell for me, would you? I should like to see the housekeeper for a moment or two.'

He nodded and, rather surprised, thanked her for her thoughtfulness. It was not until he was on his horse, having been cheerfully and properly waved off by his wife, that he realised what he could not quite put his finger on at the time.

It stung his pride that she was not weeping at the thought of her husband leaving. However much he realised that a clinging wife would be very irritating, he would have preferred her to demonstrate some reluctance at his going.

He found himself pondering the matter at Newmarket, more than he perhaps wished to. What was wrong with her? He was a handsome man, and educated enough to be a pleasing companion, he believed. Certainly his friends were glad to see him when he encountered them at the inn, and they were likely to be better judges than she. He did his best to enjoy himself with his companions. He indulged himself in the ways that he was used to, and he barely even remembered, during the daytime, that he had a wife at home. Occasionally one of his friends made mention of his once again leg-shackled state and asked if she was as pretty a creature as his first wife had been. It embarrassed him a little and he evaded the question, accusing his long-standing companion of being a very vulgar-minded fellow. Bertie laughed and ordered another tankard of ale for the table, and Sir Daniel forgot that he was put out with him. At night, however, as he lay in a state of half-wakefulness, his mind returned to the issue of Lady James's ease without him by.

It nettled him enough that on the sixth day, after his horse had run and done very badly, he bade his companions farewell and made his way home to Sedgely, curious, he told himself, to see what changes Lady James might have wrought.

Chapter Five

Lady James met him very courteously at the door.

"Sir Daniel, you have returned. All is well, I trust?" She spoke coolly but with civility. He could not quite account for the reason, but her polite enquiries bothered him. He might have preferred it if he had been met at the door by effusive pleasure at his early return or even mild disappointment that he had been gone so long.

"Ye-es, I felt I should like to come back; very flat at Newmarket at present."

"I collect that your horse did not win. I am sorry – perhaps next year."

His brows drew together, "I do not remember having mentioned the horse, my lady?"

"Oh, was it a secret? I merely noted it whilst I was looking over some accounts. It is of no great moment. Shall you come inside and have some tea, sir? I would like your view on something."

This seeking of his opinion pleased him rather better, and they headed toward Lady James's little sitting room. The room seemed cheerful and inviting; a small fire burned in the hearth and a pair of wingback chairs was positioned in front of it. An occasional table was drawn up between the chairs and a tray, already laid out with the tea things, rested upon it. There were freshly made shortbread biscuits on the tray, and Sir Daniel sat down and promptly took two. Charlotte smiled. "I noticed at Pemberley that you were partial to the shortbread, and so wrote to Mrs. Darcy requesting the recipe."

He was surprised and pleased – such a little detail in a way, but one he found very comfortable. He had not thought Mrs. Darcy was particularly pleased with him. Doubtless she thought he should be pining after her dreadful sister. That thought was quickly pushed away. He had been in error there. Settling himself back against the chair in comfort, he realised that he felt really quite satisfied at having returned home, and took a long drink of his tea. It was perfect, precisely as he liked to take it. A good wife was a delightful thing, he thought.

"What was it you wished to speak to me of, Lady James?" he asked gallantly, feeling quite generously disposed to her. It was not, after all, every wife that encouraged a husband to depart for Newmarket for a week of enjoyment.

"The housekeeper, sir. I desired her to conduct me on a tour of the whole house two days ago and was denied. She said that the mistress of the house had no business being anywhere near the servants' attics. I noticed, you see, when I was looking through the household expenditure, that you had authorised a good deal of money for the improvement of the servants' quarters – I was very pleased to see that you had done so and rather wished to look about to see what else might be done. My suspicions were aroused when Mrs. Clive was so very anxious that I not inspect the improvements that you yourself had ordered."

He was frowning now and took another shortbread; it really was delightfully rich. "And have you since been abovestairs? What is the outcome? Mrs. Clive ought not to deny you entry anywhere in this house."

"In short, I persuaded my maid to make sure that she was occupied elsewhere and went up myself. I cannot see that anything has been done, sir, to see to the basic necessities of the servants in this house. I suspect that she has pocketed the money and left the staff here to endure damp and cold conditions. It explains why so many maidservants leave so swiftly."

"But this is outrageous!" He rose and paced before the fire, agitated and a little embarrassed that she had caught out Mrs. Clive in dishonesty when he had blindly trusted the woman.

"Quite so, Sir Daniel," remarked his wife, dispassionately, "I should like to turn her off and instruct that the attics be made right before the winter. It will cost money, of course, but having made one or two changes to things, I cannot see that there will be any difficulty covering the funds from the allotted budget. You were being quite robbed by the butcher, Sir Daniel, but I have amended matters."

He looked at her with something akin to dawning respect. Lady James – Charlotte – had not exaggerated when she had claimed a knack for efficiency.

Sir Daniel sat down again and reached for another biscuit. He was particularly fond of shortbread.

"I should like to see for myself, your ladyship. It is not...please understand, not that I do not trust your account of things, but I remember quite clearly the list of instructions I gave. I should like to see if there is anything at all been done as I ordered it."

Charlotte nodded. "I am not in the least offended, Sir Daniel. You, as much as I, are entitled to go where you please in your own home, even if I would not ordinarily interfere too much in the servants' quarters – it puts them very much on edge, you know. I was wondering if perhaps a general announcement might not go amiss, once Mrs. Clive has been sent off. I should not wish there to be unease that I might turn the whole household on its head. I seek only to make things more comfortable and well run if I am able to."

"Lady James," said her husband admiringly, "I am beginning to be very sure that you are able to do many things. You are eminently capable, it would seem. Make what improvements you please – I doubt that you will beggar me. I've a mind to take you down to Dorset once you have quite finished at Sedgley – you could doubtless do wonders with the place. I've not been there for years but it's a pretty little spot. The park is a little small, being only three or four hundred acres, but you might enjoy the project of it."

Charlotte raised her brows. "Yes, I think I should enjoy that. I like to improve things. Speaking of which, sir – I have some mind, in the next few months, to do something about the home farm that lies derelict to the west of here. If a good tenant could be found, we might do rather well from it, what with eggs and honey being in such high usage at present in the more fashionable cuisines."

Her husband reached for a fifth biscuit and grunted his approval. He found himself quite inclined to remain thus in his wife's sitting room, drinking good tea and companionably hearing an account of the alterations she had made at Sedgley. Most of them were not in the least radical, she said, just minor things such as not permitting the local tradesmen to charge Sedgley above the usual price for goods, but the more he listened to her, the more he appreciated how beneficial a quality was good sense in a wife. Lady James might not be a beauty, but he found, as he looked at her, that she was certainly not an antidote. She wore her simple gowns well, and today had selected a dark silk dress in a curious shade of blue. As he regarded her, he decided that he could not say what colour it was precisely, only that it reminded him of the sea on a stormy day, and the style of it became her very well. His late wife had been very fond of pink, he recalled, and although he did not profess himself an expert in ladies' fashion, he had never been overly fond of the frills and embellishments that she had favoured.

"I like your dress," he said, feeling awkward even as he said it, as though it were too personal a thing to say to his own lawful wife.

She paused in the process of refilling her teacup and their eyes met. She did not blush, but there was that in her eyes that told him he had surprised her with the compliment and he pressed on.

"It is very...it is very elegant. You look very well in it."

Charlotte regarded her husband for a moment and then pushed the plate a little toward him. There was yet one biscuit remaining.

"Thank you. Do finish the last one, Sir Daniel – it seems a pity to send one lonely biscuit back to the kitchens. Cook has been at such pains to get them right that I feel she deserves the compliment of an empty plate."

He, feeling as though he were just beginning to take the measure of her, leant forward and took it.

Charlotte, now having a very thorough grasp of her husband's character, she felt, smiled to herself. Had Sir Daniel looked up at that moment, he might have seen in her eyes a lurking twinkle that Mrs. Darcy was well familiar with.

Six biscuits indeed! Men were so very predictable.

Chapter Six

Mrs. Clive was swiftly and efficiently dealt with, and if at first that female was relieved to be facing her calm and collected mistress rather than an irate master of the house, by the time the interview was over she stalked out of the room quite certain that she should have preferred to speak with Sir Daniel, for all he might have ranted at her. Lady James was cool, matter of fact, and utterly uncompromising in her presentation of the facts in the face of Mrs. Clive's sputtering fury that she was to be turned off, after twenty years, without so much as a character reference.

The following night, after a tiring day in which Lady James had clearly and patiently explained to the staff that Mrs. Clive had been turned off on account of dishonesty and that she herself would temporarily take on some of the housekeeping duties until a suitable replacement could be found, Charlotte found herself quite unable to sleep.

There were changes beginning to happen within her that she could not ignore. It was too soon, much too soon, of course, to even speak of such things and yet...she lay awake that night, tired as she was, strangely excited for the possibility of hope.

She attempted, for the space of an hour, to scold herself back into rationality and give herself over to sleep in the way that she knew she needed, but alas, rest would not find her. She heard the chimes of a clock downstairs and, sighing, thrust the covers from her.

Donning a voluminous white robe over the top of her nightgown (Mama had insisted that a billowing dressing robe was quite a necessary purchase), Charlotte lit a candle and made her way to the door of her chamber that led out to the hall. It was excessively draughty in some parts of Sedgley – oh, it was a pleasant enough house and she was glad to have charge of her own establishment after so long being a mere daughter, but there were surely improvements that could be made, for example, when the wind blew to the east as it did now. The chimneys, she had noticed, seemed to catch the slightest breeze, and thus a low hollow whistling howl could often be heard echoing down them. It was an eerie sound, she supposed; Mrs. Clive had jumped visibly at it once or twice, even knowing and explaining to her ladyship what had caused it.

Charlotte did not understand people like that, who frightened themselves silly even after a logical explanation had been presented to them. It was a very simple thing to accept the more likely possibility, surely? Perhaps she had not much imagination.

The door behind her banged shut and she winced. Solidly built English oak doors were all very well, but not when they were not hung quite straight. She muttered to herself that she must instruct a carpenter to come and rectify matters. Charlotte paused briefly, thinking that she had heard a sound behind the door of her husband's chamber, and hoped that the noise had not awakened him. She knew very well that she could ring for her maid to fetch the papers that she wanted from her sitting room, but it seemed too long a process to wait for the maid to bestir herself, order the maid downstairs, and then sit idly in her own chamber for the woman to come back up again. Besides, she felt like wandering this night – there was not much time to spend alone recently, she found. If it was not her husband who wanted her attention, it was a long line of servants needing advice on some matter or another. She did not mind the latter so much, for she liked to give directions and know that they would be carried out. Not everyone saw things as clearly as she did; she knew it well enough, and if she was indispensable, so much the better. Her husband was another matter entirely. She had been naive, perhaps, in thinking that theirs was a business arrangement and that he would be largely absent. It had not mattered to her, particularly, that she knew nothing of him, because there would be time enough for that. All men had their foibles; even her dear Papa, who was the most genial of men, liked to think that it was he in charge of matters at Lucas Lodge and not Mama. Mama did not correct him, of course – she was wiser than that, and Charlotte had learned from early on that there was a good deal of difference between what a man thought and what was the reality of a situation. She almost pitied them sometimes, being as they were so comfortable in their belief that they had the upper hand in all respects.

Sir Daniel was easy enough to understand; his faults were fairly readily apparent – he thought very highly of his own opinions, that was certain, and she was not surprised to encounter the occasional vice, such as a tendency toward gluttony and a liking for rather too much porter after dinner. What surprised her was that she thought him a fairly likeable man – he was clearly well disposed to her, which showed excellent judgment, and he had very sensibly seen that she was capable of managing things at Sedgley rather well. Charlotte hoped that he had been sincere in his talk of taking her down to the Dorset estate, and intended to demonstrate at Sedgley just how beneficial good management could be.

As she turned down a draughty dark corridor to pass the library and then go on to her little sitting room, Charlotte noted a noise, not unlike the clunk of metal, from behind the library door. There was no cause for anyone to be in that room at that hour of the night, and she stopped to listen attentively. Yes, she had been correct, for there it was again, but quieter this time, as though there was someone behind the door trying to be very quiet indeed. Charlotte blew out her candle and waited for her eyes to adjust to the darkness. It was difficult indeed to distinguish the shadows from what was solid, for there was no helpful moon that night to shine through a nearby window and help her on her way. She stretched out an arm to touch the wall and use it as a guide. Her hand felt the weave of one of the large tapestries that hung either side of the library door, and she noted that it felt very much as though it needed cleaning. She would add it to the list of things that must be seen to in the morning. The library door opened a crack and Charlotte swiftly ducked behind the tapestry, thinking to place herself flat against the wall to avoid detection until she had established just who was wandering about when they had no business doing so.

Unexpectedly, her back did not touch the wooden panelling as she had thought it would, and upon meeting nothing but space, she stumbled slightly and reached out blindly to stop herself from falling. Her foot met something heavy and hard on the floor but she could not make out what it was. Bending down to feel with her fingers, she surmised that the object was a short heavy chain of some sort, attached to nothing but just left carelessly lying on the floor of this dreadfully dusty recess. Thinking it might serve her well later, Charlotte picked up the grimy chain, and with one hand following the wall, walked deeper into the recess. It was not a tiny space but it felt unpleasantly enclosed, and when her hand met what felt like the hinge of a canvas-clad door that surely led into the library itself, Charlotte pushed the door open without a second thought. The painting, for she realised that it was the back of a large painting just as soon as she stepped through the opening, moved smoothly and with less noise than her own chamber door did.

There was a small circle of light in the library, and Charlotte could see quite clearly Mrs. Clive standing beside a little table loading a silver ornament into a bag. The wind howled down the chimney and the woman jumped, looking up and that instant spying a white figure stepping through the portrait of a late James ancestor.

The bag dropped with a clatter and Mrs. Clive's mouth fell open. Her eyes became wide with terror, and after a moment she let out a long, shrill, piercing scream that cracked in fright at the end as Charlotte lifted the hand not holding the chain and pointed a dust-covered grey finger at her.

Her eyes narrowed and her voice low and raspy from the filth she had breathed in behind the portrait, Charlotte spoke to the woman.

"You dare to rob my home?"

Waxen-faced, Mrs. Clive glanced back and forth between the portrait and the chain-holding figure in white. Utterly petrified, she swayed once on her feet and fainted dead away.

Chapter Seven

Charlotte, with great presence of mind, stepped forward into the room and caught the lamp that Mrs. Clive had been using to light her way. Having rescued the expensive books from possible theft, it would be a pity if they were to catch light from a carelessly positioned flame. She glanced at Mrs. Clive stretched out on the floor, and dispassionately considered whether it would be better to attempt to revive her immediately or to rouse the household first.

It turned out to be quite unnecessary to spend long in making such a decision, for very soon after Charlotte had rung the servants' bell, Sir Daniel himself came into the library and let out a shout of alarm at the sight of her.

"Sir Daniel," said his wife, "how you made me start at such a sudden noise! I have caught Mrs. Clive attempting to rob us this night as I stepped out from the entrance behind that portrait over there, and she swooned, I am afraid."

Sir Daniel James had not ever thought of himself of anything less than the bravest of men, but he laid his hand over his heart as if to slow down the thudding therein. He took in Charlotte's appearance – her hair might have been thoroughly powdered by her maid, judging by its appearance, and her face, ordinarily pleasant enough to look at, was equally disguised in the same grey-white hue.

His voice, to his later embarrassment, was decidedly fragile when he responded, "I beg your pardon, my lady. I had not intended to frighten you."

"Oh, you did not, Sir Daniel," said his wife, reassuringly. "I am not easily frightened as a general rule, you know. It was merely that I had not expected to hear such volume after the silence of the night."

"Not easily frightened. No – no, I quite see that you are not." He took a deep, fortifying breath. "Forgive me, Charlotte – are you aware of the appearance that you currently present? Did you deliberately don such a...well..." he gestured to her with a hand that was not quite steady, "in order to scare Mrs. Clive witless? I admire your ingenuity if so."

Charlotte looked down at herself, a little baffled. She saw nothing out of the ordinary, except that her hands were grey with dust. "This is my dressing robe, Sir Daniel – it is, perhaps, a little more voluminous than I should have liked it to be, but I cannot see that it should cause a thief to faint."

His heart having slowed to its usual rate, her husband's mouth began to twitch upwards at the corners, quite against his will.

"Madam, you look like the veriest spectre. I do not know what you have done to your hair to change it so, but if you glance in a mirror you will quite see why Mrs. Clive should even now be lying at your feet."

Charlotte frowned and was startled when her husband let out a hooting laugh. "But it is entirely ridiculous, sir – I am merely very dusty from having been through the passageway behind the tapestry. I was headed toward my sitting room, you see, and I saw the light in the library. There is a perfectly rational explanation."

A footman, his livery hastily thrown on, entered the door and let out a yell of alarm when he saw his mistress. This proved too much for Sir Daniel, and his loud, continuing laughter roused his former housekeeper from her faint. He had, Charlotte discovered, an infectious laugh, and she found herself nearing a grin.

"Hoburn, do control yourself; it is only I. Someone will need to be sent to fetch the magistrate. Mrs. Clive has sought to rob us this night and will need to be taken to the lock-up, I should think. I had better return to my chamber and clean this dreadful dust off. I cannot think, Sir Daniel, why the secret passages in this house are not cleaner than they are. I shall amend matters, depend upon it."

Hoburn took in the scene before him. His master had needed to grasp the back of a chair in order to support himself, and his mistress, in spite of looking astonishingly like a ghost, looked amused. Hoburn quickly crossed over to Mrs. Clive and assisted her, none too gently, to her feet. He had heard that she had pocketed the money intended to improve the servants' accommodations, and he resentfully attributed many a freezing night to her.

"I'll take her to one of the cellars for now, madam – there's an empty one with a good lock on it. She'll not get out of there in a hurry."

"Thank you, Hoburn. Do send me my maid, would you, and ask her to bring a large pot of hot water to my chambers. I must try at least to remove this dust before I sleep again. Sir Daniel, shall you want to collect any evidence?"

This sobered her husband sufficiently, and he nodded, mirth still evidenced by the broad smile that he could not quite remove. "Yes, I'll put the whole bag in the safe until morning. Permit me to escort you to the staircase, my dear – can't have you terrifying a wandering nightwatchman now, can we?"

Dryly, whilst thinking he looked endearingly boyish with his face alight with laughter, Charlotte thanked him for such thoughtfulness. "I really must write to Mrs. Darcy of this night's work, Sir Daniel. I have little doubt that she would enjoy the tale immensely. It is just the sort of thing to amuse her, particularly given that she knows full well that I would not plan such an escapade deliberately."

There was a companionable moment between the two of them as they walked the dark hallways to the grand staircase together, Sir Daniel holding her arm gently with one hand and lifting the lantern well aloft with the other. They stopped at the first step.

"You need not worry about Mrs. Clive, Charlotte – I will ensure that she meets justice for this. I will admit that my temper can be less than pleasant if I feel that I have been made a fool of, and that particular female has been taking me for a fool for many a year now. She will be handed over to feel the full force of the law."

Charlotte nodded. She knew what he meant by it and did not try to persuade him toward mercy. If she was not hanged, she would be deported. It was sobering, certainly, but she must have known the consequences of her actions when she chose to steal. She was an intelligent, well-educated woman after all.

"Law and order must be kept, Sir Daniel," was all she said, without any noticeable upset in her voice.

He smiled at this for some reason, obviously thinking her lack of sentimentality a good thing in this instance. Looking her over, he seemed disposed to talk, and, with a laugh in his voice, said, "It is a pity you are unlikely to ever be arrayed thus again, Lady James, for I should very much like to remember it. I have been thinking that I should like your portrait taken very soon, for the gallery."

Charlotte looked at him. "I have been wondering, actually, about the empty space beside your own portrait in that very room – the paper is faded elsewhere but the pattern is far stronger where another painting must have once hung."

Her husband looked uncomfortable. "Ah, yes. I ordered that one taken down once I had your father's permission to marry you, you know. I did not wish you to feel at all uneasy."

"I collect that the empty space was once taken up by your late wife?" surmised Charlotte, having suspected as much. "It must certainly be put back, you know; I am not in the least disturbed by her portrait rightfully hanging where it always has done."

"You are very good, my dear," he said a little absently, "but I do think that it is only right and proper that the current mistress of this house be put beside its master. It would not be right for your portrait to hang elsewhere in the house."

"Quite so, Sir Daniel," responded Lady James, "but then, you have two sides to you, do you not?"

She pondered this thought, as she went up to her rooms and waited for the maid to come with clean hot water. Her husband's reaction to the adventure of the night was not entirely expected. He was clearly brave enough, she thought, as she caught sight of her eerily white face and hair in the mirror, for he had not seemed overly worried by her strange appearance once he had established the facts. His hooting, infectious laughter had surprised her too, having not heard his genuine amusement so expressed before. There was a part of her that very much wanted to hear it again simply because it was such a boyish, unaffected sound. Her hand dropped to her waist as she considered the reason that she had been sleepless to begin with.

No doubt, if there was a child, she could blame it for the tenderness she felt at the thought that it too might inherit such a laugh.

Chapter Eight

The memory of that night made him smile, whenever it resurfaced in his mind, for many years more. His wife, so spectral in appearance, had been so entirely bemused by the fear she had caused that it struck him as quite irresistibly amusing. She made him curious, this practical wife of his, in a way that his late wife never had. She did not behave as he expected a female to behave. The first Lady James had been a rather more predictable creature. He had expected her to dote upon him, to hang upon his every word and opinion, and she had fulfilled that expectation admirably. Having made an effort to study Charlotte closely for the space of a few days, he wondered one night why he had never felt bored in his first marriage. Charlotte was so very unusual, he decided. Her passions, if passions she had, were directed towards the improvement of the estate. He liked her mind and the way she thought, having questioned her intentions regarding the kitchens. She had concluded that they were much too far from the dining room, and that despite the best efforts of the staff, the food was all too often cold by the time it reached the table.

He had marshalled, silently, a plethora of reasons why it would be a very bad idea to move the kitchens – the servants wouldn't like it and the upheaval would be enormous – but she had been two steps ahead of him.

"It would not do to move the kitchens," she stated, a slender finger tapping thoughtfully on the polished wood of her little table. "It would be far too costly given the minor improvement to the food. It makes far more sense to relocate the dining room – I have been considering that the Chinese salon would do very well for it, the dimensions being so favourable."

Sir Daniel James, who had been irritated by the unsatisfactory temperature of his dishes since he had been a boy, wondered why he had not thought of it, and said so. She seemed pleased by that, and he found that he liked the warming of her smile and the way the corners of her eyes smiled before her mouth did. She did not appear to be irritated when he started to linger more often in her sitting room, preferring to take his coffee in there of an evening. He thought at first that it was merely the general cosiness that she had brought about in the room that drew him there, but, having experimented in a scientific fashion, he realised very quickly that he did not like the room half so much when his wife was not in it.

Sir Daniel liked to watch her. It didn't matter that she largely ignored him if she had things to do or letters to write. It gave him a sense of peace to look at her as she went about her business, sometimes a pucker of concentration between her straight brows. He had a strong urge, one evening, to cross the room from his place before the fire and press his lips against the crease of her forehead, merely because he had grown fond of it. If Lady James looked so, whilst bent over her little table, she was doubtless doing something quite marvellous for the efficiency of Sedgley. She seemed to be good at everything, if one only had the sense to let her do as she pleased.

A curious tightness in his chest afflicted him, on the rare occasions that she smiled broadly and looked triumphant, and he found himself slower of speech than usual when that happened.

She was in a more talkative mood one evening as the nights were drawing in a little. Charlotte had just finished adding up neat rows of numbers with an air of satisfaction, and he, sipping at his cup of tea and contentedly helping himself to the plate of little cakes that was available, asked her how it was that she was as she was.

"How I *am*, Sir Daniel?" she repeated. "What can you mean?"

"I mean that you are..." he waved a hand, not entirely knowing how to phrase his inquiry, "you like to do the accounts."

A slow smile appeared in her grey eyes. "Yes. Do you find it so unusual?"

"I detest them," returned he, bluntly, "only do it because I have to and because it's expected, but you like to. I don't think you are ever happier than when you have additions to do."

"I suppose that I am not, not that I have ever thought long on it."

"Well, *why* then?"

She almost laughed, but not quite – it was a small huffed chuckle, over as soon as it escaped, and so very like her that he smiled.

"How can I say why I enjoy something, sir? I am more like my Papa than my Mama – perhaps I inherited it from him. He was used to put me on his knee when I was a small girl and he sat at his desk to tally up the numbers and spoke of his little shop before he was knighted. I used to enjoy those times, when he would show me on the accounts the cost of waste and the benefit of efficiency – perhaps that explains some of it. I imagine I saw what pride and satisfaction he took on in what he himself had built up from nothing. I like to see plainly on paper that money is being put to its best use; that is all. It is nothing extraordinary."

"I think you are too modest, Charlotte," was all he said in reply but there was something in the warmth of his tone that made her look quickly up at him. She was not an unobservant fool; she could see tender admiration in a man's gaze as plainly as the next woman – she had seen it often enough directed at others. Feeling awkward, Lady James cleared her throat, unsure of what to say to ease the discomfort of the moment. She did not care for the heat that had risen, quite unbidden, at the nape of her neck.

It was fortunate, in a way, that Mrs. Darcy sent her a letter, strengthening the more rational creature within her the very next day.

Pemberley

My dearest Charlotte,

Lydia has returned triumphant from the continent and was greatly dismayed to hear of your marriage. I do not say so to alarm you, my dear. You need not fear her envy – Lady Warwick is far, far too satisfied with her husband for anything of that ilk. You know me, my dear, and you know very well that I would easily laugh off Lydia's frown and dismiss the whole were it not for the guilty look on her face that prompted me to investigate a little further. When Lydia is sullen, it is a sure sign that she has done something worthy of guilt. Happily, managing her has become her husband's affair now. I would be a poor friend to you, would I not, if I were to withhold information from you that might be important in some way? However much I cannot tell what it means, perhaps it might mean aught to you and thus I must relate it.

Lydia informed me that whilst she was in Bath after Papa died, Sir Daniel proposed marriage to her and he did not take the rejection well. I do not suggest for a moment that he was in love with her, and Lydia was quite clear that she did not think so, but in the course of the argument, your name was mentioned. She dug her heels in quite dreadfully and would not relate the context but did say that she feared he must have deliberately come to Pemberley in some sort of effort at revenge. I must own that I do not think it a likely scenario, for how could he have known of your presence there? Perhaps her imagination has run wild – there has been a look about her that I have thought might explain the reason. How like Mama I am getting, dear Lady James! Two charming babies have I delivered and I must necessarily think myself an expert on the subject.

Her letter then digressed to a very fetching description of Mr. Darcy's great pride in announcing to his aunt that little Miss Darcy was to be named Anne, after his late Mama and his cousin. Charlotte read the letter through to the end, as ever captivated by Elizabeth's skill in narrating the events of her life.

She returned, however, to the passage that concerned Lydia, as she made her way to a part of the house that was not often used, it being so much older than the rest and not so comfortable. Charlotte could not say that she liked Lydia Bennet – she remembered too well the cruelty of her heedless words. She was not a girl who bothered to think if her words might injure. Often, in company with Charlotte, Lydia had passed some remark or another that referenced her great pity for females who were plainer than she. Charlotte, aware even then that men were equally shallow as the youngest Miss Bennet, thought poorly of her for such comments.

Naturally, Sir Daniel was entirely free to have proposed to any number of females before he had met her. Rationally speaking, it was to be expected that she should be a last resort, yet it needled her that even he, the man she had wed, should have been blinded by pretty faces before his lack of an heir bothered him enough to lower his standards to *her*.

It had stung, she admitted. She could not help that she was not beautiful or that she had a merely commonplace figure, nor could she alter the fact that she did not sparkle with wit and conversation, but she was intelligent enough, and honest. How was it that she should have been in danger of being an old maid simply on account of such a silly reason as being plain?

It didn't matter. She had what she wanted – a comfortable home and the respect of her servants. She could do as she pleased, and, if her husband would cease to be constantly about, she could be entirely content at Sedgley.

Charlotte found the portrait that she had been looking for, in a dark little sitting room that had been decorated with very little thought for good taste. Her predecessor's portrait hung on a thickly papered wall, just as her maid had said it did.

Charlotte lit a candle and studied her.

"How typical!" she said aloud, without realising that she meant to. The late Lady James had been a pretty creature, all blonde curls and limpid blue eyes, and not a bit like her.

It was fortunate, she thought with irritation, that she had never much approved of romantic love, for if she had been determined to be in love with her husband, she should have opened herself up to all manner of unnecessary hurt. She located a servants' bell that was in working order, for the older parts of the house were not so well kept up, and summoned footmen to put the beautiful first wife back where she belonged, on the same wall as Sir Daniel.

Really, marriage was much better if it was done *her* way.

Chapter Nine

If Sir Daniel had been confused by his wife's return to polite indifference, he made no mention of it to her, and remained frustratingly determined to be constantly in her company. Charlotte found her patience stretched upon realising that he either could not or would not notice any of her hints that he should take himself off elsewhere. He even rejected an invitation to spend some weeks hunting with an old friend of his, in spite of her assurances that she was entirely content to be left at Sedgley. He had even seemed annoyed when his wife had been so certain that he should not deny himself the enjoyment.

She often felt his gaze on her as she went about her work, and wondered if he noticed, as she had done, that her waist was thickening as the weeks went by. Sometimes she thought he must do, given how he intently he studied her, but at other times, Lady James recollected that it had taken her husband nearly a month to notice that the portrait of her predecessor had been returned to its original position. He made no comment on the matter but had looked quite baffled by her seeming lack of jealousy. She was glad of that, upon reflection, for if she felt a twinge of irritation whenever she happened to look up at that unquestionably lovely face, at least she had the comfort of knowing that she concealed it well.

"What makes you smile so, Charlotte?" he asked her, one late evening as she sat sipping tea with him in her favourite room. The tea had taken some weeks of careful experimenting to get exactly right, and she had enjoyed it for an entire fortnight before realising that nothing tasted pleasant any longer. There was an odd taste in her mouth that she could not like, even if she managed to ignore it for the most part. She heartily wished that Eliza were nearby so that she might ask if such a strange thing was on account of the child she believed herself to be carrying.

The babe had quickened but a half hour before, the very moment that she had sat down comfortably in her chair and taken her teacup in her hand. Charlotte had been unable to prevent the delight from appearing on her face. Her throat felt tight and she laid a hand to the place where she had felt the child move. It was a wondrous, precious thing – little point in denying it.

Waiting for her to reply, her husband watched her yet more closely.

"Are you ill, my dear? Your hand is trembling." He set down his teacup. One might believe all too easily that his care for her ran deeper than civility. She pushed the thought away.

"No, Sir Daniel – I do not believe I am ill. I am well." Charlotte raised her hand. The fingers were indeed unsteady. How had she not noticed until now? "I am well. I have good news – I have every expectation that there will be a child born at Sedgley by the time the harvest has been brought in."

She had known, of course, that he would be pleased – this was why he had married her, after all – but she had not anticipated how his silent, open-mouthed stare would fill her with fond laughter.

Eventually he managed to speak.

"Is it indeed so? My dear, *dear* Charlotte! I am in every way...and you are well? You have not been ill? My first wife – she was not well for months – but you seem to have been going about as you usually do, have you not? The autumn? We must engage a doctor. I will go to London."

He stood as though to depart immediately, and Charlotte reached forth her hand to take his and still him, trying to check her laugh.

"You do not mean to go *now*, Sir Daniel! It is late and will be dark in an hour or so. Do sit down again and have some more tea." She would have withdrawn her hand to go to the teapot, but he turned his wrist and prevented her, enfolding her fingers in his palms. Charlotte felt a lurch in her heart when he bent his head to kiss her hand. She swallowed and tried to speak in her usual steady way.

"There now – there will be time enough to find a doctor. I should not like to go to London, you know; I want to be here at home. I have not felt ill, not since the first few months, at any rate, and now that has passed I feel quite, quite well."

He bent to kiss her hand again. "An heir to Sedgley! It is all that I had wished for, my dear."

"It may be a girl, Sir Daniel," warned his wife, even as some small part of her delighted in his satisfaction.

He considered this but did not look at all unhappy with the thought. "A girl is as good a start as any, Charlotte. We will buy her an old tumbledown estate somewhere, and if she is anything like her Mama," he said with pride, "she will have the fattest dowry in England by the time she has overhauled it. What is it?" he asked, concerned, seeing that her eyes had dampened.

"Oh, you must not mind me; I am a little tired, perhaps, or I would not weep so easily." Lady James's heart felt full in her chest and she tried to calm herself. She had not expected that he should be so unruffled about the possibility of a daughter, nor had she been prepared for the compliment he had bestowed upon her, particularly in that admiring, tender tone of voice. He spoke as though she were some accomplished and talented delight, rather than merely Charlotte who made herself useful.

Her guard, which had been very firmly in place since receiving Elizabeth's warning, began to drop over the following weeks, and given her husband's unexpected indifference to the deliberate mention of Lady Warwick, Charlotte found contentment as her time drew nearer.

When she had referred to the former Lydia Bennet, she had done so against her own better judgment. One day, however, she had been feeling unusually low in spirits and spoke to Sir Daniel of Elizabeth's letter.

"Mrs. Darcy wrote to me some time ago, my dear," she said, as they wandered the apple orchard on a bright afternoon. She had taken to calling him such, after doing so quite by accident one day, and he had looked so pleased that she had rationally told herself that there could be no harm in doing so more often – it was such a small thing, after all. "She was informing me of Lydia's return to England with her husband; apparently she made quite a stir on the continent."

"Unconventionally behaved titled women generally do, my dear. I believe England has rather *higher* expectations of the nobility than do those across the channel."

"Do you dislike her then, Sir Daniel?" she could not help but ask – he did not seem angry at the name but certainly there was some contempt there.

"Dislike her! No, not really, Charlotte – she is well enough, but I cannot help but think that her manners ought to be curbed. I doubt Warwick will trouble himself to do so."

Charlotte thought of what Elizabeth had said about how amused the earl had looked at his wife's antics, and nodded. She had often thought similarly about Lydia Bennet herself, in times past.

Sir Daniel paused to examine a green apple on a low-hanging branch and stopped to look at his wife.

"By the time these are picked, my dear, our household shall have increased." He seemed content to change the subject, and Charlotte allowed it.

They walked arm in arm in silence for a few moments. The wind, which had been blowing gently until now, suddenly grew more intense and one end of her shawl blew from where it rested on her shoulder. Her husband caught it and arranged it about her again. She looked up at him and smiled her thanks.

The smile fell from her face when he did what he had never done before and cupped her face with his hand. She looked at him in puzzlement as he stood still, gazing at her. He was not by any measure an ugly man, but neither were his features uniform in the way that was so valued in society. His nose was not quite straight, and his smile, when he smiled, was a little twisted. She wondered at herself, that she should think his face so very pleasing at that moment. He frowned a little later, and she felt acute disappointment. Had he been examining her face and suddenly found it wanting? After many months of marriage, it was becoming increasingly difficult not to care.

He spoke then, and her fears subsided. "I have been growing concerned, my dear," he said slowly, as though searching for the right words, even weighing up the wisdom of speaking them, "that some harm might come to you when the child comes. I cannot like the thought of it."

Her head whirled and she held onto his arm for balance. She tried very hard to think clearly but her voice shook a little when she answered him.

"It is a risk all we women must take, Sir Daniel – we all of us know how it might end." She did not scold him for raising such an unpleasant subject.

"Ye-es, I suppose you are right, but I...Lady James, you know – she was not very like you."

Rather more tartly than she had intended, Charlotte responded, "Yes; I have seen her portrait, remember."

Frowning more deeply now, he lowered his hand from her face and took both her hands in his. The wind blew a little harder and the lace frill on Charlotte's cap fluttered madly.

"What can you mean?" he asked her.

"Not a thing, Sir Daniel. Shall we go back indoors? This wind will bluster yet for a while."

He did not move, merely kept possession of her hands. "No, not yet, my dear – I am not the quickest to understand you, I know that, but I feel that you meant more by that than you will readily admit."

Her own brows were now drawn together and she tried unsuccessfully to disengage her hands once more. Charlotte eventually answered him honestly, with as studied an air of indifference as she could muster.

"Your wife was very beautiful."

Sir Daniel was silent for a few moments, considering his reply. "Yes, I daresay that she was. No, don't try to pull away, my dear; I had not...no, I will be brave and speak. It was a very sad thing when they died – the child and my wife, I mean. For many months I was quite unhappy with the waste of it; she was not a bad sort of girl, for all that she was not so clever as you. I have been increasingly worried about...that is...I should be quite disconsolate to lose *you*, Charlotte."

Chapter Ten

Charlotte looked at her husband, taken aback by the sincerity of his declaration. He was not merely being gallant – that she could have dismissed very easily – but his earnest tone and serious expression gave her pause. It seemed that Sir Daniel, for all his air of self-importance, had decided that she was indispensable to him.

It was, perhaps, not overly tactful of him to have mentioned the likelihood of her dying in childbirth, but the very fact that he spoke so thoughtlessly made her believe him when he held her hand and candidly told her that he did not want her to die.

She returned the pressure of his hand and swallowed down the lump that had risen in her throat. Impending motherhood was turning her into a sentimental girl – which she had not ever been. Her husband's hands were warm about hers, but when the wind whistled its way through the apple trees and whipped about her head, she could not repress the shiver that ran through her.

Sir Daniel did not seem to expect a reply, which was fortunate, because she had none to make. He could not expect her to lay bare her heart to him, surely; she could not even determine her own feelings toward him except that she knew she wasn't in love with him or any such nonsense as that. Charlotte had seen love and it looked excessively silly. Her heart did not deviate from its steady rhythm when he entered a room, she did not spend her idle minutes sighing at the thought of him, and she certainly did not have any desire to beg him for his continual company.

"Come inside, Lady James," said Sir Daniel. "You were quite right, as usual; the wind is quite abominably strong now. Take my arm, my dear."

Still, she thought, as they walked slowly back to the house, he was solicitous of her comfort, he so carefully matching his pace to her odd swaying gait. If she did not love him, neither did she wish him gone. It was a pleasant thing to be liked for the things she prided herself on. He had not, thankfully, tried to flatter her by saying that she was classically beautiful, or delicate and charming; no, he seemed to appreciate in his wife that most mundane of virtues – common sense. She leant heavily on his arm and he looked down at her.

"I have had a letter from Bertie – well, a note really; he doesn't write lengthy epistles. He wants me to go down to Cedars for a week or so, for the hunting. He says he is getting up a shooting party."

Charlotte nodded, even as she felt a vague prickle of disappointment. She answered him in her usual, collected manner, "Well, then, you must go, my dear, and enjoy yourself as you please."

Sir Daniel frowned.

"What if I do not please?" He sounded peevish, for some reason that Charlotte could not begin to fathom. She felt on edge and her back was beginning to ache dreadfully.

"I rather thought you liked hunting, Sir Daniel?"

"Well, of course I do, same as any other man, but you are very likely to enter your confinement soon!"

Charlotte paused and laid a hand on her lower back, feeling a little relieved by the pressure of her hand when she pushed against it. She winced a little, but smiled when her husband noticed and looked concerned.

"I spent too long last evening bent over my sewing, my dear. I am not the same shape as I once was – it is not so comfortable to sit for long periods of time any longer." Sir Daniel, still frowning, moved her hand from where she pressed it into her back and laid his own there. The warmth of it made her sigh with relief and she continued on with their previous conversation. "I do not see that it will make any difference to the child coming if you are at Cedars or at Sedgley – it is not as though you will be present in the room at any rate, and you are far more likely to enjoy yourself if you are with your friend, are you not?"

The irritation in his voice was noticeable when he answered her. "I wish you would not send me off quite so readily, Charlotte, as though I were some neighbourhood acquaintance."

"I was merely…."

"I do not please!" he repeated, interrupting her. "I would far rather remain at Sedgley and take care of you."

"I hardly…."

"Yes, I know very well that you need no such taking care of – of all the women I have ever met, you are the *least* likely to require cosseting, but did it never occur to you that I might *wish* to be needed?"

They stood by now on the steps that led up to the principal entrance to the house. A footman had noticed their approach and opened wide the doors for them. Charlotte stared at her husband for a moment before answering him in a low, sombre voice.

"No – it had not."

He regarded her for a moment then released her. He bowed in her direction before addressing the footman.

"Fetch her ladyship's maid, Shoreton."

"Very good, Sir Daniel," answered the servant, before walking off at a stately pace toward the door that led belowstairs. Sir Daniel moved toward the hall that led off to his study but was checked by Charlotte.

"My dear!" she said, "I…forgive me, I should not have been quite happy to see you go to Cedars."

The frown that had made him look so severe lifted, and his expression softened.

"I will see you at dinner, my dear. Try to rest until then."

She sat in quiet contemplation in her room for the remainder of the afternoon. Her maid had draped a thick blanket over her knees and attempted to protest when her mistress demanded that she be brought her work basket. Charlotte set about threading her needle with great industry, and even went so far as to pick up a tiny gown that needed finishing. Her little one would not lack clothes; she had been steadily stitching away at similar gowns for many months now, and although she did not often hold them up and smile fondly, occasionally she stopped in her sewing to wonder what the child would be like.

On this particular afternoon, there were very few stitches made – her desire to be usefully employed had quite deserted her, and she found herself staring out of the window toward the apple orchard and dwelling on the expression on her husband's face when he had said that he worried for her. It warmed her that it was so, and having considered the matter, Charlotte realised that she now thought of him with more tenderness.

An uncomfortable tightness spread across her middle and she grasped the arms of the chair for a moment, quite surprised by the discomfort. Her maid, entering the room to bring in some mending, looked carefully at her mistress.

"Lady James? Shall I send for the doctor?"

Charlotte shook her head, "No, it was a momentary thing – quite gone now. You had better help me dress for dinner; I shall need to go down shortly.

She ate well that evening. The veal was tender and the fish course dressed very well – even her husband remarked upon it, and in general he did not concern himself overly with the details of a dish, so long as there was sufficient food before him. When she rose to leave him to his porter, she felt another similar discomfort spread across her torso, this time with a sharper edge of pain. He watched her make her way across the floor. The evening sunlight filtered in through the long windows that graced the entire wall of the new dining room. Charlotte was vastly pleased with the change – what better way to dine of an evening than with such a view as Sedgely could boast.

In the drawing room, she had barely had time to pour out a cup of tea for herself when another pain came and she recognised it for what it was. Her husband, evidently more observant than she had given him credit for, entered the room and took her cup from her when he saw her falter.

"I had thought you were not feeling well – is it the child, do you think?" He laid his hand on her shoulder and she leant into it, feeling for a moment as though she badly wanted him to reassure her.

Charlotte was not a female who gave into wild fears; she had, granted, feared for her future before her marriage, but aside from that did not spend much time in contemplation of those things which were generally held to be frightening. Fear gripped her now, though, as she understood that she was about to endure the pain and danger of childbirth. The pain across her middle receded and she reached for his hand.

"Yes, I think it very well may be – but I do not believe it will happen so very quickly – the pains – there have not been many."

He held her hand and ran the other through his hair, sending it into disorder. "I will send for the doctor regardless, Charlotte, and perhaps you would like your maid?"

She reached for her tea that he had set down. "Send for the doctor, by all means, my dear, but for now, once you have done so, sit with me a little while and have your tea."

Having completed his errand, Sir Daniel returned to her and regarded her gravely, his brows knit together.

"Do you want more tea?"

Charlotte gestured to her half-full cup. "Not at present, thank you, Sir Daniel."

He paced to the window and looked out, standing beside her little round table. When he spoke, he did not turn to face her. Perhaps he was afraid to.

"Do you love me, Charlotte?"

Her brows rose and she sipped her tea, trying to think how she might answer him.

Sir Daniel evidently grew impatient quickly, and turned his head to her even as she was framing her reply.

"I had not thought of it." Carefully considering the matter, she kindly added, "I like you well enough."

"You like me."

"Yes."

"But you have not thought on whether or not you love me. Why not?"

She twisted a little in her chair in order to look at him more easily. Another fleeting pain came as she did so, and she waited until it had passed before responding.

"It seemed unreasonable to think of it, given that we married for convenience – I did not suppose that you were much likely to fall in love with me and so I did not contemplate the possibility of doing so with you."

He looked away from her then, back to the window, and then studied the toes of his boots carefully, his mouth pursed in thought.

"Yes, yes. Of course, you underrate yourself – but you must pay me no heed, my dear." He waved his hand, dismissing the subject, and came to sit beside her. "No, do not pour my tea, Charlotte – I am able to do it. I should hope that the doctor will not be above an hour or so."

Unexpectedly, tears sprang to her eyes and he looked up from the teapot to see her dashing them away.

"Charlotte!"

"Oh, I know – I do not weep very easily. I am feeling frightened, that is all."

"And I, my dear. Come here to me," he said, rising and holding his arms out in invitation.

Charlotte, feeling much in need of kindness, stood also and stepped into her husband's embrace, barely giving any thought to the fact that they had never stood thus before. His arms folded about her and she sighed a little, feeling no less afraid but comforted nonetheless.

He spoke plaintively into her hair, "I cannot get on without you, Charlotte. I do believe I love you."

A small sob escaped her, and if her trembling voice was not quite rational, her words were. "I am a good mistress of your house, Sir Daniel, and I am unexpectedly useful to you. Finding someone useful is not at all the same thing as love."

His arms tightened about her when she laid her head on his shoulder. "No, for I am not in love with my steward, after all."

That made her laugh but it was cut off at the hitch of her breath when another pain came, and he continued on.

"I had far better say all that is in my heart to you now, Lady James, or I may face the regret of having been silent when I ought to have spoken. I love you – perhaps not in the same way as one finds in novels and the like, but mayhap you will not mind that, for I have never yet seen you read one. I would have you know it – that you are needed, even if it is only by your poor bumbling husband."

Charlotte stood in the circle of his arms for some time without speaking. She heard the clock chime in the hallway and registered that her pains were seeming to last a little longer now. She extricated herself from him when she heard the knock at the door and the doctor was announced.

"Thank you, Shoreton; send my maid to my rooms, please. Doctor O'Brean, Shoreton will direct you. Sir Daniel will see me safely upstairs."

Her husband did so, not minding that it took quite three times longer than usual to mount the staircase and walk the short distance to Lady James's chamber. Before going in, she turned and quickly kissed his cheek; when she entered the room, she did so with rather more courage than she had thought she might earlier in the day – it was an uplifting, happy thought, to know that she was loved.

Her labour went hard, for many long hours. Her maid stood by her and whispered encouragement, even as she manoeuvred a small piece of wood for Charlotte to bite down on. It was slow, and it was painful. There was a moment when Charlotte had pleaded for it to be over, telling the women present that she could not do any more, and the doctor had spoken firmly.

"Do not give up just yet, Lady James; the hardest part is now done and you have only to bring the child forth entirely and your husband shall have the heir he has so much desired."

The thought of it encouraged her, and she summoned up the very last reserves of her strength, thinking dimly that if this was to be her end, at least she could make him happy by giving him a child.

Not ten minutes later, Charlotte lay back against the pillows in exhaustion, feeling all the relief to be expected from the cessation of pain. The wail of her baby met her ears and she smiled. Wearily she turned to her maid, who, with uncharacteristic cheer, told her that she had done very well and that she should soon feel quite well again now.

She was gently tended to by the servants and given the babe to hold. Doctor O'Brean had left the room to inform Sir Daniel of the news, and Charlotte, quite overwhelmed with happiness as she looked into her child's face, waited for him to come.

He did so very soon. She heard his quick step outside the door and smiled broadly at him when she saw him.

"Well, my dear – Charlotte – let me see her then! Ah, she is quite, *quite* lovely, Lady James."

"I suppose we have to find a suitable derelict estate for her to transform, Sir Daniel."

He laughed, the sound making her smile widen. "Yes, I will begin searching tomorrow if it will please you. You look tired, my dear."

She tore her eyes away from her daughter and nodded. "Yes, I doubtless look quite unkempt but I wanted to see you, and for you to see her, so I told the doctor he might invite you in."

She watched him trace a featherlight fingertip across their daughter's frowning brow and smiled when the same finger touched the similar crease on her own forehead. He bent his head to kiss where his fingertip had rested on the both of them.

"She is like you. I had hoped that she might be."

"My dear, what you said, after dinner – that you loved me...."

"Yes?"

"I found it so very comforting when I was in here and feeling quite alone. It helped me through the trial of it all, knowing that you care for me – as I am. I believe that I like you very well indeed; perhaps it will grow to be more – maybe it already is a little of love that I feel for you. I admit that I do not much like to think that there might have been a third Lady James to take my place."

Accepting this almost declaration with another kiss to her brow, Sir Daniel leant back more comfortably beside his wife and stared contentedly at his daughter.

"Tell me, my love, what sort of estate do you think Lottie will like to have? It must be nearby. Perhaps something a little more modern than Sedgley."

Charlotte smiled. It was not romantic – but it was enough.